A Man of Value

The Montbryce Legacy~II

ANNA MARKLAND

ISBN:987867369
ISBN-13: 978-0-9878673-6-0

Try not to become a man of success,
But rather try to become a man of value
~Albert Einstein

For my father William Gaskell
~A Lancashire lad through and through,
Honest, loyal and true

PROLOGUE

Edwinesburh, Scotland, 1087

Caedmon Brice Woolgar liked the sound of laughter, and savored the guffaws of his friends, already well into their cups. He parted his long hair down the centre, gathered the thick black locks into two bunches, and pulled back tightly. Sticking out his tongue, and rolling his eyes, he continued his mockery. "They say William Rufus, the new King of the English, wears his long blond hair parted in the centre, and off his face, which is always red, as if he's angry. That's why they call him Rufus."

Edgar choked on his ale. "Don't let the fair Aediva see you making that face, Caedmon," he teased. "She'll no longer love you."

Caedmon felt his face redden. "Aediva doesn't love me, though she thinks she does."

"And what of the beautiful Audrey, and the voluptuous Coventina—and the well-endowed—"

"Cease! Can I help it if these women lust after my handsome face?" Caedmon interjected good-naturedly, wiping his mouth with the back of his hand after taking a long swig of his dark ale.

"It's not your bonny face they lust after, my brawny friend," Leofric Deacon commented sardonically, bending his long arm to his head and looking cross-eyed at his own bulging bicep. "It's those impressive muscles."

1

"Aye!" was the jovial agreement, as tankards clinked together and laughter rang out.

"I hear Rufus is a dandy who dresses in the height of fashion, however outrageous," Edgar Siward cooed, prancing foppishly around the crowded alehouse.

Relieved the jesting had turned back to Rufus, Caedmon carried on, "Rumor has it the new king's eyes are threatening, his voice strident, as if he's trying to intimidate. They say he's a bully who easily takes offense."

Leofric imitated the features Caedmon described, giving rise to further fits of laughter.

Despite their levity, Caedmon knew they were all wondering if the son of the hated Conqueror would be as ruthlessly cruel as his recently departed father.

"The Normans have their problems with all William's ambitious sons. Robert Curthose won't be content to be the Duke of the Normans. He thirsts for Rufus's throne," Edgar opined. "Did you know that when they were boys, Rufus and his brother Henry once stood on a high balcony and dumped a full chamber pot on their brother Curthose's head? Playing dice must have become too boring."

General comments of disgust ensued.

"Perhaps, while they are busy trying to steal from each other, we can help our King Malcolm regain Northumbria?"Caedmon slapped his friend on the back. "Pray you're right, Leofric. I too would like a piece of Northumbria to claim as my own."

"As would any one of us," Siward agreed. "It's ironic all of us were born in this barbaric country, yet we're outcasts, the sons of Saxons who fled the Conqueror after Hastings."

"Aye, and most of us fatherless, our heroic sires dead at Hastings, or Dover, or any one of the innumerable merciless skirmishes with the brutal Normans," Leofric lamented.

"And listen to us. 'Aye,' Leofric says, as if he's a Scot," Caedmon said. "We sound like Scots, though we're Saxons. We've had to learn the tongue of the Gaels to survive at King Malcolm's court. Aye, we sound like Scots, though any Scot knows we're not."

"At least we haven't been forced to learn the hated Norman French," Edgar offered.

Eivind Brede came over from another table and joined the conversation. "Here we are, landless and powerless, but looked upon by our exiled forebears as the hope of the future, the pride of our race. We burn to liberate a country many of us have never set foot in."

Caedmon's Saxon mother, Lady Ascha Woolgar, took such pride in him, and he'd always admired her bravery at risking the flight to Scotland after the death of his father at Hastings—a pregnant woman, with no one but her brother, Gareth, for sustenance. Even after Gareth's death, she'd prospered in Scotland, and become a respected pillar of the exiled Saxon community. His mother made sure everyone recognized him as the son of a martyr of Hastings.

"I wish with all my heart I could restore my mother to her own country, the land of her birth," he declared solemnly.

His friends nodded in silent agreement, and not a word was spoken for several minutes.

They all seethe with the same longing, an England ruled again by Anglo-Saxons.

"Now we're getting too serious," he said finally. "We've sworn to help King Malcolm oust the Normans, at least from Northumbria. Let's drink to that."

He leapt up onto his seat. "King Malcolm *Cenn Mór!* Malcolm, the Great Chieftain," he shouted, raising his tankard.

"Northumbria!" came the echo.

"Aye!"

CHAPTER ONE

Bolton, Northumbria, March 1093,
Sixth Year of the Reign of William Rufus

Agneta Kirkthwaite crouched in terror in the abandoned hayloft, shivering, despite the warmth of her mother's arms clasped tightly around her. Her father, Sir Eidwyn, had hurried them into hiding as soon as the outriders had raised the alarm.

"Make sure you have your dagger, Ragna," Eidwyn told his wife, his voice strained.

The barbaric Scots had been increasing their murderous raids on Norman holdings in Northumbria, and though the Kirkthwaites weren't Normans, their manor in the tiny village of Bolton, more prosperous than most, might tempt raiders. Over the years since the Conquest, their isolation, and alliances with the Normans, had spared them many of the ravages experienced by other Northumbrians. Now, in defense of their home, Eidwyn and his sons, Aidan and Branton, had armed themselves and the villagers and were ready for an attack.

Unholy battle cries heralded the arrival of the marauders, raising the hairs on the back of Agneta's neck. Ragna Kirkthwaite pressed her eye to a crack between the old planking of their hiding place.

"God save us," she breathed, making the Sign of the Cross. "They're naked!" She looked away, and dragged Agneta across the rough floorboards, further from the wall.

"Who are they, Mamma?" Agneta whimpered. "Why are they attacking us?"

"Barbarian Scots," her mother spat. "Will they never give up their claim to Northumbria? Stay here."

Ragna crawled back to the chink, and peered out again. She gasped, and scurried back to Agneta, who grasped her mother's sleeve. "What is it?"

"There are Saxons with them."

"But father is a Saxon. Why would Saxons attack us?"

Ragna took a deep breath. "I don't know, but your father and brothers will fight them off, with the help of the villagers."

The mayhem below continued for a long while. Agneta winced at the harsh sounds of metal on metal, screams of pain, and shouts of triumph. Then suddenly—nothing. She clung to her mother for long anxious minutes, until the faint smell of smoke wafted up to them.

Ragna inched closer to the crack. She choked back a whimper and her forehead slumped against the wood.

"What's wrong? What is it?" Agneta whispered frantically.

When her mother didn't reply, Agneta crawled over to the crack and looked.

The house is on fire.

She was about to look away when new shouts came to her ears, and she caught sight of her father. Sword drawn, he fought with two naked raiders whose bodies shone eerily. Were they covered in grease?

"Papa looks tired," she whispered. She turned to look at her mother, and saw a tear roll down her cheek. She looked back through the crack. No one!

Suddenly, Aidan, her beloved seventeen year old brother, one year older than she, staggered into view and fell to the ground, clutching his chest. A shrieking marauder appeared, leapt onto Aidan, and plunged a dagger into his back.

"*Aidan*," she rasped, her throat dry as dust. She furrowed her brow in anguished disbelief, and rocked to and fro, hugging her knees. "They've stabbed Aidan."

Her mother crawled away from the wall, and curled up, whimpering.

Where are Papa, and Branton, and the villagers?

Agneta couldn't help it. She was drawn to look back at the slaughter. Before long, she'd witnessed the murders of Branton, and her father. Bloodied, broken bodies lay all over the courtyard. The only sounds were the crackling of the burning timbers, and the victorious laughter of the barbarians who'd perpetrated this horror.

Fear gripped her and she couldn't stop the tears streaming down her face. Her mother had gone strangely quiet. Agneta sniffled, wiped her runny nose with her sleeve, and looked through the crack again. Her stomach clenched and she blinked rapidly. A man in chain mail was crouched beside Aidan. He turned the boy over, and dragged him into a sitting position, cradling Aidan's shoulders with his arm. Agneta fisted her hands against the wall, her fingernails biting into her palms.

Please don't hurt him.

The warrior smoothed the hair off the boy's face then lay Aidan down again. Agneta flattened her palms against the wall and clawed at the splintering wood. Everything seemed to have tilted and she was afraid she might swoon.

Aidan, Aidan—

Unexpectedly, the man rocked back on his heels and slowly stood, brushing the dirt from his leggings with his gauntlets. With the back of her fist she strangled a cry that threatened to burst from her throat. Even seen from her high perch, he was a giant.

Oh God! He's looking up.

Her insides pitched and rolled, but she willed her body to be still. The man removed his helmet and wiped the sweat from his brow with the back of his hand. Black hair fell to his shoulders. She couldn't look away. Soon another man came to stand beside him, similarly clad.

These are the treacherous Saxons.

The two men conversed together quietly, still looking up. She couldn't move, transfixed with fear and fascination. The man with black hair shook his head when the other put his hand on his comrade's shoulder. Both seemed troubled. They put their helmets back on, turned and walked away.

She swooned against the wooden wall.

***

The first grey streaks of dawn were lighting the sky when she woke to find she was alone. The voices had fallen silent, and the house had burned to the ground. The stench of smoke filled her nostrils. With trembling hands, barely able to cling to the rickety ladder, she climbed down slowly from the loft, forcing her numbed legs to move, and went in search of her mother. Though some deep longing wanted to believe her father and brothers might still somehow be alive, why then wouldn't they have come for her? How would she and her mother cope without the protection of their men?

Wandering in a daze, rubbing the smoke from her eyes, she was vaguely aware of other shuffling figures. Suddenly, she caught sight of her mother, slumped over a body. She came closer. Her mother was slumped over her father's body. Agneta shook her by the shoulder. "Mamma, Mamma," she coaxed, looking into the dead eyes of her beloved Papa. A choked gasp escaped her lips.

There was no response. Had her mother fainted? She took hold of her shoulders and eased her up. Blood trickled from the corner of her mother's mouth and dripped on her bodice. Her father's blood? Bile rose again in her throat. "Mamma—"

She must have screamed when she saw the ceremonial dagger she recognized as having belonged to her Danish grandmother. It was embedded to the hilt in her mother's breast. "No," she shrieked in anguish. "What about me? What about your little girl?"

She pulled on the dagger in her mother's hand, desperate to plunge it into her own heart, but death's grip held firm. She despaired that she lacked the strength to prize open her mother's petrified fingers. Hurling hoarse curses at the grey sky, she buckled, collapsing to the hard ground, her hands tearing at her hair, retching uncontrollably.

Later that day the nuns found her curled up in a tight ball beside her brother's body and took her to the nunnery.

CHAPTER TWO

Edwinesburh, Scotland, October 1093

Lady Ascha Woolgar worried for her son. He and a group of his friends had joined forces with a band of Scottish marauders and they'd been raiding deep inside Northumbria. None of her entreaties would change his mind.

"Caedmon, you are too stubborn. The poor people of Northumbria suffered enough from the brutal harrying carried out by the Conqueror all those years ago. The land, and the people who did manage to survive, are only now recovering from what I've heard. Now you're intent on raiding there?"

"We only target Norman holdings," he reassured her. "King Malcolm *Cenn Mór* isn't prepared to attack now, so skirmishes are what we have to content ourselves with for the moment."

Each time they returned from their forays, they were dirty, bruised and exhilarated with the Norman plunder they hauled back. They outfitted themselves, like their Scots comrades, in leines and brats, though Caedmon told his mother once that some of the Scots stripped naked when raiding and greased their bodies. "They say it makes them more terrifying. They're right. Sometimes they terrify me."

"You're a Saxon knight, Caedmon Brice Woolgar, not a barbaric Scot."

"Mother, this will be good training for when King Malcolm launches his next offensive. We mostly use pikes and axes. I'm already skilled with the sword and this provides me with more choices. We don't take as many chances as the Scots. They're the fanatical killers. We Saxons concentrate on relieving the Normans of their ill-gotten gains. And don't worry, I'm not likely to strip off my clothes when I go into battle."

Ascha shook her head. "You speak as if it's an outing."

"Mostly that's what it is—though—"

Ascha waited. He couldn't be pushed, if he didn't want to talk. She watched him bite his lip and scratch his head. When he spoke, his words terrified her.

"There was one raid, a few months ago, when I first joined them. It didn't go the way Leofric and I anticipated."

Ascha looked hard at her son, afraid to ask, "In what way?"

"They weren't Normans."

Ascha sank into a chair. "Caedmon! You raided Saxons? Tell me you didn't."

Caedmon went down on one knee in front of her and took hold of her hands. "I wish I could. We were near Alnwick, where the Earl of Northumbria's castle is. We assumed from the Scots that all the estates in that area were held by Normans."

She gripped his hands. "But they weren't?"

Caedmon hung his head. "One turned out not to be."

Again Ascha waited. Though Caedmon was a warrior, he wasn't a brutal man, unlike his supposed father. Her son had morals and she recognized his need to confide in her. They'd depended on each other for many years.

He stood and walked away to the hearth. "By the time it became obvious they weren't Normans, the Scots couldn't be dissuaded. They murdered the lord and his family. They may have been Danes—or Saxons. He and his two sons fought bravely, but they were no match for the barbarians. There was nothing we could do. Their bloodlust sickened me."

Ascha's hands had gone to her mouth and she couldn't speak.

He knelt again before her, his hand over his heart. "I killed no one, Mother, I swear. I admit I plundered their manor, but I didn't kill anyone."

She took his hands and squeezed them tightly. "Caedmon, this is much too dangerous. What were you doing close to a Norman stronghold like Robert de Mowbray's castle? It's foolhardy in the extreme."

He frowned and rose to his feet. "Mother, what other choices are open to me, other than to be a mercenary? I have no lands, no titles. I must make my own way in the world. My skill as a warrior will perhaps bring me wealth. Otherwise, I have nothing to offer any woman if I wish to marry."

"There's the manor house at Ruyton." As soon as she said it, Ascha wished she'd bitten her tongue.

He turned to look at her. "Ruyton?"

Ascha bit her lip. "Shelfhoc Hall was your father's estate. It's mine now, and has been administered for me by a steward since I left."

"A steward?"

She couldn't meet Caedmon's enquiring gaze. "Yes, Ruyton is in the Welsh Marches. After your father died the Earl of Ellesmere offered to administer and protect Shelfhoc, to safeguard it from the Welsh."

"The Earl of Ellesmere? A Norman? A Norman Earl administers your estate?"

She rose from the chair and walked over to the window, fidgeting with her wimple, her back to him. "Yes, Caedmon. Not all Normans are monsters."

"Huh! Show me one that's not. This has been the source of your income all these years? It never occurred to me. I assumed the money came from Uncle Gareth's estate."

She turned to face her son. "Some of it did. As you know, when my brother Gareth and his son Gawain were killed fighting to restore Edgar the Aetheling to the English throne, this house devolved to me. But Shelfhoc is *your* birthright, Caedmon."

Caedmon scratched his head. "What fee does this great Earl impose for his Norman benevolence?"

Ascha sensed her face must have reddened in the course of the conversation but she was determined to keep her voice steady. "There's no fee, Caedmon. It would be vulnerable to the Welsh without his protection."

He slumped down into a chair, stretched out his legs and put his feet on a stool. "Well, mother, I'm not interested in riding off to live in the Welsh Marches. There's work to do here for King Malcolm. He'll need strong warriors for his next attack on Northumbria. The rumors are it will be soon."

Should she weep or rejoice that he wouldn't go to Ruyton?

***

"Sire, your Queen lies gravely ill, surely you don't intend to leave her to attack Northumbria now?"

King Malcolm *Cenn Mór* sighed. His emotions were in turmoil. Duncan Kincaid, the man who stood before him as he sat in the Chart Room of his castle, was one of his most trusted advisors. "My beloved wife's illness breaks my heart. She will not recover."

He stood and banged his fist down on the map table. "But I must strike now, Duncan. It's not enough that King William Rufus has cut us off from parts of Cumbria we've held sway over with his damned castle at Carlisle. No, he insults me at every turn, like his father, the Conqueror."

Duncan shifted his weight from side to side, plainly ill-at-ease. "But we're not prepared. The Saxons in our ranks are an undisciplined lot, and our own Scots have no sense of unity."

Malcolm looked Duncan in the eye. "We must regain Northumbria," he said slowly, drawing out each word, but he could see Duncan remained unconvinced.

"Your Majesty, the Earl of Northumbria, de Mowbray, has a highly trained and well equipped force waiting for you there. They have been strengthening the border for several years, especially after the recent bloody raids by those renegades and their Saxon henchmen. You'll be marching into disaster."

Malcolm snorted with contempt. "De Mowbray can't be everywhere in Northumbria. We'll use evasion tactics and march right past him, deep into the heart of Norman territory. My mind is made up. It will be a glorious victory. Northumbria will at last be ours."

Duncan shook his head, and Malcolm wondered briefly if he should continue. "My son Edward will accompany me, to experience how it feels to grind the Normans into the dust. He can return home a hero, and lighten the heart of his ailing mother."

Duncan looked shocked beyond belief. "But sire, he's Queen Margaret's eldest son. You've named him your heir. If anything happens to him—"

Malcolm held up his hand in a dismissive gesture and sat down again. "I'll hear no more objections. My mind is made up. Summon the chiefs, and the Saxon leaders. We've battle plans to lay."

***

Three sennights later, the Scottish court, dressed in deepest mourning, grieved the Great Chieftain's death. Malcolm *Cenn Mór*, and his son and heir had both been killed in a bloody ambush in Northumbria, their army decimated. There were whispers of treachery. Roger de Mowbray had lain in wait at Alnwick.

"Queen Margaret has sent for the Black Rood," Lady Ascha Woolgar murmured tearfully to Enid, leaning heavily on the trusted maid who'd been her confidante for many years. "It's the most precious of the possessions she brought from Hungary—a fragment of the True Cross, encased in a gold cross, with an ivory image of Christ," she whispered, as if in a trance. "She won't last the night. Her heart is broken. The Black Rood will bring her consolation as she faces death."

Enid struggled to control her tears, wondering where her beloved mistress would find consolation for her own broken heart. Lady Ascha's only son, Caedmon, had not returned with the few mangled and maimed Saxons who had barely survived the trap at Alnwick.

CHAPTER THREE

Alnwick, Northumbria, November 1093

The handful of nuns and monks from the religious community, accompanied by villagers from Alnwick, made their halting way through the piles of already decaying bodies, strewn like broken puppets across the field. The earth had been churned to mud, now hardened to ruts by the frost. They'd all but given up hope of finding anyone else alive amid the carnage of the bloody slaughter by de Mowbray's army.

Despite the cold air, masses of buzzing flies, drawn by blood and the stench of corruption, swarmed around them relentlessly. Mangy dogs sniffed the distorted corpses. Buzzards floated ominously overhead, waiting patiently. Braver crows were already pecking out eyes and tearing at fingernails. Ragged human scavengers picked over the remains of the dead.

"Quick Sister, o'er 'ere," came an unexpected shout. "I found one alive. I think."

Numbed by the horror of the gruesome reality through which she staggered, terrified of falling on the fallen, Agneta fought to hold down the acrid bile rising in her dry throat. She would have to point out to Thomas Swineherd she wasn't yet a Sister, only a novice. The final vows would be made once she came of age. She'd been at the nunnery for —how long was it now—eight months—since the murder of her parents?

Then her paralyzed brain absorbed the significance of what Thomas had shouted. Raising the edges of her habit, already caked with mud and gore, she stumbled over to where a nervous horse snorted and shied, its eyes wild. A wounded man lay completely covered by the mutilated corpse of another fallen warrior. The bodies were tangled, muddied and bloodstained and it was impossible to tell on which side they had fought. Was this man a Norman, a Saxon or a Scot? She didn't care. None of them were worth saving. If she nursed them back to health, they would leave and kill again, or be killed. It was the way of men.

"'E's badly wounded, Sister," said Thomas, shooing away a persistent crow. "We mun get t'others off 'im. Don' look like a Scot—don' wan' save a curst Scot. Blest be God their curst King Malcolm died 'ere. Mebbe now the raidin'll cease. Wouldna foun' thisun if t'weren't fer 'is 'oss standin' o'er 'im like a sad dog."

Agneta felt she should say something pious about God not caring on which side mortals fought, but the words stuck in her throat. She did care.

Thomas and another villager, Gilbert, struggled to lift the rigid corpse off the fallen warrior, and Agneta fell to her knees on the frozen ground beside him. She clenched her fists on her lap, hesitant to touch him, and looked him over for signs of life. The odor of his body assailed her nostrils. She straightened her back and wrinkled her nose.

"Are you sure he's alive, Thomas?"

"Looks like he's pumpin' air, I reckon. Smells like it too," he chuckled.

She wondered how anyone could keep a sense of humor amid all this sorrow, but noticed the rise and fall of the warrior's broad chest. Convinced it was the cold seeping into her knees causing her to tremble, she reached out her hand to place it near his lips and felt a faint wisp of air caress her frozen fingers. He moaned suddenly and she snatched her hand away, toppling over.

"Nowt to be 'fraid of, sister. 'E's in no fit state to do thee any 'arm."

She reddened, feeling foolish. Thomas was right. What was there to be afraid of? If the wounded man wasn't lying here half dead, she would be terrified of him. He was big and likely intimidating to behold. But he was hurt, and his life was in her hands now. She was in control. It was a not altogether welcome feeling and blood rushed to her head.

Don't swoon, don't swoon.

Pulling herself together, she placed her palm on his forehead, then pressed the backs of her fingers to his neck. Heat from his skin warmed her frigid hand. "He's alive," she said quietly.

And in need of soap and water.

The nervous stallion backed away.

"Reckon 'is 'oss 'as the stench o' dead 'orseflesh in 'is nostrils."

The warrior's iron helmet was badly dented and partly knocked off and she suspected a blow to the head had taken his wits. A livid gash snaked from his right temple down to his chin. It had bled, but wasn't deep and the blade had missed his eye. The purple bruising made it look worse than it probably was. She couldn't tell if any bones were broken beneath his heavy, blood-stained hauberk. The worst injury seemed to be a deep, angry wound to the front of his right thigh. It still oozed blood through the slashed leggings.

She held out her hand and Thomas helped her to her feet. "I can't do much in the field, Thomas. He's obviously a knight. We must get him back to the nunnery. Carry him over to the haywain. Can you pry his hand from his sword? It might take three of you to lift him. He's not a small man."

There was something vaguely familiar about him. An acquaintance of her father's maybe? Perhaps this one was worth saving? She hoisted her habit, slogged her way back across the field, and stumbled into the oxcart.

"Lay him with his head on my lap," she instructed. She would be uncomfortable, sitting on the rough planking of the haywain with the knight's heavy weight on her. The villagers, already exhausted by the difficult expedition across the field, struggled to lift the warrior. His helmet fell to the ground, and Thomas, breathing hard, stooped to retrieve it, tethering the reins of the warrior's horse to one of the rough hewn wooden slats. The animal was further alarmed by the proximity of the oxen, and pulled away, jolting the cart and causing Agneta's hands to fly to her mouth.

The man filled the two-wheeled cart. She felt overwhelmed by his size, pinned against the side by his malodorous body. She pushed against the rough wood, trying to shift her weight, her bottom already feeling numb. A spile of wood pierced her hand. She resolved to deal with it later. "Gilbert, please tell Mother Superior we're taking a casualty back to the infirmary. Go, Thomas. Quickly."

Thomas led the beasts along the rutted track at what seemed like an interminably slow pace. The lumbering dragons snorted frozen breaths on the frigid air. Agneta peeled off the hood of the knight's hauberk. His long black hair was plastered to his head with sweat. There was no blood. She felt a large swelling on the back of his head.

"He has the look of a Norman, though his hair is too long," she mused, brushing back a strand from across his face. She was calmer now, more in control. Detachment, mantra of the nuns, took over. She assessed the man's pallor. Careful to keep his head cradled on her lap, she used her other hand to press the linen cloths from the infirmary against his wounded thigh, trying to stem the blood. She shivered as the cold November wind gusted around them, but felt the warmth of the warrior's head on her thighs. "Looks like rain," she suddenly shouted to Thomas, who peered at the sky, coughed, spat and grunted.

A deep groan emanated from the man's throat, reverberating through her, destroying her fledgling confidence and making her sweat despite the cold. Sixteen when she was brought to the nunnery, she had no knowledge of men, except for her darling brothers, brutally slaughtered by the likes of this warrior. She looked down at him and noticed his lips were parched. She licked her own. She had to get his weight off her—soon.

When they arrived at the community, monks and laymen hurried out to assist in carrying the man to the recently constructed infirmary. She breathed a sigh of relief as the weight was lifted from her, but missed the warmth on her legs as the cold trickled back into his sweat on her habit. They laid him on a raised pallet.

Agneta found fulfillment in her work in the infirmary and Mother Superior had told her she had a way with healing. It had saved her from madness, given her a purpose. Others recognized her talent and acceded to her.

"We must get his hauberk off to see the extent of his injuries. Take care. I believe his ribs are broken." She was surprised at the note of urgency in her voice.

Remember, a nun must remain detached.

The idea of detachment appealed to Agneta. If she could ever achieve it, never again would feelings destroy her.

Two monks helped raise the man's upper body, and two others dragged the bloodstained and muddied hauberk over his head. Agneta and another novice cut away the sweat soaked padded clothing beneath it. Mayda wrinkled her nose.

"I know it's not pleasant," Agneta said with a wry smile. "We must be grateful to God it's the healthy odor of male sweat, and not putrefaction."

The knight's broad chest and well-muscled arms were covered in livid bruises, but no wounds. A close inspection did reveal broken ribs, but seemingly no other major bones broken. They unlaced his boots and eased them off, then two monks stripped off his mailed leggings. Agneta looked away, admonishing them needlessly to be careful not to inflict further damage to his thigh wound.

The monks set to work bathing him. Agneta kept her eyes on his face, and applied salve to the gash, judging it wasn't deep enough to stitch.

"Cover him as soon as you can," she said over her shoulder to one of the lay helpers. "We mustn't let him get chilled. But leave the thigh wound uncovered. I'll stitch it once we've bound his ribs and set poultices on the bruises."

The wound still bled, and required pressure. She felt the sticky warmth of his blood on her hands, and hastily wiped them, one at a time, on her habit. The sight of blood had never bothered her before, except when—no, she would not resurrect that buried memory. Once the bleeding stopped, she sewed up the gash with the smallest silken stitches she could contrive, her hand shaking. Then she bound the wound with the help of a monk.

"It's fortunate he's still in a stupor, Brother Manton," she remarked, trying to sound calm.

For me as much as for him.

"His fever worries me. He lay for hours in the wet mud. I hope the metal of the hauberk may have protected him from the damp."

Despite being naked and injured, the warrior exuded masculinity and power, and she found working on him exhausting. She'd tended other men in the infirmary, farmers with broken bones, old men with rheumatism, boys with scrapes and bruises, serfs with the ague or the bloody flux. She'd done it all dispassionately, devoid of feeling since the bloody massacre of her family and her mother's betrayal. Why did this man bother her? He was a man of violence. Perhaps that was the reason? Or had the horror of the scene she'd walked through worn her out?

She wanted to get nourishing liquids into him. Brother Manton crooked his arm under the man's head, and she poured cooled vegetable broth into his mouth. He had difficulty swallowing and started to cough. "He'll do more damage to his ribs," the monk remarked quietly.

Agneta longed to sleep, but sat by the warrior's side for a few hours, trying once in a while to drip broth into his mouth. Desperate for sleep, she left him in the care of another novice and sought her bed. She was to be called if he worsened.

In her cramped dormitory cubicle, she kicked off her boots, untied the cord at her waist, and removed her rosary and cross, kissing them reverently and placing them carefully in her tiny dresser. She peeled the soiled scapular over her head, barely able to lift her arms. The black wimple came off next, and then she breathed a sigh of relief as she dragged the starched coif off her head, releasing the pressure on her neck and cheeks. She rolled her head back and forth. The tunic followed quickly, and lastly the stiff black underskirts. The nuns had cropped her brown hair when she'd entered the novitiate. She hadn't cared. Nothing mattered. Each month, one of the older sisters sheared the hair of the novices.

Once she'd freed her tresses from the coif and wimple, the candlelight reflected on the golden highlights of what remained. Mother Superior often lectured her charges on the sin of pride, but Agneta couldn't deny the guilty pleasure she felt as she ran her fingers through her loosened hair, and smoothed her hands along the developing curves of her body. Her breasts, concealed when she wore the habit, had grown to be firm and round. The cold air teased her nipples to tautness. She was thin at the waist. Her mother had been fond of telling her she had beautiful eyes that were neither brown nor green, but a combination of the two.

Memories of her mother conjured a vision of the ornate steel blade of the Danish dagger. The weapon reposed in a place of safekeeping known only to Mother Superior. Agneta had wanted to hurl it into the depths of hell. She stretched to rid her slim body of the tension of the past few harrowing hours, then washed with a cloth and water from the ewer, anxious to be rid of the lingering smell of death. The cold water raised goosebumps on her skin. Quickly she slipped on the simple linen chemise, her teeth chattering. She succeeded in wiping most of the mud from her only habit, but wasn't sure how to remove the bloodstains.

Warrior's blood. Always so much blood.

Climbing onto her pallet, she tugged the rough woolen blanket over her to ward off the chill night air. The stricken knight occupied her thoughts. She'd allowed herself to care about another human being. She would have to be sterner. If he lived, he would probably kill again, for she had no doubt this warrior had killed. Then she wondered if he had a family, perhaps a wife. Would someone be grieving for him as she'd grieved?

"Dear Lord, give me the knowledge I need to heal this wounded man and help me overcome my hatred of the Scots. Forgive me, if I pray he's not a Scot."

Exhaustion soon claimed her.

***

"Agneta, Agneta," murmured the novice she'd left with the knight. Had she slept? She heard faint snores. She sat up slowly, her body stiff.

"What is it, Beatrix?" she whispered, rubbing her eyes, trying not to wake the other novices who would have to rise soon enough for Lauds after little sleep.

"The knight. The fever has him in its grip. He needs to be cooled, but—"

Fear curled in Agneta's belly. "I'll be there in a few moments."

She dressed quickly in the still damp habit, shoved her feet into her boots, and picked her way in the dark through the partially built cloisters, trying unsuccessfully not to make noise. She went as fast as rules allowed, her hands tucked into her sleeves, hugging her body against the chill. She was frozen to the bone by the time she reached him. The beleaguered knight's fever was worse and he thrashed about, moaning.

She blew on her fingers, rubbed her hands together and instructed Beatrix. "We'll need to bind his hands to the pallet. Bring the linen strips."

She couldn't get her fingers to thaw and it was a difficult task to bind him. "It will make it hard to change the linens, but he'll be safer."

As she surveyed their handiwork, she had a sudden feeling of pity. Such a man should not be bound.

She nursed him for two long days and nights while his fever raged, trying to get ale or broth between his lips, cooling off his body with wet cloths, tending the wound in his thigh, now left unbound to benefit from the healing properties of the winter air. Agneta couldn't understand why she was compelled to stay with him as long as she could. Was it a holy obligation she felt? Offers of assistance from others were politely declined. She gazed at him for uncounted minutes, listening to his breathing, trying to make sense of his ramblings. To her surprise she found she was willing him to live.

Heat assailed her whenever she cleansed him. Thank goodness most of his chest was covered by the bindings. She was petrified the linens covering his torso would slip and she would see—that was one area of his care she willingly left to the monks. She'd seen her brothers naked, but feared this would be—different.

"You're far too attached to your patient," Mother Superior scolded her. "You must give more of his care over to the others. Remember, detachment."

"Yes, Reverend Mother," she replied, her head bowed, only too guiltily aware she was consumed with his wellbeing, but unable to conceive of trusting anyone else with it. "The gash in his thigh and the cut on his face are healing, which is a good sign, but still the fever ravages him, and I can't understand why."

On the third day, in the evening, Agneta dozed fitfully by the knight's pallet, her head nodding. Something caused her to wake. He was staring at her, a trace of a smile on his face. Was she awake or dreaming? His eyes were blue, soft like bluebells, and she felt he was looking deep into her soul. Her throat constricted. She leapt to her feet and nervously felt his brow.

CHAPTER FOUR

The stricken warrior judged he must be in hell. Some sharp-toothed creature gnawed at his thigh and he was being stretched on a rack, his wrists bound. Yet, beside him an angel dozed. Perhaps purgatory then? He stared at the angelic face haloed by the flickering flames of distant candles. He must be in heaven and this was his beautiful madonna.

Then the angel stirred and opened her eyes. She touched his forehead, but it felt like the caress of a woman.

"Are you an angel?" he whispered, casting his eyes into the gloom around them.

"I'm Agneta," she whispered back. The words seemed to catch in her throat.

He closed his eyes, confused, and a little afraid. The vision was still there when he opened his eyes again. "Why are my hands tied, Agneta?"

He saw the beginnings of a smile, but then her eyes widened and a frown creased her brow. Had he said something wrong?

"You have broken ribs, and other injuries, including a blow to the head. You were feverish, thrashing about, and we were afraid you might fall from the pallet."

She was nervous, evidently wrestling with some indecision and he wanted to ask for more candles to be lit so he could see her eyes more clearly.

"I can untie you now, if you wish?"

He nodded, and watched as she untied the knots with some difficulty.

"My hands are cold," she murmured.

He had an urge to take hold of the slender fingers and warm them with his breath. Her voice was cold too. What could he do to warm that? Why wouldn't she look at him?

Once the knots were undone, he raised each of his hands slightly then looked back at her. Pain snaked through his chest with the movement and he hoped his face hadn't betrayed him. She flushed, and he felt a wave of heat roll over him.

It was clearer to him from the moans, movements and shadows, that he wasn't dead. His angel *was* a woman. Her hair was completely covered, her body concealed by what he now saw was a grey habit, stained with what he hoped wasn't his blood. Why could he not take his eyes off her? His twitching fingers itched to reach up and remove her wimple. Was her hair brown or blonde? A nun. He was excited by a nun. He felt ashamed.

Forgive me, Lord.

But she'd said her name was Agneta, not *Sister* Agneta. He'd somehow been delivered into the care of a woman whose face alone drew him like a lodestone. But she'd spoken of a blow to the head. Perhaps that was his problem. He licked his lips and she scurried off, returning a few moments later, a tankard clasped in her delicate hands.

She steadied his head, and held the tankard to his lips. "Drink. Your body needs liquid." Her hand on the back of his neck was indeed cold and he shivered. He drank, tentatively at first then greedily when he tasted ale.

The effort exhausted him, but she was the one shaking. He looked over the lip of the tankard to catch a glimpse of her eyes. They were downcast, but definitely green, or perhaps brown?

"Thank you, Agneta," he rasped, wiping his hand across his mouth. "That was good—Sister."

She laid his head back down and he closed his eyes.

Agneta wasn't sure if she should have untied him? Was it too soon? He seemed calmer.

His voice sounded like the deep, low drumming of a moorland grouse, calling its mate. But her attraction fled quickly when she heard the brogue of the barbaric Scots.

"What's your name?" she'd whispered, flustered by the feel of his eyes on her as he drank. His hair had felt silky beneath her hand, but her cold fingers had been a shock to him. Looking around furtively to make sure none of the lay workers were still in the infirmary, she wondered how they would react, if he proved to be a Scot? How would she react? Would she still want to heal him? The nuns taught that God loves everyone. Could she feel love and compassion for a Scot? Aware of the answer, she hunched her shoulders.

She'd asked him a simple question, why didn't he answer? He opened his eyes and reached up to his forehead, as if to find his name there. He touched the newly forming scar at his temple. She reached to stay his hand and explained in a whisper that he had a wound. "It's healing, but you'll open it if you rub it."

As she touched him, a wave of heat surged through her and she snatched her hand away. The blanket tented near his groin, and she averted her eyes quickly, but not before his face reddened as his eyes dropped, and his hands went to the bulge in the blanket. She retreated back to the stool, knocking it over.

He now knows he's naked.

"I am—my name is—I don't seem to recall—my name," he stammered. "Perhaps it's because I'm tired. Every bone in my body feels like it's broken. Where am I?"

"You're in the infirmary of the Abbey being built near Alnwick. We brought you here after we found you wounded, on the battlefield."

"I was in a battle?"

How could he not remember being in a battle? If only she could forget her terrible memories.

"Yes. You were badly hurt. Besides the blow to the head and the wound on your face, you have a gash in your thigh, the damaged ribs and several deep bruises. You became feverish after lying on the muddy ground for hours before we found you."

"And you've nursed me?" he whispered.

"Yes," she murmured, keeping her eyes on where she supposed his feet were under the blanket.

There was an uneasy silence. Then he asked her, "Who won the battle?"

"The Earl of Northumbria. He defeated the cursed Scots and killed their King, Malcolm Canmore, and his son. Perhaps we're finally rid of their attacks."

He became pensive and she could see he was trying to put the pieces of information together.

"You're hoping I'm not a Scot," he said finally.

"Yes," she admitted, then against her better judgment added, "But you sound like one, though you look like a Norman nobleman, except your hair is long—" She stopped, aware she was babbling, and felt a twinge of foreboding that she hoped her eyes didn't betray.

He glanced around the room. "I should perhaps stay silent then," he murmured.

She didn't reply, but nodded slightly. "Sip more ale."

At a loss for what to say after several minutes of awkward silence, she ventured, "We retrieved your sword. You were grasping it tightly. We might never have discovered you, if not for your horse. But your hauberk and helmet are not in good condition. We had to cut off most of your clothing."

She blushed. He would now suspect she'd helped to strip him. Should she ease his embarrassment by assuring him she'd looked away? Or would trying to find the words increase the discomfort for them both? In an effort to change the subject, she reached underneath the pallet to grasp his sword. It was heavy, and she needed two hands.

He laughed, which caused him to wince. "Such a delicate nun, wielding such a large sword."

His laughter warms me.

He took the sword from her with both powerful hands, and held it up in front of him, examining it in the dim candlelight. A spasm of pain ripped through him as he raised the weapon, though he masked it. She dared a glance. Was there a glint of a memory in his blue eyes? The sword swayed, and she had to take it carefully from his hands. She brought out the damaged helmet. He looked at it, laid it on his belly, closed his eyes, and fell asleep with his hands on it.

He dreamed of a desperate battle, an intense struggle. But who was his enemy? He felt the despair of a cause lost. Mangled bodies, parts of men, shrieking horses. Blood, a river of blood. Axes chopping off heads. Screams of terror. The rank smell of death. A suspicion of betrayal. A sword raised high against him. He turned his body and the blow glanced off his helmet. He fell, felt his opponent's sword slice into his leg and pain sear through his chest. He awoke sweating and calling out, disturbing the handful of other patients.

Perhaps my little nun should have kept me tied up.

How long had he slept? Agneta was gone. Without her there, his befuddled mind sensed something important to him was missing. He felt an inexplicable need to look into those intriguing eyes.

"I suppose nuns are instructed to keep their eyes downcast," he muttered. "Pray God I'm not a Scot. She hates Scots."

He wondered about the cause of her deep hatred? What had happened to make such a beautiful woman sound cold, distant, and bereft? He felt ashamed he'd become aroused by a nun. What kind of man was he? Who was he?

CHAPTER FIVE

"How long have I been here now, Agneta?" the warrior asked, scratching the stubble at his chin, as he watched her approach, carrying the usual bowl and flint razor. She smiled briefly. "Ten days, and you seem much improved."

"Aye. Only thanks to you. And the food."

"I'm surprised you enjoy the food here. Men don't usually like vegetables. My father—"

She seemed reluctant to continue.

"I love cabbage, and garlic and leeks, and onions," he interjected, sensing her unwillingness to continue.

The tension seemed to leave her. "And we throw in the occasional salted herring."

He laughed, and now there was less pain. He liked the way she smiled when he laughed. She didn't smile enough. "I do feel better. When I first stood, with the help of the monks, it took all my strength to relieve nature's needs."

He smiled, remembering how discrete the pious monks were when they removed the jordans filled with urine. "They carry the jordans away as if they held gold," he jested.

"In a way they do," she explained timidly. "They use the—contents—for making vellum."

The silence stretched between them as he digested what she'd said.

"Now I can walk, albeit slowly, with some assistance. I want to remember who I am. It's infuriating, like a tapestry with all the wrong threads. But, enough about me. If I stop trying to remember, it will come back. Tell me how *you* came to be here while you shave me."

She was nervous when she shaved his beard. At first he'd been afraid she might cut his throat, but her hand was steadier now and she'd evidently come to accept she would actually have to look at him while she did it. If he kept her talking while she worked it seemed easier for her, though that was risky in itself. He was strong enough now to shave his own beard, but didn't want to give up the pleasure he felt when she performed the task.

Taking a deep breath she wet his face, began the ritual and shared with him in whispers how she came to the nunnery. "My parents and brothers died in a raid carried out by Scots and their Saxon allies. I watched them butcher my father and brothers."

She swallowed hard, and it was a few minutes before she could continue. "And then my mother—she—she died too."

She trembled, making him nervous. He reached out to still her hand. She pulled away. "I'd nowhere to go. The few villagers who survived were taken in by this religious community where work has been underway for years on the building of an Abbey. The orphans are still here and they'll become nuns or monks. Most of them are simple folk from the village. I'm the only one of genteel birth, and Mother Superior has high hopes and big ambitions for her protégé."

She smiled bleakly. "I'm a young woman alone in dangerous times. The Church will protect me."

He wondered why she felt it necessary to add, "I pray daily for a true vocation."

"I understand now your deep hatred of the Scots," was all he could say.

Agneta nodded, and turned his face to shave the other side. "Here in Northumbria the people are a mixture of ancestries, some Danes descended from the Vikings of the Danelaw, like my mother, some Anglo-Saxons, like my father's family, the Kirkthwaites, and now Normans after the coming of the Conqueror."

He rubbed his hand over his newly-shaved chin, wishing her hands were still on him. "But you said Saxon allies killed your family?"

She nodded. "They were most likely Saxons who had fled to Scotland after the Conquest."

He shook his head. "Northumbria?" he murmured.

"Alnwick is in Northumbria, in the north of England."

27

"Go on," he said, wanting to keep her by his side as long as he could. "When did the Normans come?"

"In the Year of our Lord, One Thousand and Sixty-Six."

"And what year is it now?"

She stopped in her task of gathering up the shaving materials, and thought for a moment. "It's a score and seven years since."

"Seven and twenty?"

Agneta wiped his face with a drying cloth. "Yes, and now Normans hold all the power. Roger de Mowbray is the Earl of Northumbria. His castle is nearby in Alnwick. The Conqueror wanted to hold Northumbria against the Scots. The Scots consider it theirs. King William Rufus, the Conqueror's son and now the king, has seemed unable to stop the incursions by the Scots, who are often aided by these exiled Saxons. We're caught in the middle of the conflict. But we're not Scots."

He admired the pride with which she spoke about her people, her heritage. He regretted she'd suffered such pain and loss and he wished he could offer solace.

Agneta Kirkthwaite. I love the sound of her name.

He felt she desperately wanted to impart to him why she had such strong feelings, but none of it resonated with the warrior—though she'd said *Rufus*. Something about that name niggled at the back of his mind, one of the tangled threads of his forgotten life, but why? "I was obviously involved in this important battle, but on whose side did I fight? And why?"

"I don't know," she replied wistfully. "Perhaps, I don't want to know." She reddened and left abruptly.

His name eluded him, but he had no doubt whatever about his feelings towards the young novice who tended him. "I can't remember who I am, but I'm unable to hold chaste my thoughts about a nun."

He berated himself that the sight of her aroused him and his imagination ran amok when she touched him with her cold hands. If only he could draw those cold hands to his—

He loved to breathe in the clean scent of her. The ugly habit had hidden her body, and he had no idea of the color of her hair. But those eyes—oh, her beautiful eyes—he still couldn't decide if they were green or brown, or both? Those eyes had him imagining. "Whoever I am, I seem to be a man without honor. A man who lusts after nuns."

But she'd admitted to not having a true calling. She would become a nun because she had no choice. It was a great loss and, for some reason, a personal one.

When she deemed him fit enough to walk outside, she brought simple clothing from the alms cupboard—a linen shirt, woollen tunic and hose, braies, and a sheepskin jacket to protect against the December wind blowing off the North Sea. "They're rather worn," she apologized.

"Better than no clothes at all," he laughed, then saw her blush.

"The boots are your own. We cleaned them."

He tugged them on, feeling only a slight spasm in his ribs. In an effort to ease the tension, he said, "They feel good."

She braced his arm and helped him walk to the knot garden. He could feel the strength in her small fingers as they pressed around his bicep. The weather was cold and the garden barren, but he was happy to be in the fresh air. She shivered involuntarily and he put his arm around her waist to warm her, drawing her close to him. She flinched away, looking around nervously. "Sir," she stammered.

"I'm sorry, Agneta," he replied, cursing himself for a fool. "I wanted to warm you."

But touching her had aroused him, and he couldn't stop. He enfolded her in his arms, pulled her body to his arousal, and rested his forehead on hers. The feel of her breasts against his chest was as he'd imagined it a hundred times. He wanted this woman, and breathed into her ear, "I want to warm you forever."

Feeling his hard body pressed against her, seeing his warm breath on the frigid air, Agneta reddened and pushed him away, mortified in case anyone should see, and shocked too that her own body had responded with sensations she'd never felt before. Despite the chill she was on fire. She should have been outraged. It was blatant, yet enticing. She scurried away in confusion and left him standing alone in the garden.

After that, Agneta avoided accompanying him, and he spent hours outside alone, sitting on a stone bench in the bitter cold wind. She was afraid he would catch a chill if he stayed outdoors too long, but had seen how the long hours of inactivity frayed his nerves if he stayed indoors. He fell into the habit of taking his sword out with him, sitting with it in his lap. As he grew stronger, he practised movements, slicing and thrusting at an imaginary enemy. She winced when he flinched at the lingering pain in his ribs. Though the deep wound to his thigh hampered his stride, it was evident he'd been an agile warrior, a man to be reckoned with.

One day, after Yuletide, he limped in hurriedly from the garden, very excited. "I've remembered my name," he shouted. "I am Caedmon Brice Woolgar."

It surprised her that she was thrilled at his progress and happy for him. "That doesn't sound Scottish to me," she laughed.

"It's good to hear you laugh, Agneta."

She sobered, but he was right. It had been a long time since she had laughed. "I'm relieved for you—but—"

"—But I still sound like a Scot, don't I?"

"*Aye*," she whispered, mocking him. Relieved as she was he'd recalled his name, she still felt uneasy about his identity. "Have you remembered where you're from?"

He took her hand, and she felt the gentleness of his touch, saw the kindness in his eyes. She wanted desperately to believe in his innocence.

"No, but it will come. I'm confident now that it will."

That night, in her dormitory, she prayed, "Dear Lord, I'm confused about this man. I pray my feelings not turn to hatred, if he's a Scot. Help me. *Kyrie eleison.*"

***

Two days later, Caedmon sat in the garden bemoaning his ludicrous fate. His heart was heavy. He would have to tell a woman he was drawn to what he'd recalled, and it would hurt her. He went back inside and sat on the edge of the pallet, bracing his feet on the stone floor, his thighs tense. The injured muscle throbbed. Agneta looked up from the patient she and Brother Manton were tending.

He strove to sound more confident in the outcome than he felt. "Agneta, may I speak with you?"

She nodded and approached him. "You sound serious and your tone is formal. I won't like what you have to say, will I?" she asked nervously.

He was afraid to share with her the memories that had rushed back. The tapestry had rewoven itself into an image he'd rather forget. "Agneta, I need to tell you some things I've recalled. My name *is* Caedmon Woolgar. I'm the son of Lady Ascha Woolgar. I was named for my father who died at Hastings, fighting against the Conqueror."

"You're a Saxon then?" she whispered hopefully, swaying slightly towards him.

He wished she would look at him. "Aye, but I was born in Scotland. My mother lived in Ruyton in England, in the Welsh Marches. She was alone, expecting a child. She had a brother, Gareth, who decided to flee to Scotland. She went with him. They couldn't abide living under Norman rule. Then King Malcolm married the Saxon princess, Margaret, Edgar the Aetheling's sister. They nurtured Saxons at their Court in Edwinesburh."

She moved away. "I'm nervous. That's why you speak like a Scot. You were born there."

"Aye, but I've remained a proud Saxon. However, I need to tell you—I fought on the side of the Scots in the battle here. We've naturally been their allies against the Normans."

He held his breath. She was silent. Perhaps she knew what he had to tell her next. He took her hand in his. His heart thudded so loudly he was sure she could hear it. "I also need to tell you, Agneta, with deep regret, that I took part in the raid on Bolton."

"No," she gasped with an anguished sob, looking directly into his eyes for the first time. "Why, why would you do such a thing?"

She pulled her hand away from his firm grasp, but he wouldn't let go. He'd longed to look into the depths of those intriguing eyes, but now he was ashamed and had to look away from the condemnation and hatred burning there.

Forcing himself to keep his voice low, he ground out, "Agneta, I'm a landless Saxon knight living in Scotland with nothing to offer to anyone. I'd hoped if the Scots were successful in wresting some of the border lands from the English, I might benefit from a reward of land for myself, for my heirs. It's the reason many men take up arms. Agneta, I swear, on my honor, I killed no one that day. I plundered, I destroyed, I created mayhem, but I didn't kill. The bloodlust sickened me. I didn't know it was a Saxon manor. You must believe me."

Her face reddened with anger, and through her tears she stammered, "Your honor? Whether you struck the fatal blows or not matters little. You were there. You abetted the crime."

Suddenly, the color drained from her face, and in a whisper so low he barely heard, she said, "I saw you. It was you. You looked up at me, you and your companion. I was in the barn."

His heart broke. Should he fall to his knees and beg her forgiveness? She would deny him that. He let go of her hand.

She stood and lifted the edge of her habit slightly, but stopped suddenly and turned. "It would be better for you to leave. You're fit enough to ride. People here will be angry when they find out who you are. Go to the kitchens, ask for food for your journey. Your horse has been taken care of in the stables."

"I'll go, Agneta, but—" he faltered, stunned by the ice in her voice. "I don't want to leave you. You've become important to me. I owe you my life."

"What do you expect me to do? Leave with you? I'm a nun, Caedmon Woolgar, Saxon traitor. I'm the daughter of a family you had a hand in annihilating. Go now. I can't bear to look at you any longer. I hate the sight of you."

She fled.

Dazed, Caedmon did as she'd commanded. He slowly gathered up his belongings from under the pallet, made his way to the kitchens for provisions, saddled his horse and rode out towards Scotland and a New Year.

CHAPTER SIX

Agneta filled Caedmon's' thoughts as he rode as fast as his weakened condition would allow to Edwinesburh, to reunite with his mother. She would be devastated to believe he'd died in battle. She had no other relatives, and had devoted her life to his upbringing.

The few people he saw in the desolate winter landscape fled from him, until he reached Lothian. After several gruelling days in the saddle, he rode into the courtyard of the only home he'd ever known, his mother's house in Edwinesburh, the house she'd inherited from her brother, Gareth. A hue and cry went up from the servants, one of whom ran inside to tell Lady Woolgar.

"Caedmon," she cried, as she burst from the house. He limped to embrace her, his lacerated leg stiff from riding. "Caedmon, you're alive. I knew you were. I had faith you would return. I never lost hope, even when we heard the devastating news of King Malcolm's death. His poor saintly Queen Margaret died of a broken heart, only a sennight later. To lose her son at the same time—"

She laid her head on his chest and sobbed, and he comforted her. He loved his mother dearly.

"Where did you get those clothes, Caedmon? Are you limping? Where have you been all this time? Oh dear, I'm rambling. It's such a relief to see you. I thought I'd lost you."

He put his arm around her shoulder. "It's a long story, Mother. I'm relieved to be home. I'll tell you about it over dinner. I'm looking forward to a good meal."

His mother wrinkled her nose and smiled. "Let's get you into a bath, and you can change into some decent clothing. Now we have reason to welcome the New Year."

They walked into the house, her arm linked in his. He smoothed his free hand over the sheepskin jacket, suddenly reluctant to remove it.

When he came to his chamber, conflicting emotions assailed him. He was overjoyed to be back in the safety and comfort of the room he'd slept in since he was a child. But without Agneta, it seemed empty.

Enid, the maid who'd accompanied Ascha from England many years ago, ordered the other servants about, chivvying them to hurry with Caedmon's bath water, smiling broadly, obviously delighted to see him home.

After bathing, Caedmon joined his mother for dinner. He told her about the battle at Alnwick and what had happened to him afterwards. He mentioned Agneta, but referred to her as *Sister Agneta* and said nothing about his feelings for her. Nor did he mention the connection to the raid on Bolton. Did his perceptive mother sense there was something he wasn't telling her?

Ascha raised her finger to her own temple and traced a line to her chin. "The new scar makes you look like a scoundrel," she teased. "You'll have more beautiful Saxon girls lusting after you."

Caedmon winced at her reference to his reputation with women. Could he help it if they found him attractive? It was ironic that the one woman he ached for—

He stared at his food for a while, then suddenly blurted out, "Mother, did you—did you love my father?"

Ascha was taken aback. Not only had she not been in love with her dead husband, he wasn't the man who'd fathered Caedmon. But her son didn't know this, didn't know he'd been conceived during a brief but treasured encounter she'd experienced with a man betrothed to another, a man she'd fallen in love with at first sight, but could never have. A Norman Earl.

Her husband had been an insensitive brute who had died at Hastings. Caedmon Brice Woolgar was the living image of his real father, an everyday reminder of her joy and her shame and she thanked God he'd met neither his supposed sire nor his actual one.

Unable to give him a Norman name, she had named him for her dead husband, in order to further the belief among the exiled Saxon community that he was indeed the son of a Saxon hero. But she had given him the second name *Brice*, which in her language meant *son of a nobleman*, and she smiled inwardly when she thought of how cleverly she had acknowledged his real lineage, that of the Montbryce family.

She was cautious in her reply. Why had her son asked such a question? She wondered about the nun he'd mentioned with such glowing words, but resolved not to lie to him. "Sir Caedmon fell at Hastings," she said. "We weren't together long. Most people of noble birth don't marry for love. Why do you ask? Are you in love?"

"I don't know if I'm in love, Mother. I only know I've met a beautiful woman I can't imagine living without."

Ascha dawdled over her food, suddenly finding it unappetizing. "Is she free, Caedmon? Free to spend her life with you?" She was desperately afraid for him, not wanting him to live the aching existence she'd lived, destined never to be with the one he loved.

He took a deep breath. "She's a nun."

"Agneta?"

He nodded. "Aye. You're right. Typical of me to want something I can't have. But she's a novice only. She hasn't taken her final vows, and is only becoming a nun because she has no choice." He gradually told his mother the whole story about Agneta, including that she'd seen him at Bolton.

Ascha felt the tears well. "Caedmon, you can't spend your life pining for something out of reach."

As I have.

"She may not share your feelings, and your role in her parents' demise will make her resent you. When you told me about that ill-fated raid I was afraid it would have dire consequences."

Caedmon too seemed to have lost interest in his food. He pushed his chair away from the table. "There must be a way."

"There are many beautiful Saxon girls here and, I'm sorry to say, not many young Saxon men after Alnwick."

That seemed to jolt her son from his thoughts. He leaned forward. "Who survived? Who came back? Leofric?"

Ascha fiddled with the edges of her bread trencher. "Yes— Leofric returned—but—well, you'll see him soon at the New Year's festivities, such as they are this tragic year."

"You say Queen Margaret died too? Who rules Scotland now?"

Ascha shook her head. "King Malcolm's brother, Donald, immediately laid siege to Edwinesburh and seized the throne, then exiled Malcolm and Margaret's sons. He wants to rid Scotland of what he calls *the English*. It's enough to keep all Saxons here awake at nights."

Caedmon's face registered surprise. "Donald? But he must be an old man by now? And unmarried, as I recall?"

"Yes, three score years, and no heirs. More trouble ahead. They call him *Domnall Bán*, Donald the Fair."

***

"Is it absolutely necessary we attend these New Year festivities tonight?" Caedmon asked for the third time.

Lady Ascha sighed, as Enid helped her don her cloak. "Yes, it's necessary. Please, Caedmon, for my sake. You were lost and now you're found. Let your fellow Saxons, including me, rejoice in that small victory. We've all lost a great deal. These are uncertain times and a piece of good news gladdens the heart."

Caedmon shuffled his feet. "I know. It's that I would rather—"

Ascha put her hand on his arm. "You would rather stay home and pine for your Agneta. There will be many young women happy to see you tonight. They'll take your mind off Agneta. You need to get on with life and start a family."

He shrugged. "It will be good to see Leofric. He'll be there, won't he?"

Ascha hesitated. "Yes, but he's changed, Caedmon. Be prepared. He didn't return whole from Alnwick. I don't want to say too much. He's your friend. He'll be glad to see you."

Caedmon nodded. "It's a pity the celebrations aren't being held at Court."

Enid fastened Ascha's cloak around her. "Thank you, Enid. It's a hostile place for us now, unfortunately. We'll all feel safer and more welcome at the home of the Beasants. They have plenty of room for the few of us that are left."

The torchbearers were waiting, sent from the Beasants to accompany them, and they made their way on foot the short distance to their destination.

Caedmon couldn't conceal his shock when he saw his old friend, Leofric Deacon. The once burly, jovial and handsome lad had become a gaunt shadow of his former self. His right ear was gone, his right eye covered by a patch. The mutilated side of his face bore a thick, heavy scar from his hairline, through his eyebrow to his chin. It had twisted his mouth into a permanent grimace.

"Leofric, old friend," Caedmon rasped, extending his hand.

Leofric's gloved right hand remained at his side, but he offered his left to Caedmon. "Sorry, Caedmon, my right hand doesn't work well. *Godemite*, it's good to see you, even with one eye."

The two men embraced. Caedmon could barely speak, imagining the horror his friend had suffered. "Leofric," he managed. "How did you survive these wounds and get back here?"

"I was lucky. Eivind helped me. His injuries weren't as serious. You'll see him later, I'm sure. He looked for you without success, and, to be frank, I was in no fit state."

"I was found under another man's body. Wyvern drew their attention to me. What happened to your hand?"

Leofric shrugged. "Burns. You don't want to see. It's not a pretty sight. Ah, here comes your mother, with Kendra Beasant in tow. Lady Ascha will no doubt be busy trying to find a wife for you."

Caedmon turned his mouth down at the corners and shook his head. "I'm not interested in Kendra."

Leofric slapped Caedmon on the back and chuckled. "Why not? She's a beauty. Look at those breasts! What I wouldn't give to be suckling on those, wrapped in her long blonde tresses. She always did prefer you."

"Leofric, how nice to see you," Lady Ascha said when she and her companion reached them.

Leofric nodded and kissed Lady Ascha's hand. "Lady Ascha."

"Caedmon, you remember Lady Kendra?"

Caedmon turned to the well-endowed girl he remembered as empty headed. He forced a smile. "Yes, of course. Lady Kendra, I'm glad to see you again."

Kendra gave him her hand and curtseyed. He bowed and helped her to rise. When she didn't remove her hand from his, he felt obliged to give it a perfunctory kiss. She blushed. "We're all ecstatic to see you safely returned, Sir Caedmon. When we believed you were dead, it was a great loss for all Saxons. I myself cried every night for sennights."

She still hadn't removed her hand and her bountiful breasts were thrust towards him. Leofric stifled a chuckle. "I'm flattered, Lady Kendra. I'm sure there was much weeping for all the brave Saxon knights who didn't return from Northumbria."

He dropped Kendra's hand and turned to his friend. "Leofric, who else came back?"

He didn't want to continue the conversation with Kendra. He was sorry to disappoint his mother, but he would much prefer to talk with Leofric and seek out old comrades. However, Lady Kendra wasn't easily put off. "Eivind Brede, of course. He was heroic, dragging poor Leofric back."

Leofric winced. His mother reddened.

"Bernhard Blakemore has a nasty scar, though not as bad as Leofric's, and Dalston Garthside seems to have gone a little bit mad. Thomas Chadwicke's broken arm wasn't set right and looks strange, and—"

"Yes, Lady Kendra," Ascha interrupted. "I'm sure Leofric will make sure Caedmon sees his old comrades again. They too will be anxious to see him. Here comes Eivind now."

Thank you mother.

Eivind strode over to Caedmon and embraced him warmly. "Caedmon. *Oli Crosse.* It's good to see you."

Caedmon slapped his old friend on the back. "Eivind. I never thought to see your ugly face again."

"Aye. Uglier now with this cursed scar. But I was lucky." He glanced at Leofric. "I'm sorry we left you behind, Caedmon. We truly thought you must be dead. We didn't have much time to hunt for you. The Normans were making sure no survivors left that bloody field. If it hadn't been for the heavy mist, none of us would have made it back."

Caedmon nodded. "I understand, Eivind. I wouldn't have expected you to risk your lives looking for me."

"How did you manage to survive?"

Caedmon told the story of how he'd been found and nursed back to health. Kendra made her excuses part way through the story, giving the excuse she had to greet guests as her father's hostess. Ascha shook her head and followed her.

Caedmon breathed a sigh of relief and winked at Leofric. "Did anyone see Malcolm fall?"

They all looked at their feet.

"No, but I saw his son Edward die at the hands of the Earl," Leofric murmured. "I was distraught and took my attention off protecting myself, and—well—you see the results. Anyway, back to this nun you talked about in such glowing terms."

Caedmon felt his face redden. "She was a special person. If she wasn't a nun—"

"Ho, ho. Our friend Caedmon has fallen in love at last."

CHAPTER SEVEN

It seemed to Caedmon his mother would never run out of candidates for him to consider as his wife. For four months she arranged *chance* meetings. He'd known these women for years, grown up with most of them, and his heart told him he didn't want to spend his life with any of them.

Lady Ascha often voiced her opinions of his attitude at table as they supped. "But they were girls then, Caedmon. They're women now. Some of them lovely women. Kendra isn't suitable, but Aediva Newberry cares for you, and—"

Caedmon bristled. "Mother, please. Aediva is sweet. She will make someone a wonderful wife, but that someone isn't me. Please stop trying to marry me off."

Ascha ate some of her pigeon pie. He expected she would try again. "I don't want you to be alone, Caedmon. I won't be here forever."

"I would rather be alone than spend my life with a woman I don't care for."

"But you care for Aediva."

The pie had suddenly lost its taste. "Not that way."

"You mean the way you care for Agneta, your little nun?"

"Aye," he replied wistfully, excusing himself from the table.

He complained to Leofric one day as they shared a jug of ale.

"Tell someone who cares," his friend retorted jovially. "You're surrounded by beautiful women, all lusting for you and you don't want any of them. None of them take a second look at me. I'm too repulsive. No woman wants to wed a monster."

Caedmon felt great sorrow for his friend, who'd been such a handsome knight, before Alnwick.

Perhaps I'm being too selfish, wanting too much. But—Agneta.

"I know, I'm selfish, but Agneta is special."

"You spent little time with her, during most of which you didn't know your own name. From what you've told me, she isn't likely to want to marry you after what we did at Bolton."

Leofric was the only other person aware Agneta had seen them at Kirkthwaite Hall.

The alehouse was full and noisy, and Caedmon had to shout to be heard. "I helped to destroy her life, Leofric. I owe her."

Leofric shook his head, and cupped his hand to his mouth. "But that doesn't mean you have to marry her."

Suddenly there was a lull in the noise. People were staring at them. Caedmon gazed into his tankard, feeling his face redden. "I don't want anyone else. It's much more than that. She haunts my dreams. I'm obsessed with her." He took a long swig of his ale.

"I dream of a woman too," Leofric said wistfully, then stopped, and looked warily at Caedmon, whose attention was abruptly on him.

"Who?"

"It's of no importance. It was before—this." He indicated his disfigurement with his gloved hand.

"Did she care for you—before?"

"Aye. But that's the past. This is the reality. I've come to accept I'll be alone. But *you* don't have to be. Marry one of these hearty Saxon wenches, and live happily ever after. I'll be *Uncle* Leofric to your many offspring." He clinked his tankard against Caedmon's.

"I suppose—"

Their conversation was interrupted by loud shouts from the street. "Siege! An army at the gates! Normans!"

The two friends jumped to their feet and ran out of the alehouse. Panicked people scattered hither and thither. Caedmon grabbed a boy by the arm as he ran by. "What's the alarm? What's happening?"

The lad tried to pull away, on the verge of tears. "The city's under siege. Let me go, I beg you, sir."

Caedmon clamped his hand tighter. "Be calm. Tell me who is laying siege." He already had an idea who it might be. Rumors had been rampant for weeks that one of Malcolm *Cenn Mór's* sons would try to wrest the throne from Donald *Bán*.

"They say it's Duncan, son of our good King Malcolm, and his first Queen, Ingibiorg. He has a mighty army with him, Normans and Northumbrians."

"Normans?" Leofric exclaimed.

"Northumbrians?" Caedmon said quietly. He let go of the boy's arm and the urchin sped away. "We'll go to my mother's house, Leofric. Saxons must decide what to do in the face of this new threat. Our decisions now could be crucial to our future here. Edwinesburh has suddenly become a more dangerous place."

When they arrived home, Enid told them Lady Ascha had already gone to the Beasant home where most Saxons were gathering. They followed her there.

Edgar Beasant addressed a restive crowd. "It appears Duncan is in league with his half brother, Edmund, son of Malcolm *Cenn Mór* and Margaret. As you know, Edmund fled to England when Donald *Bán* seized the throne. Now King William Rufus is aiding him in this bid to wrest the throne from Donald."

Caedmon wished he could get his mother's attention across the crowded room. "This is a kettle of stinking fish," he exclaimed to Leofric. "Malcolm and Rufus were bitter enemies, and now Rufus is helping Malcolm's two sons."

"Where does that leave us?" Leofric wondered aloud.

Beasant had continued speaking. "It's my opinion that for the moment we do nothing. The siege may not be successful. If Duncan and Edmund do succeed in taking the throne from Donald *Bán*, I suggest we form an emissary committee to convey our assurance of support."

"Aye," everyone shouted.

"I will volunteer to head the Emissary Committee, but we need younger men, young knights."

"Caedmon Woolgar," someone shouted.

Caedmon's mother scanned the hall for a glimpse of him.

"Sir Caedmon, are you willing?" Beasant asked.

Ascha's eyes found his. She hesitated, then nodded slightly.

He nodded back, heartened by the pride in her eyes. "Aye. Willing. I propose Sir Leofric Deacon, a knight who sacrificed much for Duncan and Edmund's father, Malcolm *Cenn Mór*.

"Sir Leofric, are you willing?"

Leofric didn't hesitate, only nodded to Caedmon. "Aye. Willing."

"Any other names to propose?"

There was a pause. People murmured quietly, shaking heads.

"Hearing none, settled then. Sir Caedmon and Sir Leofric. If you please. My library, forthwith."

Caedmon liked the look of pride on Leofric's face, instead of the desolation he usually saw there.

***

After Caedmon's departure, life in the convent became a numbing, monotonous round for Agneta. She'd previously taken secret delight in being able to use her work in the Infirmary as an excuse not to attend all the recitations of divine office required of the other novices. Now, despite the fact she'd been appointed Infirmarian and given full control, she determined to be present at all the services, unless it was a matter of life and death in the Infirmary.

She was determined to banish thoughts of Caedmon from her life. First up for Lauds at two hours after midnight, she went back to her pallet in the dormitory after that, until first light when she rose for a breakfast of bread and ale. If all was in order in the Infirmary, she offered assistance to the Sacrist with the books, vestments and vessels.

After Prime she met with other nuns in the chapter house where chapters from the Bible or the writings of saints were read out. Then it was Tierce, after which she worked in the hospital, or helped with the washing or cooking. She learned how to make wine, ale and honey, and as the spring of the Year of Our Lord One Thousand and Ninety Four arrived, assisted with the planting of vegetables and herbs.

She often struggled to stay awake during the service of Sext at midday, but the dinner served after that revived her somewhat, and she went back to work until Nones, three hours later, then Vespers two hours after that, and finally Compline. She rarely had any idea of what was served at the light supper served between Nones and Vespers.

As the days passed, the round became a daily grind, Lauds, breakfast, work, Prime, work, Tierce, work, Nones, Vespers, work, Compline, work, work, work, sleep, work. After Compline she collapsed, exhausted, onto her pallet. She came to an understanding of why nuns were detached. They were too numbed by fatigue to feel anything.

Yet, every night, Caedmon came to her.

I want to warm you forever.

He pulled her body against his.

I have to tell you—I took part in the raid on Bolton.

In her dreams he cradled her dead brother, practiced with his sword, held his helmet on his belly, crowded her in the oxcart, breathed his warmth breath on her, brushed his lips against hers, looked up at her hiding place in the barn.

It's good to hear you laugh, Agneta.

The memory of his husky voice washed over her. "I'll never laugh again," she whimpered, awakened once more by her dreams, curling up, hugging her body, trying to get back to sleep.

She was ashamed when she dreamed of Caedmon touching her, holding her, stroking her hair. Sometimes his presence felt real enough that her own sighs woke her up.

Pray God no one heard me.

She fought to still the aching throb arching into her core, and often awoke hot with shame, her hand between her legs, her pillow wet with tears of longing. Whenever she shaved a patient, her hand shook and she had to abandon the task, often to Brother Manton. She craved Caedmon's return, and hated herself and him for it.

"You look unwell, Sister Agneta," Brother Manton whispered to her one day, keeping his eyes on the patient they were tending.

"I didn't get much sleep last night," she replied.

The monk shook his head. "It's more than that, isn't it child? You're unhappy here."

"I've nowhere else to go."

"That's not a reason to take final vows," the old man whispered softly.

Agneta felt her whole body tense. She wanted to scream, but murmured, "I'm trying my best, brother. I'm trying to be a good nun."

"You should speak to Mother Superior. She can perhaps help you with whatever is making you unhappy."

Agneta shook her head, panic in her eyes. "No, she can't help me."

"It's the Saxon knight, isn't it?" There was no accusation in the monk's voice.

Oh God, is it so obvious?

She gasped and their eyes met for the briefest moment. He'd seen the truth. She felt the tears welling.

"I will pray for you, Agneta."

"Thank you, Brother Manton. Please excuse me, I must see to the child with the broken arm."

CHAPTER EIGHT

"Your Majesty." Edgar Beasant bowed low to the new King, Duncan. He effected a slightly less deferential bow to Duncan's half-brother, seated in the lesser throne beside Duncan's. "My Lord Edmund."

He turned back to Duncan. "May I introduce my comrades who have accompanied me on this mission from the Saxon community to bring our good wishes on your accession to the throne?"

"Proceed," Duncan replied. Edmund nodded.

Edgar indicated the two knights who'd accompanied him. "Sir Caedmon Woolgar and Sir Leofric Deacon are both Saxons born in Scotland after their parents fled the Conqueror. Both fought valiantly for your Father, King Malcolm *Cenn Mór* at the Battle of Alnwick, and, as you see, both bear the scars of their sacrifices for Scotland.

While Edgar talked, Caedmon watched the new King Duncan. He seemed ill-at-ease and obviously aware of his half-brother seated beside him. Though they shared the same father, they didn't look alike. Caedmon wondered if they trusted each other. What had they done with their uncle, Donald the Fair, whom they'd deposed?

When his own name was mentioned Caedmon bowed with great deference, aware his actions and those of Leofric and Edgar, would have an impact on the exiled Saxon community. As Edgar continued to extol the loyalty of the Saxons, Caedmon sensed Edmund growing impatient and suddenly King Duncan raised his hand.

"Enough, Sir Edgar. We're already aware of your efforts over the years on behalf of my Father. Sir Caedmon, Sir Leofric, we thank you for your bravery and your sacrifices for Scotland. However, we must also respect the feelings of our new allies, King William Rufus and the Northumbrians who have aided us to regain the throne. We must have assurances there will be no further attacks by Saxons against Norman holdings and interests."

"I, like my fellow Saxons, seek only to protect the interests of Scotland, the land that has afforded us protection since the Conquest," Caedmon replied.

"Aye, well, we all seek to protect Scotland's interests," Edmund suddenly interjected. "We need your oath there will be no attacks against Normans."

Caedmon raged inwardly, but he had no choice, any more than the two royal princes who sat before him. What price had Rufus exacted for his support?

"On behalf of the Saxon community, I swear there will be no attacks on Norman interests and holdings," Edgar solemnly intoned, his hand on his heart.

They were dismissed. As they left, Caedmon whispered to Leofric, "I predict the reign of Duncan the Second to be a short one."

***

As the days blurred into each other, Agneta lost track of how old she was. She wouldn't be required to make her final vows until she reached her majority, but exactly when that would be wasn't clear in her mind. Since she didn't want to think about the finality of that event, she made no great effort to clear the fog. She was grimly certain Mother Superior had the matter in hand.

One day, in the early autumn, a man came to the infirmary with a deep sword wound to his upper arm. It wasn't a new wound, but had been poorly treated and there were signs of putrefaction. He was feverish. Agneta quickly had him assigned to a pallet and she and her helpers tended him.

"Where did this happen? This blow came close to cleaving your arm in two. Who sewed your wound?" she asked him.

"Edwinesburh," he rasped. "One of my comrades did the stitching, just so's I could get back home."

"You're from Northumbria?"

The man nodded, wincing at the pain.

"What were you doing in Scotland?"

The man looked around nervously, then seemed reassured. "Helped with the siege."

Agneta's had to wipe her sweaty palms on her habit. "Siege?"

He nodded. "Went with Rufus's army to help depose King Donald."

She swallowed hard. "Was the siege successful?" Her hands shook and she had to stop her ministrations. She saw the questioning look of concern in Mayda's eyes.

"Are you all right? You look like you might swoon," the novice whispered.

Agneta nodded, and wiped her brow with her sleeve.

The injured man continued, "Duncan's king now, but more or less shares the throne with his half-brother, Edmund. They're the sons of King Malcolm, you know, the one killed near here, at Alnwick."

To Agneta's surprise, it was Mayda who asked, "But you say the Normans helped them capture the throne?"

The man nodded, gritting his teeth against the pain. Agneta could see he was close to swooning as they laved the putrefaction from his wound.

"Was it a long siege? Did many die?" she stammered.

He had to wait for the spasm of pain to pass. "No, it was enough that we threatened. Donald the Fair couldn't withstand our army and gave up quick. Saved his own neck. I was unlucky. Too cocksure of our success."

Agneta had to get away, before she did indeed fall to the stone floor. Caedmon wouldn't sit idly by if he had a cause to fight for and he hated Normans. "Sister Mayda can finish taking care of you. Hopefully, the wound will heal properly now. Watch his fever, Mayda," she whispered, unwilling to look her friend in the eye. She fled to the sanctuary of the chapel, and fell to her knees.

"*Pater Noster*," she sobbed. "Please—please protect him. Keep him alive. I can't bear the thought he might be dead. Please."

CHAPTER NINE

"Many Saxons have already left, mother. We must do the same. This country is no longer safe for us. We have no future here. Duncan's flimsy hold on the crown won't last now that his foreign allies have had to return to their own lands to put down a rebellion."

"You're right, Caedmon. I'm too old to start again," Lady Ascha replied sadly, slumped in a chair. "This house has come to be home for me."

"But you have another home. In Ruyton. We must go there."

Ascha shook her head, apparently unwilling to think about it, but said, "Shelfhoc is your birthright, Caedmon. I suppose you're right. I've been away for a long time, and the memories—"

He took his mother's hand, and bent his knees to hunker down beside her. "It won't be easy. You already know it's a long, hard journey. But I'll be there to help you and Leofric has already said he'll accompany us. There's no reason for him to stay, now both his parents are gone. I believe many more will want to accompany us. We'll seek shelter in monasteries and abbeys along the way. We can make a new life in the Marches. From what I hear, your *valiant* Norman protector, the Earl of Ellesmere has the area under control, and you've said yourself his stewards have kept up Shelfhoc."

"Yes," Ascha whispered.

"It's ironic, isn't it? The Normans stole everything from us, yet it's thanks to a Norman we have a manor to return to in England. I'll set about organizing our departure."

Ascha looked around, her eyes wandering over the furnishings, the drapery, the warm wooden panelling. "What about this house? Can we sell it?"

Caedmon clenched his jaw. This was the only home he'd ever known. "We can try. I'll speak to some people at Court. Though in these unsettled times—"

He pondered the possibilities. "Edgar Beasant *might* be interested. He's decided to stay here, and has mentioned buying a house for Kendra and Eivind, now they're married." He shook his head. "What is Eivind thinking? Being married to Kendra would drive me mad."

"Perhaps he loves her," his mother said.

Caedmon shook his head. "Eivind isn't a man who would marry for love."

"Not like you, my son? Will you not choose a bonnie Saxon girl to take with us as your wife? There are many who would wish you as their husband."

"Mother, there's only one woman I will consider marrying, and that's Agneta."

"But she may have made her final vows already."

He shook his head. "She's not old enough yet. Anyway, when we travel through Northumbria, I'm determined to try to change her mind about me."

"She may not be glad to see you."

"I have to try, if it's only to say a last goodbye."

***

Caedmon and Leofric set about making clandestine arrangements for their departure. The three surviving members of the Brightmore family, Coventina and her mother and aunt, had decided to join the Woolgars in their flight. The three women had come to assist Ascha with packing.

"The morrow will see a twelvemonth passed since Alnwick," Leofric observed, as he and Caedmon were examining the latest charts they'd procured, planning a route. "Hard to believe a year has passed since that bloody day when life changed completely."

"Aye," Caedmon agreed. "And isn't it ironic the same thirteenth day of November is the feast day of Saint Brice?"

He turned to his mother. "Why *did* you pick that as my middle name, mother?"

Lady Ascha reddened, muttered something about having to finish packing, and left abruptly. The elder Brightmore women went with her.

"It's more than a fitting day for us to leave this cursed country, make a fresh start," Enid, Lady Ascha's maidservant said. "I'd better go help your mother."

Caedmon wondered exactly what Enid meant by her unusual outburst, but his thoughts were interrupted.

"You have to admire Enid's loyalty. She's not a young woman and yet she's been willing to follow your mother and serve her for many years."

Caedmon looked at the person who'd spoken. Coventina Brightmore was a shy, quiet girl, not beautiful, but pleasant, with a good figure, and what Leofric described as *voluptuous tits*. It was rare for her to offer an opinion. Caedmon nodded, and then happened to notice Leofric also stared at the girl, clenching his good fist nervously.

I wonder.

"Let's go over the plan again, Leofric," Caedmon suggested.

"What? Oh—yes—the plan. Everyone who is assembled here at dawn will be making the journey. Each traveller has been told they must have their own healthy horse and sufficient provisions for a sennight, at least. There will be only one wagon, which has been generously provided by Edgar Beasant, and each family will be allotted a space in it. No furniture, chattels or the like. Warm winter clothing and boots. Sufficient funds to support your family—well concealed, of course."

"How many have committed?"

"Fifteen."

Caedmon was about to reply when he was interrupted by a commotion, and Eivind Brede burst into the room. Lady Ascha, the Brightmores and Enid followed right behind. "They've butchered Duncan."

Lady Ascha's hand flew to her mouth in shock. "The King?"

"Aye. The treacherous Edmund has joined forces with his uncle, Donald the Fair. They've had Duncan murdered, and Donald the Fair is back on the throne. The old man has named Edmund his heir."

"Rufus won't be happy about all this," Leofric suggested.

"Will we still leave on the morrow?" Lady Ascha asked worriedly.

"We must," Caedmon replied.

I hope my little nun is praying for me.

***

Agneta's patient with the putrified sword slash proved to be an excellent source of information about the goings-on north of the border. He recovered after a fortnight in the Infirmary and she visited him and his family often in their cottage near Alnwick, on the pretext of making sure his wound had not reopened. She always took another novice with her. As she carefully examined the scar, she learned, one cold November morning, about the murder of King Duncan a sennight before.

"Ironic it was on the eve of the twelvemonth anniversary of the battle here, when his father Malcolm and his half-brother died," he told her.

Agneta was startled. "Twelve months? Since Alnwick?"

Oh God. Has it been that long?

"Yes. Feast Day of Saint Brice."

It suddenly came to her she'd been immersed in the ritual of the divine office and paid no attention to which saint they were honoring. Her head spun.

My name is Caedmon Brice Woolgar.

She made a great show of examining the man's scar. "What's happening there now? Has there been bloodshed?"

The man looked at her strangely. "You're mighty interested in all this."

"I have a friend who lives there, a Saxon."

"They say the Saxons are leaving in droves."

"Leaving?"

He nodded. "I expect many will come to Northumbria. The people I'm in contact with are already on their way here. You'll likely be seeing refugees at your Abbey soon."

Agneta could hear her heart pounding in her ears. She rose to her feet unsteadily and bade her patient goodbye.

"His wound seems fine to me. It's long since healed," Mayda suggested as they made their way back on foot to the Abbey.

"Wound? Oh, yes. It's healed well. You're right."

Agneta looked at the threatening clouds and drew her cloak around her.

It was on such a day as this.

As she crossed the very moorland where she'd first seen Caedmon the memory of the sights, sounds and smells of that fateful day assailed her, but the one predominant image was of Caedmon, lying helpless, tied to the pallet, yet exuding strength and power.

Are you an angel?

"Do you think he'll come?"

Agneta stopped abruptly and stared at her fellow novice. "What?"

"Your knight. Will he come?"

Agneta hunched her shoulders against the wind and clutched the cloak. "My knight? I don't know what—"

"Agneta, we all know. We all sense why you're unhappy. None of us can understand why you didn't leave with him."

Agneta found it hard to believe the wail she heard came from her own throat. "I sometimes can't understand it myself," she choked.

Her friend embraced her as she wept. "We must pray for him, Agneta."

"I pray for him, but I don't know what to do if he comes."

They stood for long minutes, buffeted by the cold wind, then walked back, arm in arm to the Abbey. Thank goodness her friend said nothing more.

As if the mercenary's words were prophetic, there were indeed newcomers seeking sanctuary at the fledgling Abbey when they arrived back. Mayda squeezed Agneta's hand in reassurance as they entered the Infirmary. "Trust in God, Agneta."

There were ten refugees, all cold, hungry and dirty. Caedmon wasn't among them. The nuns offered food and shelter for the night. The group intended to move on the next day, bound for Sussex.

"You've a long journey ahead of you," she said to one of the older women, determined not to ask about Caedmon.

"Do you have any news of a knight named Caedmon Woolgar?"

Agneta looked daggers at Mayda.

The woman nodded. "Yes, I know his mother, Lady Ascha. My daughter knows Sir Caedmon. In fact she never stops talking about him. He's a handsome devil, a hero returned from the dead, so to speak. All the young women have set their cap at him. The Woolgars were still there when we left, but they intend to flee."

Mayda smiled at Agneta, but it did nothing to calm the conflicting feelings racing through her. Caedmon probably had a thousand women falling at his feet. Why should she care? "So, he's not married, this Sir Caedmon?" She wanted to kick herself.

"No, unless he married someone in the last few days. Many of those fleeing did that, for the sake of propriety. Sweethearts didn't want to be left behind. It's been a terrible time. Reminds me of when we fled the Conqueror, all those years ago."

Agneta could see the woman had reached the limit of her endurance, and didn't envy her the long journey to Sussex. "Sleep now. You need your rest."

The group left after Prime the following day. Agneta watched the horizon, willing more refugees to appear, but none came, until the day after.

***

"How far are we from the Abbey at Alnwick now, Caedmon?" Lady Ascha asked wearily.

"We'll be there in about two hours," he replied curtly.

Ascha bit her lip. "What's your plan?"

He grimaced. "I'll beg."

"I have a better plan."

He reined his horse and rode back to where she'd stopped. He could see she was worn out. She'd shown a moment of tearful elation and gasped when he'd told her they'd crossed into England an hour earlier. The whole group had come to a halt, dismounted and gathered for a moment of prayer. But now the strain of long hours in the saddle showed in them all.

They'd been on the road from Scotland for ten days. It had taken them longer than anticipated, problems with the wagon slowing them down. Then, Coventina's mother had become unwell and the Brightmores had to stay behind at a monastery until she recovered. Leofric had volunteered to remain with them, prompting Caedmon to wonder again about his friend's relationship with the girl. Leofric's distorted face had given nothing away when Caedmon smiled at him and arched his eyebrows.

Now, he stood in the stirrups, taking advantage of the pause in their journey to rub his sore saddle muscles. "Plan? What are you talking about?"

"We have money, Caedmon." She patted her belly, where the money belt she wore made her look rounder than she was. The person of an older woman had been deemed the best hiding place for the proceeds of the sale of the house to Edgar.

He looked at her blankly. "I don't understand."

"Didn't you tell me Alnwick is an unfinished Abbey?"

54

"Aye—but—"

She wagged her finger at him. "My son, I'd wager there isn't an Abbey, monastery, convent, priory or church in the whole of England that has sufficient money for its needs. All those mouths to feed, buildings to keep up, good works to be undertaken."

Caedmon now understood.

She smiled and continued. "The Abbey near Alnwick, in addition to all those expenses, must find funds for building a great edifice."

He smiled. "You're right. I remember talk when I was here of how difficult it was to keep the construction going. When money ran out, the work stopped."

Ascha raised one foot, and appeared to be studying the toe of her boot. "How long do you estimate it will take to finish, if they go on at the present rate?"

He rubbed his chin. "Fifty years, at least."

"This Abbey has something you want, does it not?"

"Aye—but if she ever found out—"

"Who will tell her? You said yourself she doesn't want to become a nun. You can offer her a better life, at Ruyton."

He looked his mother in the eye. "You would give me your money for this?"

Ascha smiled. "Caedmon, money means nothing to me compared with your happiness. It's obvious you're smitten with this woman. I'm selfish. I can't be happy if you're unhappy."

Though he longed to see Agneta again, Caedmon had been feeling pessimistic about the reunion, but now his heart sang with renewed hope. He dismounted and went to kiss his mother's trembling hand. "My gracious Lady Ascha Woolgar, whatever did I do to deserve a mother like you? I thank you from the bottom of my heart."

She shifted nervously in the side saddle. "It would be better if I speak with the Superior. Woman to woman."

"I agree. I might make a detour, to a nearby lodging house, when we get closer. I'll catch up."

***

As she entered Vespers, Agneta heard the Almoner welcoming new refugees. Her feet itched to run out, to see if Caedmon was among them. All through the office, she fidgeted, alternating between hope and dread. Instead of the *Magnificat*, she recited her familiar exhortation regarding Caedmon's health. Mother Superior looked down her nose at her more than once.

Be still.

As they filed out of the chapel the Almoner gave Mother Superior a message. The woman went off in the direction of her office and didn't join them for supper. Agneta cast a glance at the newcomers who were nodding their grateful thanks to the nuns serving them. No Caedmon. Her heart plummeted. She could barely get the food past her lips.

She noticed one of the older refugees, in the garb of a maidservant, examining the faces of all the nuns with great interest, as if looking for someone. When her eyes caught Agneta's, the woman smiled. She managed to return the smile. After all, this poor woman had undergone a long, difficult journey. No-one in this group was in need of attention in the Infirmary and Agneta had no opportunity to speak to them before entering the chapel for Compline. She thought she heard the Almoner welcoming someone again, but it seemed late for that.

As she left the torment of Compline, the Sacrist whispered a message. "Mother wants to see you. In her office."

"Now?"

"Immediately."

CHAPTER TEN

"I don't understand, Mother. Why am I being denied final vows? You wanted me to become a nun." Agneta was at a loss to comprehend why the stern woman had told her bluntly she wouldn't be making her final vows. Inwardly it was an immense relief. The idea of living out her life in the remote abbey filled her with dread, though she enjoyed tending the sick and injured in the infirmary. But where would she go? What would she do? She had no family to turn to.

The woman's mouth was stern. "I did, my child, I did. But to be a good nun, a woman needs to be detached from worldly things. You've had difficulty with that. You become too involved with people."

"But I—"

The Superior raised her hand. "The decision has been made, my child. Gather your things together, if you wish, and make plans for yourself. You can stay here as long as you need refuge. We won't turn you out to be destitute, but you'll not be joining the community."

Agneta was thunderstruck. She felt the same lonely desolation she had on the day of the raid on her home, and cried herself to sleep that night, desperately trying not to let the other novices hear her sobs.

Mayda appeared at her side. "What's wrong, Agneta?"

"The nuns have rejected me. I'm not to be allowed to make my vows."

Mayda put her arm around Agneta's trembling shoulders. "Oh, Agneta. Why?"

She rested her head on her friend's shoulder. "I don't know. I've tried hard to be a good nun, haven't I?"

Mayda rocked her and she must have fallen asleep, exhausted. She woke before two in the morning and started to dress for Lauds, then remembered and fell back on her pallet, sobbing. At dawn, an elderly nun came for her habit and gave her an outfit of lay clothing. It felt strange to put on the simple chemise and dress. There was no wimple, only a hooded woolen cloak. She suddenly missed the hated coif and hoped her ugly hair would grow quickly.

"Perhaps Mother is right. I care too much about worldly things. She must have noticed how unhappy I've been since Caedmon left. I can't understand why my thoughts keep drifting to a man I should hate."

She decided to go to the garden. Caedmon had found some answers there, perhaps she would too. She sat shivering on the cold stone bench, beneath a leafless willow tree, staring at her hands clasped in her lap. How long had he been there before she felt his presence beside her? She sensed who it was before she looked up. Her heart thudded in her ears.

"What are you doing here, Caedmon?" she asked, struggling to make her frozen legs work as she stood, fretting over her clothing and her hair. She drew the hood tighter.

"I came for you, Agneta."

He moved towards her, but she backed away. "I told you I wouldn't go with you. There's too much hatred between us. I could never love you."

He moved quickly to place his hands on her shoulders, and drew her to his body. "I don't ask for your love. Only that you agree to spend your life with me. I need you. Please say you'll fill my need. I want no other—only you. Say you'll become my wife. You need me."

What to do or say in reply? Her head throbbed as much as her heart. She was cold, and his body radiated heat. He alone had managed to break through the icy numbness in which she'd been encased for too long. The nuns had cast her out. She'd nowhere to go, no one to turn to. Now, suddenly, here was a man she'd been attracted to proposing marriage in the husky voice that beguiled her. She'd lain awake at nights trying to recall the sound of it. But what did he mean about knowing she needed him?

How could he know about the Abbey?

"How do you know my needs, Caedmon?" she asked suspiciously.

He cupped her face in his warm hands. "I know you long for my touch, as I long for yours."

Oh God.

"You long for my lips, as I long for yours." He brushed his thumbs along her quivering lower lip. "You long for my body, as I long for yours." He put his hands back on her shoulders and bent to kiss her, gently at first and then his tongue coaxed her lips. His mouth was warm in the chill air. She'd tried not to dream of his kiss. She couldn't kiss him, wouldn't kiss him, and didn't know how to kiss. He licked the corners of her mouth, nibbled her bottom lip and kissed her again. "Open for me, Agneta," he breathed.

His words washed over her like a warm summer breeze and she was lost. Sighing, she opened to him and shyly put her arms around his neck, arching her body to his, tears streaming down her face. The hood slipped from her head.

He licked the tears from her cheeks, and again put his hands on either side of her face, then ran his fingers lovingly through her hair. The sensation echoed in her toes.

"I knew it. Your hair *is* brown—and short. It's the most beautiful hair I've ever seen." He sighed and leaned his forehead against hers. "Agneta, please say *aye*."

She was relieved he'd uttered no words of love. It could never be a marriage of love. But he was right. They were attracted to each other. Perhaps that could take the place of love. "But where would we dwell, Caedmon? I could never live in Scotland."

"We're bound for my manor in England. My mother tells me it's a beautiful estate with five hides of good land and its own church. It earns a dependable income. It's in Ruyton, in the Welsh Marches. We can ask the Abbot to wed us before we leave. When we get there, I'll make myself known to my mother's protector, the Earl of Ellesmere. Then he can be assured I've returned to take care of the manor myself."

Agneta felt like she was in the grip of mysterious illness, one that had dulled her brain. She was overwhelmed by many conflicting feelings. "I remember you told me a Norman earl is your mother's protector."

"Aye. It seems strange, I know."

Suddenly something he'd said a few moments ago penetrated the fog. "You said *we?*"

"Aye. My mother is with me, and her maidservant, Enid. My friend, Leofric, isn't far behind us with another family, the Brightmores. And we've travelled part of the way with two other families bound for Kent."

She had a man embracing her who was the embodiment of masculine beauty, a man who was what women dreamed a knight should be. He was begging her to marry him, but she understood, from what her mother had told her of men, that they were driven by needs different from a woman's. Ragna Kirkthwaite had often boasted her husband still loved her and was faithful, even after the years and the birth of three children had taken their toll. But she'd cautioned Agneta not to expect that in a man. It was wise to be prepared for a man's eye to wander, once he tired of his wife.

She'd seen only the kind, gentle side of Caedmon, but he had the heart of a warrior. Look what he'd done at Bolton. Warriors were hardened men. Caedmon burned with hatred for Normans, as her desire for vengeance made her loath the Scots. Would hatred bind them together? She had to make a decision. She had no trust in men, but—

"I will marry you, Caedmon," she whispered, relieved to be rescued, but resenting she had no choice.

He picked her up, laughing and whooping, and twirled her around until they were both dizzy.

"Caedmon, this is a nunnery."

"It's of no import to me!"

She managed a smile, her heart lifting to see him exhilarated. Perhaps he did care for her?

"I love to see you smile," he said with a grin. "Come, I want my mother to meet you."

"But my clothes, my hair."

"That won't matter to her. She's anxious to meet you."

He strode off and returned a few minutes later, with an older woman. Her hand rested on his arm. Her bearing bespoke nobility and pride.

"Mother, may I present my betrothed, Lady Agneta Kirkthwaite. Agneta, my mother, Lady Ascha Woolgar."

She heard the pride in his voice. Her first impression of his mother wasn't what she'd expected. The still-beautiful woman greeted her with great warmth, though there was something about her grey eyes—loneliness. Lady Ascha had been a widow since before Caedmon was born. She shuddered at the thought. She saw the love and respect that Caedmon shared with his mother and admired the courage of this woman who had fled to Scotland and raised a child alone.

At least I won't be alone when I marry Caedmon.

"We've spoken with the Abbot, Agneta," Lady Ascha explained. "He has agreed to marry you after banns have been read out three times, but has suggested he'll do it in one day at the Morrow Mass, High Mass and Vespers."

Agneta nodded.

"Now, Caedmon," his mother suggested, "Why don't you take Agneta and introduce her to the others in our party?"

All her new acquaintances attended the ceremony. Agneta had to smile when she recognized Enid as the maidservant who'd been searching the group for her.

Mother Superior forbade any of the novices to attend. She acted as Agneta's sponsor, and Leofric, who'd arrived in time with the Brightmores, stood with Caedmon. Agneta greeted Leofric coolly. She recognized him instantly, despite his disfigurement. This was the man who'd stood at Caedmon's side looking at the barn.

The ceremony seemed to be over quickly and Agneta didn't recall much of what was said or done. Everything was happening too fast. She felt breathless. The one image she would remember was her new husband's smiling face, and his chaste kiss after the Abbot gave permission.

Their meager belongings had been readied for departure, and as she and Caedmon were preparing to leave the Abbey, Agneta was summoned by her Superior. "Come with me, child. I've something to give you."

Once they reached the private office, the woman held out an object wrapped in sacking. Agneta's heart raced. She didn't need to unwrap it. She stepped away. "I prefer not to take it."

"You must take it, Agneta. It can't remain here. It belonged to your grandmother, and your mother. It represents pain and sorrow for you, but sometimes it's good to have a reminder of those things. It's part of your heritage. Something to pass on to your children."

And what will I tell them? My mother took her life with this dagger.

Reluctantly, she took the bundle, but didn't unwrap it. The religious smiled weakly and gave Agneta a perfunctory kiss on each cheek. "Go with God, child."

As she walked back through the cloisters, Agneta remembered how pleased her Superior looked. Caedmon had never questioned why she was no longer wearing a habit when he returned, never asked about her hair being uncovered, or about her vows. "He knew," she whispered. "He knew I'd been shunned. How could he? How could Mother Superior have known he would come?"

When she reached the courtyard, Caedmon's voice interrupted her musings. "I've only the one horse, my love. We'll have to share Wyvern. Will you ride before me?"

"Put this in the saddle bags, please, Caedmon."

He took the bundle she thrust at him, tucked it away, and eased back in the saddle, to make room for her.

"Where are the others?" she asked.

"You and I will go to a nearby lodging house for our wedding night. We'll return here on the morrow and all travel south together."

As they rode away from the fledgling Abbey that had been her sanctuary, Agneta turned to look back.

"Tell me your thoughts," Caedmon commanded softly.

She fingered the coarse woolen cloak. Without emotion, she said, "The nuns gave me shelter, clothing, and sustenance, but it was a strict, Spartan life, a life of poverty, without love and affection. The focus of a nun's life is to be the Bride of Christ. But, working in the infirmary, I learned a great deal about healing, and it used to bring me special privileges. I was appointed Infirmarian after you left."

"Special privileges?"

"I was often excused from the soul destroying monotony of daily masses, prayers and rituals that usually started in the hours just after midnight."

Caedmon laughed. The deep rolling chuckle of his laugh warmed her.

They rode in silence for a while. Once again, Caedmon's husky voice broke into her reverie as he nuzzled her neck. "It's a good thing we're going a short distance to the lodging house today, Agneta. It's sweet torture to feel your body pressed against me in the saddle. But, you seem preoccupied?"

She blushed. She'd striven to ignore the evidence of his arousal by not allowing their bodies to touch, but that had become a back-breaking physical impossibility. She decided to face him with her concerns. "We may not have love between us, husband, but I hope we'll have honesty."

He remained silent.

"How did you know they'd turned me out?"

"You're right. We have to have honesty. I made them an offer they couldn't refuse."

"An offer? I don't understand."

Caedmon hesitated before continuing. "Every abbey, priory, and convent needs money to continue its existence. None of them have enough of it. Your Abbey had something I wanted desperately. They wanted money more than they wanted you, so they can continue with their building."

"You bought me?" she screamed, swiveling round in the saddle to face him.

He grimaced. "Agneta, did you want to stay there? Are you telling me you would rather stay there than live with me?"

She turned away from him. "Where did you get the money?"

"My mother gave it to me."

"Did she know what you planned to use it for?" she asked sarcastically.

He reined the horse to a halt. "Look at me, Agneta. I'm not a man who lies to his mother, or tries to bilk her out of money. My mother has made many sacrifices for me and, only God knows why, but she loves me dearly. It was her idea. She gave me the money gladly. It was she who spoke to your Superior."

She felt instantly contrite. "I'm sorry. Your mother is a loving person. I didn't mean—"

"Agneta," he said, urging the horse forward again, "Be happy. I'm happy we're married."

"So am I," she conceded regretfully.

Caedmon cursed inwardly, afraid what he'd told Agneta could interfere with his plans for their wedding night. As soon as the words about the Abbey were out of his mouth he regretted them. They rode the few miles to the large lodging house where he'd made previous arrangements for a private room.

"There are other establishments closer to the Abbey," he explained, after they'd climbed the stairs to their chamber, "But I wanted to make sure the room was spacious, the bed comfortable and vermin free, the food good and the linens clean."

Agneta took off her cloak. "Thank you," she murmured. "It's a nice chamber."

As he shed his warm jacket, he noticed she didn't look at the bed. "My Scottish burr at first made the landlady cautious, but when I explained it was for my bride, she couldn't do enough to accommodate us."

A buxom maid entered a few minutes later, carrying a tray laden with something that smelled delicious. She eyed Caedmon with appreciation, but looked at Agneta's hair with undisguised scorn.

Slumping into a chair, Agneta tried unsuccessfully to fashion a braid at the back of her neck. "I hope my hair grows quickly. It's ugly, and I have only this one dress and chemise, as well as my cloak."

Caedmon went to stand behind her, took her hands from her plaiting, combed his fingers gently through her hair and inhaled the scent of it. "Your hair is the color of chestnuts."

It was good she was in front of him, and couldn't see his body's response to touching her. "We'll get you more clothes when we arrive in Ruyton, if you can manage until then. Though, I'm hoping you'll not be spending much time clothed."

He felt her flush at his suggestive remark. How to get through the supper without tearing off her clothes and taking her right away? The surcoat the nuns had given her wasn't a flattering garment, but it revealed curves the habit had hidden. He sensed his Agneta had a body that would more than fulfill his needs and he longed to join it to his own. He only hoped he could satisfy the passion he was sure was part of her nature. He'd seen it in those incredible eyes.

They ate the tasty food prepared by the cook. The roast chicken was tender and juicy and they had to lick the greasy goodness off their fingers. He looked away when she turned her gaze on him, sure his eyes would betray his burning need to taste her. He poured each of them a goblet of wine, hoping to relax her. She sipped it, peeking at him over the top of the goblet, her long lashes fluttering as she tested the unaccustomed taste. His heart raced and his arousal throbbed. She was an innocent. He would have to be gentle. He'd never bedded a virgin. He prayed he would do this deed right. He'd long dreamt of it.

He rose from the table and took hold of her hands, pulling her up to his body. He kissed her lovingly and she gradually responded by licking him tentatively with her tongue. He sucked it into his mouth.

Slowly, he cupped his hands around her tiny bottom, and pulled her tightly to his body.

She whimpered then whispered his name nervously.

Go slowly.

His hand wandered over her body, touching the curve of her breast, the contour of her hips. He kissed her neck, then her throat. He lifted the dress from her body, and she stood before him wearing only the thin linen chemise the nuns had given her.

She was shivering, her eyes fixed on the wooden planking at her feet. "It's not a very elegant nightgown for our wedding night."

"I couldn't ask for a more beautiful bride," he whispered.

He slipped the chemise off her shoulders and bared her breasts. She gasped as the garment bunched at her waist, but didn't raise her eyes. He fought the desire to lick the dark nipples as he slid the chemise over her hips. It pooled on the floor. He stood back to look at her. She wrapped her arms around her breasts. His breath caught.

She's afraid.

He took hold of her wrists and moved his hands slowly to coax her arms away from her body. He kissed the inside of each wrist, watching her face. She'd lifted her head, but now her eyes were closed. The enticing scent of female arousal invaded his senses.

She desires me.

He had an urge to put his fingers between her legs, sure she would be wet for him. He swallowed hard at the sight of her perfect breasts, the taut dark nipples with their large haloes, the flat belly and curvaceous hips. She was trembling, her eyes open now, but still downcast. "Oh, Agneta," he murmured.

She thrust her head back. Their eyes met for an instant then she looked away shyly and stared at his feet. "I don't know—"

He came close to losing control.

My little nun is trembling because she's unsure, not because she's afraid of me.

"Don't worry. I'll show you."

She nodded, and watched him, wide-eyed, as he tore off his clothes and soon stood naked, his need obvious.

She whispered shyly, "I've glimpsed male parts before, Caedmon, in the infirmary. But yours is—"

Though she'd nursed him, she'd never seen his manhood before! He felt like strutting like a cockerel. "Agneta, I'll spill myself soon, like some green youth," he groaned. He could tell she didn't know what he meant. He swept her up and carried her to the bed.

Nudging her legs open, he knelt between them, cupped her face in his hands, leaned over and kissed her deeply. She arched her body to his. His hand found her breasts and tenderly rolled a nipple between his thumb and forefinger, teasing. A sound emerged from deep in her throat, and she arched again.

He suckled one nipple and she screamed a loud throaty yell as her first release took hold. He'd not yet touched her most intimate female flesh and she'd released already. He'd been right in his assessment of her passionate nature.

"My beautiful Agneta," he rasped, his heart bursting with the knowledge he'd been the one to give her the first taste of ecstasy.

When he stroked her female bud with his fingers, her eyes widened. She keened cries of pleasure and he felt her wet heat. She was ready. He didn't want the pain to be too great, but couldn't wait any longer. "Open your legs wider for me," he breathed. She spread her legs and he slid his swollen phallus into her and pushed past the barrier. It felt right.

This woman was made for me.

***

There was some pain, but Agneta's building need outweighed it and she curled her legs around his body to drive him deeper. He found his rhythm and she matched it stroke for stroke. She was as astonished at the force of her passion as he seemed to be. She felt the sensation of his essence pumping into her and decided, in her near delirium, it was the most fulfilling thing she'd ever felt. She tensed the muscles of her sheath to hold on to him and felt her muscles throbbing involuntarily against him long after they'd both found release.

He must feel it too.

She twirled her fingers in his hair as he lay atop her, breathing heavily.

"I'm surprised no one came to see what the screaming was about. The landlady must have warned everyone there were newlyweds upstairs," he laughed. "I never want to leave this bed."

After a while he rose and went to get water and a cloth. He cleansed his own body then came over to the bed. "Would you like me to cleanse you, my lady wife?" he drawled.

"You don't have to do that."

"But I want to do it," he replied, gently wiping the blood from her thighs. "You took care of my bodily needs. Now I want to do the same for you."

She tugged the linens around her shoulders, to ward off the chill. "I didn't know a man and a woman could—could share—something so—"

She couldn't express her feelings, couldn't look at him.

He put his arm around her shoulders, and smoothed her disheveled hair off her face. "We're lucky, Agneta. Not every man and his wife experience what we've found. You and I fit together perfectly. You were made for me. I've always had the feeling my own mother didn't share with my father the pleasurable passions we've shared this night."

Agneta's thoughts went to her dead parents, and the love her mother boasted of fiercely. Had Ragna Kirkthwaite experienced with her Saxon husband the same heart-stopping ecstasy she'd enjoyed?

No wonder she couldn't bear the thought of life without him.

This was dangerous. Agneta never wanted to be hurt again by the loss of someone she loved. Better to be detached.

CHAPTER ELEVEN

"**I** want to go to Bolton one last time before we leave Northumbria."

Caedmon hesitated then cinched the girth around Wyvern's belly. They were preparing to leave the lodging house. "Are you sure that's a good idea?"

"I have to go, Caedmon. You know I do."

"Very well."

She could tell he was none too pleased as they set off. She too dreaded the idea of going back to the manor where her world had ended. She was entrusting her future to Caedmon in another border region where life might be as unpredictable as it had been in Northumbria. But Northumbria was her homeland and for some reason she didn't understand, she had to see Bolton one more time. It wasn't likely she would ever return to the north. Would she want to?

Caedmon's tension increased as they neared the village a short time later.

"Don't worry. I won't betray you," she murmured to the back of his head. His shoulders stiffened.

On the outskirts she noticed with surprise that several cottages had been restored and rethatched. They looked clean with their fresh whitewash. The gazes of a few villagers followed them as they made their way towards the manor house.

"Lady Agneta?"

Caedmon reined the horse suddenly and she came close to toppling off. Clutching Caedmon's jerkin, she turned to see who'd spoken her name. "Desmond!" she cried in recognition, taking the hand the young man proffered. "It's good to see you. I'm relieved you survived the raid. Your parents?"

"The brutes killed my da', but ma still lives. We thought you were in the convent, at Alnwick."

"I was—but now I'm married. This is Sir Caedmon I ride with, my husband."

The boy eyed the knight, and nodded, then looked back to Agneta. By now a crowd had gathered. "We wish thee well, then, Lady Agneta," said Desmond's mother. "It's glad we are you're still alive, after—"

She looked curiously at Caedmon. "Your husband is a Saxon?"

"Aye, I'm a Saxon," Caedmon replied.

"Huh. Ye sound like a Scot," someone in the crowd murmured.

Caedmon was about to reply, but Agneta interrupted. "We're headed for my husband's manor, in the Welsh Marches. I wanted to see Kirkthwaite Hall, one last time."

"Not much left," Desmond said dispiritedly. "Earl of Northumbria came to look at it, but the Normans don't seem interested in the ruin. They leave us alone, more or less, so long as we pay their taxes."

"Let's go, Agneta. Let's get this over with," Caedmon whispered, urging his horse forward to crest the rise. The villagers watched them go.

Agneta steeled her body, sure he must feel her fingernails digging into his waist. Yet the sight of what remained of her childhood home still made her cry out. Caedmon tensed.

"Stay here," she told him, sliding from Wyvern's back.

It wasn't the charred timbers that bothered Caedmon. A host of bad memories swept over him as he sat atop his horse, watching Agneta pick her broken way around the outskirts of the ruined manor. The faint odor of smoke still clung, borne, he thought, on the swirling clouds of black dust whipped up by the wind. His wife fell to her knees beside the untidy mound where her family had been buried, the crude marker now overgrown. He would remember the faces of the gallant defenders interred there to his dying day.

The hardest sight of all was the tumbledown barn he and Leofric had looked up at, full of regret and self-loathing at what they'd witnessed, what they'd been an unwilling part of. It still stood, a gaunt memorial of his sin. "What a naive, idealistic fool I was," he said aloud.

Agneta had lain hidden there, watching him, after seeing her father and brothers murdered. How could she not judge him to be like those maniacal Scots marauders? How could she ever come to love him? It was a forlorn hope. What was she remembering as she walked slowly around the ruin? Childhood games with her brothers? Love and laughter with her parents? Feasts in the Great Hall?

"Thank God we didn't burn the barn," he muttered with a shudder.

No, Agneta would never love him, though he loved her, burned for her with a passion he'd never known. He'd helped to destroy her life. Now he felt honor bound to ensure her future was secure, that she wouldn't want for anything. They would go to Ruyton and build a good life together. She would never forgive him, but he would try his best to erase the terrible memories.

I so swear, Agneta.

As Caedmon offered his firm hand to help her remount the horse, Agneta couldn't look into his eyes. Hers watered and burned with the grit from the smoky dust. She was afraid she would feel hatred when she looked at him again, but she didn't. It was something else she felt as his strong fingers closed around hers and heaved her up. It was hope and longing, grief and fear, regret and expectation, all mingled together. But it wasn't hate. She found she couldn't hate this warrior she'd married, try as she might.

She sat behind him, rigid as a post, her hands resting lightly on his hips. He made no move to set the horse in motion. "We won't go until you're ready, Agneta," he rasped. She felt the tension in his body, heard the deeper hoarseness in his voice.

"I'm ready," she murmured, leaning forward to rest her head on his back, looping her arms around his waist, pressing her breasts to his comforting warmth.

"To Ruyton, then."

She heard the deep sigh he exhaled, as if he'd been holding his breath, and felt his body relax as they rode away, back to the Abbey to meet up with the others. She didn't look back as the silent tears rolled down her cheeks.

CHAPTER TWELVE

The journey to Ruyton took twice as long as it should. With two of them on the horse they didn't want to tire out their mount. They rode slowly and every mile was pleasurable torture for Caedmon. His manhood rioted against her bottom when she sat before him.

Occasionally she rode behind. "I love the feel of your arms around my waist, and your body pressed up against my back," he told her. He didn't tell her he'd money enough for another horse, hoping the enforced closeness might help ease the rift that stood between them. Nor did he want to draw the attention of any ne'er-do-well who might judge them rich pickings.

Their route took them south to the River Tyne.

"The Normans have built a wooden bridge at the easiest point to cross the river," Caedmon explained. "They have a fort there, but hopefully we won't attract their attention. We aren't carrying anything they can tax. My mother and Enid will cross with us, Leofric with the Brightmores. The others aren't going west but continuing south from here. They'll take the wagon, then we should make better time."

Agneta suddenly tensed. "Pass me the bundle I gave you at the Abbey."

"The bundle?"

"Quickly, Caedmon, pass it to me. I want to conceal it, under my skirts."

"What?"

"Just pass it to me."

He was perplexed at her urgency. He passed her the bundle and she concealed it, a moment or two before a Norman sentry blocked their path.

He held up his hand. "*Arrêtez!* Where are you bound, Saxons?"

Caedmon fought to control his ire at the disparaging way the man spoke to them. "My wife and I journey to Ruyton, in the Welsh Marches."

"A long journey—on one mount. Who are the old women?"

His mother bristled and looked away from the sentry, her nose in the air. "My mother and her maidservant."

The sentry's eyes wandered over the horses, looked Caedmon over, then lingered on Agneta. He barely glanced at the others. "Why are you going there?"

"We're *en route* to Shelfhoc Hall, it's my—it's a manor house, under the protection of the Earl of Ellesmere. I'm to be the new steward."

"The Earl, eh? A steward who sounds like a Scot?" Once again the sentry's eyes wandered over Agneta. "*Allez.* Safe journey to you, then."

His mother's lips twitched into an imperceptible smile. He urged the horse forward across the bridge and felt the tension leave Agneta's body as she sucked in a deep breath. He wondered what was hidden up her skirt that had her in such a state.

"The Normans and their much vaunted *Peace of God*, my arse," he whispered. "Saxons are only safe if they can lay claim to a Norman protector. I wanted to rip out his cursed Norman eyes for the way he looked at you."

Agneta cuddled into him more tightly and he pressed his arms over hers. "Once across, we'll follow the river and the Roman Wall westward, to Carlisle."

Agneta shivered. "I daren't look down. I hate water. I'll feel safer once we've crossed, and I can hand back this burden. The sackcloth is chafing my skin."

But Caedmon sensed there was much more to it than a minor discomfort. Would she ever allow him to share her burdens?

***

In the tiny village of Wylam, the lodging house didn't have enough room for all of them. Caedmon, Leofric and Agneta slept in the stables. A beck ran behind the building. The current was too swift for them to enter the water, especially since Agneta couldn't swim, but Caedmon was able to draw water for drinking and washing. Agneta wouldn't go near the water.

"This isn't very grand, I'm afraid," he lamented.

"It's all right, Caedmon. We have no alternative," she replied coldly.

"I'll keep you warm," he offered.

"I'm not concerned about warmth. I just don't like things that scurry and crawl and stables are full of them."

He teased her by walking his fingers up her arm. "Don't worry, I won't let the wee beasties bite you."

She pushed his hand away with a grimace. "Stop that!"

He could see she wasn't in a good mood. In an effort to lighten it, he suggested, "Let's go inside and at least sample their ale."

"Will we be welcome?"

"I think so. It's an old Saxon village. Haven't seen any Normans about."

"Aye, the cursed lord of Balliol gave our village to the Priory at Tynemouth," one of the villagers complained, once the travellers had been judged acceptable, and the conversation inevitably turned to the invaders. "Nigh on eight year sin'."

"And do the monks ever come here?" Leofric asked as he joined them.

"No, *Godemite*, but they take their due from us. Curse the Normans."

"Aye. I'll drink to that curse," Caedmon replied, raising his tankard.

"But you're Scots. What do you care?"

"No. We're not Scots. We're Saxons. I'm the son of a hero of Hastings, a *housecarl* to King Harold," Caedmon retorted proudly. "My fellow knight here, Leofric, is a hero of Alnwick. And my wife is a Northumbrian girl, born and bred."

"Northumbria? One of us then? Whereabouts?"

"Bolton, near Alnwick," Agneta murmured, looking uncomfortable.

Caedmon's heart lurched. Why had he mentioned Agneta was from Northumbria?

"Ah, de Mowbray's territory," one of the villagers observed.

"Aye," Caedmon replied, unable to look at Agneta.

"God go with thee, then, young Saxons."

***

"My father told me of this Hadrian's wall, but the height and length of it is astounding," Agneta remarked as they continued their journey. "It must have taken years to build?"

"Aye, I estimate it's about ten feet wide and we've passed many ruined forts built into it. The Romans surely wanted everyone to recognize they held the power. Just like the Normans. After hundreds of years, you can still see the whitewashed plaster in some places. The sun on it would have made it visible for miles. Arrogant bastards!"

"Caedmon," Lady Ascha remonstrated.

"Sorry, Mother. I'm used to the company of men. My tongue ran away with me. You'd think I *was* a Scot."

He regretted his jest as he felt Agneta stiffen behind him. She kept her hands on his hips, but withdrew her body, and sat rigidly.

"Keep tight hold," he tried. "The going here is treacherous in places on these moors. They say it will improve once we reach the old Roman road at Corbridge. The Stanegate will take us all the way to Carlisle."

They rode in silence for a while, and Agneta slowly relaxed. "I love this landscape," she mused.

"But these Pennines are bleak and barren," Caedmon replied.

"It's true, but there's a wildness, an earthiness to the hills and moorlands. Look at the all bracken and heather. I suppose I'm a child of the moors."

Caedmon pointed to a group of sheep in the distance, clustered near a gnarled tree. "They seem to like it, but they're lucky to have thick woolly coats. Too cold, windy and wet for me. Though I must admit, the hare I've snared are tasty—lots of flesh on their bones."

"You're right. I've enjoyed them. Your snares are effective. You're a good provider, and a good cook."

Caedmon flushed at the rare words of praise and recalled how he'd become aroused watching her bite into the succulent meat with such relish, licking her lips and fingers and flashing one of her infrequent smiles.

They encountered many becks and streams and, despite the icy lick of the water on their skin, Caedmon and Leofric often took advantage to cleanse themselves at the end of a long day. Only a few lodging houses had a bath available. But Agneta was afraid of the swift rushing waters that teemed out of the crags and fells. She made the excuse she didn't like cold water, but he sensed it was fear kept her crouching nearby, hugging her knees, longing to be clean.

"Come on, Agneta. I'll keep you safe. Leofric will give us privacy. Come join me. It feels good."

She always shook her head.

The lodging house in Corbridge did have baths available and Agneta asked, "Do we have enough money? I'm freezing, and badly in need of a bath."

"Aye. We do, and we'd both benefit from a good scrubbing."

"I'm definitely ordering a bath," Lady Ascha told them.

"Me too," Leofric laughed.

"I'd love one too," Coventina Brightmore murmured.

Her mother bristled. "It's not seemly to say such things in front of Sir Caedmon and Sir Leofric."

Coventina blushed and gave Leofric a strange look as her mother hurried her away.

Now, in the warmth of the cozy room above the lodging house, barefoot and stripped down to his braies, Caedmon watched Agneta lather her body in the soapy water. He abruptly peeled off his last piece of clothing and joined her. She squealed in surprise. The water slopped over onto the floor as he sat facing her. The size of the tub forced him to bend his long legs, and his knees stuck up out of the water.

"Caedmon! What are you doing?"

"I'm taking a bath with my wife." He dunked his face and came up covered in suds.

She laughed and wiped his face. It lightened his heart. He opened his legs wide and reached out to feather his thumbs over her nipples. They hardened more beneath his touch.

"Caedmon," she whispered, half closing her eyes.

He took hold of her hand and drew it to his shaft. "Touch me, Agneta. Take me in your hand." He curled his hand around hers and moved it on his arousal.

"It's silky," she whispered.

"Move your hand on me," he rasped. "That's it, oh God, that feels good. Keep going."

His thumbs went back to her nipples, and he squeezed them between his thumb and forefinger.

"I like that, Caedmon," she whispered. "It makes me feel—oh—" She parted her lips and threw back her head.

Caedmon couldn't resist leaning forward to kiss her, sucking her lower lip into his mouth. "We're clean enough," he rasped, lifting her and striding out of the tub. He laid her on the bed.

"We'll get it all wet," she protested, laughing.

"I don't care, wetness pleases me, and you *are* wet—and warm."

***

The winding old Roman Stanegate did indeed provide a smoother journey as it followed the easiest gradients and they came at last to Carlisle. The town was teeming with Normans, all seemingly occupied with the construction of a motte and bailey.

Caedmon clenched his jaw. "This is what infuriated King Malcolm, the thing that drove him to the ill-advised foray into Northumbria that ended in his death. He was maddened that Rufus was determined to cut the Scots off from their traditional influence in Cumbria. I'm glad I didn't see him fall at Alnwick. He was a good man."

Agneta said nothing.

"In a way, if the Norman king hadn't undertaken this fortification, you and I might never have met."

Agneta remained silent.

"We won't stay in Carlisle itself. Too many Normans."

Agneta stiffened. "Sometimes I get tired of your constant complaining about Normans, Caedmon."

This time Caedmon kept quiet, seeing no point in bringing up her resentment of him and his Scottish allies. He was an optimistic man at heart, but despaired she would ever forgive him. Did she care for him at all?

***

"Are we far from the sea?" Agneta asked. "I've never seen the sea."

Caedmon sniffed the air. "I can smell it."

Lady Ascha smiled. "Reminds me of the smell of the Firth, back home."

Lady Ascha's mouth dropped open and a look of resignation passed between Caedmon and his mother.

"We might be well advised to head in that direction and avoid Lancaster," he suggested.

They turned west after seeking directions from a villager and after about two hours, came to the sands of Heysham. They sat for a long while perched on their horses atop the cliffs overlooking the beaches, gazing out to sea.

Agneta found it soothing to watch the waves curl and break on the beach. She tightened her arms around Caedmon's waist, using him as a shield against the wind. "Can we go down there?"

"We'll stay with the mounts, Caedmon. I've no wish to get sand in my boots," Lady Ascha said.

Caedmon, Agneta and Leofric set off to look for a path, but Leofric stopped and came back to the group. "May I ask Lady Coventina to join us?" he asked her mother.

Coventina's eyes lit up. "Please, mother," Coventina begged.

"Very well, since Sir Caedmon and Lady Agneta are accompanying you."

Leofric assisted Coventina to dismount, and the four of them hurried off to find the way down. Once at the beach they took off their boots and prepared to walk along the wet brown sands, rippled into ridges by the tide. Coventina offered to assist Leofric with his boots.

"Don't worry, Coventina, I'll do it," Caedmon offered, and Agneta admired her husband for trying to spare Leofric's feelings.

"I can manage it myself," Leofric objected, but she could see he was grateful for Caedmon's offer of help.

"The sand feels strange," Agneta murmured. "It sticks to my feet."

Caedmon took her hand and the four walked briskly. The wind whipped the wimples off the women's heads. Coventina gasped and looked worriedly at Agneta, then struggled to adjust the flapping wimple back around her hair. Suddenly Leofric took her hand. The girl glanced up at the cliffs then smiled at Leofric and the two kept walking.

"He'll have to marry her now," Caedmon whispered in his wife's ear with a grin. "Not only has he seen her hair, he's holding her hand."

Agneta pulled Caedmon to a halt. "Does she know? About Bolton?"

Caedmon looked down at the sand. "I'm not sure. But if not, please let him tell her."

Agneta nodded. "I want to go in the water."

She shivered in the winter breeze and Caedmon wrapped his arm around her waist, bringing the hand he held to his lips. "You taste salty. The water will be cold this time of year," he warned.

She pouted. "But I want to at least put my toes in. We might never see the sea in Ruyton."

He pulled her to the water. She squealed when the cold waves lapped her feet, and ran away from the incoming tide. Instantly she missed the warmth of Caedmon's hand, the comfort of his arm around her.

"You're a coward, wife," he taunted, reaching down and playfully splashing water towards her.

She tiptoed back to join him, holding the edge of her dress out of the water, and put her hand in his again. They stood watching the water suck the sand from beneath their toes as the waves rolled in and out.

"Let's walk along the beach. I'm getting cold, and walking might warm us."

"I'm warm already, Agneta," Caedmon whispered in her ear, moving her hand to his groin and pressing it against his arousal. "You look beautiful with the wind in your hair."

She drew her free hand through her locks. "At least it's getting a bit longer."

Their eyes met, and she pressed her hand on his hard maleness. He gathered her to his body and kissed her deeply. "Mmm. Salty. I want to make love to you, but it's too cold here—and too sandy."

"Leofric," he shouted. "Let's go find a place to stay nearby."

Turning back to her, he murmured in her ear, "We can make love to the sound of the sea."

CHAPTER THIRTEEN

Days later they were following the River Dee, south of Chester, another town they'd skirted because of the likelihood of a heavy presence of the Earl of Chester's soldiers. The older members of the company were finding the pace taxing. Lady Ascha had intimated to the others that they give Caedmon and Agneta some time alone together and the newly-weds were a fair distance ahead. Leofric had agreed to stay with the women. Caedmon and Agneta were tired and hungry after an early start and decided to stop for a midday meal.

"It will give the others a chance to catch up. I'll try for some fish in the river," Caedmon told her.

Agneta glanced over at the river. "We have food enough left. It looks treacherous."

Caedmon shrugged. "I'll be fine. I'll go out on that fallen oak over there. I won't even get my boots wet."

Agneta was nervous. The water was flowing swiftly, and the tree Caedmon climbed onto looked none too safe to her. She set about preparing a fire, unable to watch him as he made his way out to the large branches that stretched over the river like the gnarled hand of a giant. She heard him whistling and peeked over her shoulder to see him drop his line into the water.

"There's a nice deep pool under here. Should get some brown trout, or maybe a grayling," he shouted to her. She waved and then looked away.

A loud crack, followed by a splash, caught her attention. She cried out in horror as Caedmon grasped desperately at the remains of the tree limb that had broken off, catapulting him into the water. The current took him quickly. He disappeared beneath the waters, and she screamed as she hurried along the bank, trying to keep pace.

"Caedmon, Caedmon, oh God, no! Caedmon!"

He resurfaced, but she could see he was having difficulty holding on to the branch. He went under again, then the current carried him closer to the bank where he was able to grab hold of a half submerged tangle of tree roots. The water buffeted him, and then rammed a huge log right up against him, but he held on for dear life, struggling to catch his breath. Blood oozed from his forehead.

"Agneta," he spluttered, coughing up water. "My legs—"

She screamed as he disappeared again, only his arms visible, his white hands clamped onto the roots.

"My legs—caught—beneath the water," he yelled when he resurfaced.

"Caedmon—I—" she choked, staring at the swirling black water.

"Can't hold—on—much longer," he rasped.

A memory of the first time she'd ever seen him on the battlefield at Alnwick flashed before her.

"I didn't save your miserable life for you to drown here," she cried.

She struggled along the muddy bank, holding up her skirts, until she was close to where he held on. Already up to her knees in the frigid water, she stretched out her hand. He took one hand off the root and reached for her. As their cold, slippery fingers meshed, their eyes locked. There was fear in those blue depths, and a surge of energy went through her.

I will not let him drown. Where is Leofric?

She took hold of his numbed hand in both hers and pulled with all her might. She could tell the blow from the tree and the repeated dunking had weakened him.

"You have to help me. Not strong enough to heave you out. You're pulling me in deeper."

She lunged then and latched one hand onto the back of his sodden jerkin.

"Push!" she screamed. "Push!"

Caedmon struggled to free himself, to no avail.

"Let go, Agneta. If I'm—to drown, I don't want to drag you with me."

Their eyes locked again. This time, Agneta saw resignation.

Don't let him die not knowing you love him.

"No! Caedmon, I—"

"Hang on there," came a strongly accented voice on the wind. Agneta turned her head, hoping at last to see Leofric, but through her tears saw a blurry image of several men running towards them.

"Help," she sobbed, on the point of exhaustion, relief washing over her. "My husband's legs are caught fast—under the water."

"We'll get him out of there," one of them shouted.

Strong hands dragged her away from the water. They had to pry her frozen fingers from Caedmon's hand.

"It's all right. You can let go of him now. We have him," one of them coaxed.

Someone took hold of her hands and rubbed them. She looked up into the eyes of a smiling lad of about four and ten years, kneeling at her side. "I'll soon have your hands warm again," he said with a lilt.

One of the three men held Caedmon firmly around the chest, while the others dove to free his legs. Gradually, they were able to pull him up onto the bank. On hands and knees he coughed up water then collapsed beside Agneta, trembling and gasping for breath.

"Good knights—I thank you—I was a dead man."

The men nodded.

"You saved my life, Agneta. Don't cry. You were brave."

Agneta's teeth chattered. "No, it was these good men saved you. Thank God you came, sirs."

Caedmon looked into her eyes. "But you kept me afloat."

Sobbing, she followed as the men hauled Caedmon further from the water. She fumbled to unfasten his clothing, but her fingers were too cold and she was trembling.

"I've never seen you in such a hurry to undress me," he jested.

She scowled at him. "You need to get out of these wet clothes, Caedmon. You must get dry and wrap yourself in blankets."

"She's right," said one of the men, a black-haired giant, who seemed to be the leader. "You need to keep warm."

The three had pulled bundles of dry clothing from their saddlebags, and were stripping off their wet clothing as they headed to the trees. Agneta turned away and looked at Caedmon, her face grim. "You scared me to death, silly man, taking such a foolhardy risk for a fish." She whispered so the lad couldn't hear. He was busy building up a fire.

Caedmon grimaced. "I have to admit, I scared myself."

When the three Welshman returned, Caedmon proferred his hand to their leader and said hoarsely, "We're in your debt, sirs. I'm Caedmon Woolgar. Agneta is my wife."

The giant took his hand. "Good thing we came along when we did. I'm Rhodri ap Owain, Prince of Powwydd. These good men with me are Aneurin and Andras. And this bright lad is my son, Rhys. We're part of a band paused in yonder copse. We heard the commotion."

"You're Welshmen then?" Caedmon asked.

Rhodri nodded. "We are. And you're Scots?"

"No, we're Saxons."

The Welshman arched his brows as he crouched by the fire. "Where are you bound?"

"My late father was the thane of Shelfhoc Manor in Ruyton. I'm returning there to take up residence. I was raised in Scotland."

Rhodri looked surprised. "Ruyton? Isn't that a protectorate of the Earl of Ellesmere?"

"Aye. Do you know him?"

The Welshman smiled. "Yes, we've met. My wife, Rhonwen, is a friend of the Countess, Mabelle de Montbryce. In fact, we named our daughter Myfanwy Mabelle. Rhys has been to Ellesmere Castle several times."

The Welshman winked at his son. Rhys nodded and returned his father's enigmatic smile, but she paid no heed, busy as she was trying to strip off Caedmon's wet clothing and tend the wound at his temple, which had stopped bleeding. "It shouldn't scar," she said. "It's not deep."

The tree branches in which he'd become entangled had left livid scratches along her husband's calves and thighs. She wrapped a blanket around him and rubbed his arms to warm him up.

The Welshmen turned their backs and walked away while Caedmon held a blanket around Agneta and she removed her clothing. They wrapped themselves in their blankets and huddled together by the campfire Rhys had built. Agneta couldn't stop trembling, but felt calmer after she'd eaten some of the delicious fried fish Rhodri's men caught and shared with them.

"You don't have dry clothing?" Aneurin asked.

Caedmon shook his head. "The others are carrying some of our goods. They should be here soon. None of us are carrying much."

"A good idea. The less you have, the less can be stolen from you in this land the Normans boast of having made safe," Andras remarked sarcastically.

"Aye, that's the sum of it," Caedmon agreed.

The Prince of Powwydd gave an imperceptible signal to the others, and they all rose as one and started to mount their horses.

Caedmon asked, "Won't you stay and meet the rest of our group? My mother would surely like to thank you for saving my life."

"No, my Saxon friends. We thank you, but we never tarry long in England. Too many Normans. We'll follow this river *Afon Dyfrdwy* back into Wales this day," Rhodri replied with a chuckle. "I bid you farewell, and good luck in Ruyton. Your mother, you say? Woolgar? Yes, I recall the name now. Strangely enough, Ruyton is where I first met the good Earl of Ellesmere. You remind me of him somewhat. Give him my regards if you see him."

Caedmon got to his feet. "I will. Farewell, and our thanks again, Prince of Powwydd. There will be a welcome for you at Shelfhoc Manor."

Rhodri smiled and the Welshmen disappeared into the forest as quickly as they had emerged.

"That was a strange look he gave you as they rode off," Agneta remarked.

"Aye. Who knows with the Welsh?"

They clung together in silence by the fire, waiting for the others to arrive.

"I'm sorry, Agneta. You're right. It was foolhardy."

They didn't speak for a while, then he quipped, "And now we have no fishing line."

He was trying to cheer her, but her heart broke when he murmured, "Thank God I have a courageous wife. You tried to save me despite your fear of the water."

"You're all I have. What would become of me if I lost you?" she whimpered. She would be haunted by the fear she'd seen in his eyes. It was a rare glimpse of vulnerability in him and he was aware she'd seen it. The depth of her love for him struck full force, confusing her to the point of total exhaustion and she was asleep when the rest of their group arrived to be told the tale.

Caedmon cursed over and over to Leofric as his friend helped him unpack their dry clothing. "I'm a fool. The great warrior, Caedmon Brice Woolgar, almost drowning and having to be rescued by his wife, and a bunch of wandering Welshmen, who were no doubt outlaws."

On the other hand, he was in awe she'd risked her own life to save his. "How could I have been stupid enough to endanger her safety that way? I must be more cautious. It's no longer acceptable to behave like a fancy-free youth with only myself to consider. I'm a married man now, with responsibilities. What are you laughing at?"

"I'm not laughing, my friend," Leofric smirked. "That's the way my face is now."

Caedmon would never forget the terror in Agneta's eyes as she struggled to keep hold of his slippery hand.

But her fear wasn't of the water. It was for me.

Perhaps she did care for him. He'd all but resigned his fate to a watery grave and had been on the point of avowing his love for her when the Welshmen had ridden to his rescue.

***

Their lovemaking after his near drowning took on a new intensity. He was happy that making love to him excited her, and she seemed always to be eager for him. They made love when they had privacy, only falling asleep when their bodies' cravings were completely satisfied. On the last night of the journey, as she lay in his arms, he whispered, "On the morrow, God willing, I shall bring my bride to my estate and she'll become the lady of Shelfhoc Hall, Lady Agneta Woolgar."

"I like the sound of that, Sir Caedmon Woolgar," she replied sleepily. "It's difficult to grasp that a short time ago, I was completely alone in the world, with no prospect for the future outside the convent. Now I have a magnificent man to share my bed. Who knew such a wanton lay buried deep within? Goodnight, Sir Caedmon."

"Goodnight, Lady Agneta," he whispered, feeling smug about his magnificence.

CHAPTER FOURTEEN

Early in the afternoon, they clattered into the courtyard of Shelfhoc Hall, after apparently satisfying the visual scrutiny of a handful of men-at-arms as they passed through the fortress gate of the rampart.

They were given an indifferent welcome by the Earl's steward. He was the third steward to be assigned there since Ellesmere took over protection of the lands and had no idea who these unusual travellers could be. The man at their head shared a horse with a woman, whose alarmingly short hair was uncovered. The group looked like they'd travelled for days in the same inferior clothes. There was something vaguely familiar about the man, but he couldn't put his finger on what it was.

"I'm Sir Caedmon Woolgar. Who are you?"

It had been so long since any Woolgars had lived at Shelfhoc the name didn't resonate with the steward at first, but then something reached in and tickled his memory.

"Woolgar?" he queried.

"Aye, Sir Caedmon Woolgar, son of the late thane of this estate," the knight declared as he dismounted and helped the woman. "And this is my wife, Lady Agneta Woolgar and my mother Lady Ascha Woolgar. We've come to take up residence."

Tybaut's mind went blank. "But, my lord, if I'd only known you were coming. We could have prepared chambers, food, a hot bath. Forgive me, I'm Tybaut, your steward."

The knight laughed. "Don't worry. A bath sounds good if you could organize that. Fresh linens will do for this night, and a light meal, then, on the morrow, you can set about doing the rest."

"*Oui*, my lord. We've a small staff here, only my wife and I, and the stable boy, but we can meet your needs if you have but a little patience. On the morrow, I can go into the village to procure more servants."

"We've all the patience in the world, Tybaut," Sir Caedmon smirked as he took his wife and his mother by the hand and led them into the house. "Perhaps you could give us a short tour after you've settled our companions in their chambers? Sir Leofric Deacon will require a chamber, and perhaps Lady Coventina Brightmore can share one with her mother and aunt?"

"*Oui*, my lord," Tybaut said, trying without success to solve the enigma of who it was this man reminded him of. Perhaps it was the Scottish burr confusing him?

***

Caedmon knew nothing of the house, but now he savored every lime-washed panel, every stair, every chamber. His mother wandered off, Enid at her side. It was a grand house, two stories high, built from stout split and planed timbers, fastened together with iron nails. The interior was elaborately decorated with ornamental wood turnings, the wooden floor softened with wattle mats. The roof was well thatched. The sturdy outbuildings were framed with large timber uprights, filled with wattle and daub and chinked with moss to keep out the winter cold. The stone kitchen was set apart from the wooden house.

"This used to be the weaving shed," Tybaut explained, as they entered a long, narrow building. "Perhaps the ladies might start up the use of it again? I've kept the old looms well covered."

"Perhaps," Agneta agreed. "I like to weave."

"I didn't know my mother did weaving," Caedmon said. "How hard it must have been for her to leave all this."

Agneta said nothing in reply, probably lost in memories of her home, destroyed with his help. He silently cursed himself for his insensitivity.

There was a modest Great Hall where Caedmon imagined his father had conducted business, enacted justice and spoken judgments. Had his father sat in the massive thane's chair on the dais, his wife Ascha by his side, and signed contracts, praised good deeds, eaten with his men? The Hall was long and narrow and had two doors, one at each tapered end. The four windows had wooden shutters for defence and to keep out the cold. He felt proud of his sire who'd died at Hastings, proud to be a Saxon. He was relieved he'd not brought Agneta to a ruin.

"Imagine my parents here, Agneta, in the days before the Conquest, watching the smoke make its lazy way up from the hearth here in the middle, out through the hole in the roof."

"We had a great hall similar to this in Bolton," she replied coldly. "It had alcoves on the sides, like this. Of course, you only saw the outside."

Tybaut looked at Agneta curiously and Caedmon was relieved she said no more about Bolton. "You've done a fine job of maintaining the manor, Tybaut, and you've been meticulous in sending my mother her revenues from the tenant and church income. Why is it the Earl never takes a commission or percentage of the revenues?"

Tybaut scratched his head. "That's been the way of it since the outset. I wasn't here then, of course."

"The Earl's generosity amazes me, I must confess," Caedmon said sarcastically. "There has never been any charge levied for the services of the stewards nor for these Ellesmere men-at-arms who guard the manor house. Perhaps Normans aren't as greedy as I thought, or perhaps there's something I'm missing. There has to be some reason for the Earl's uncommon generosity to a Saxon family?"

Tybaut shifted his weight from one foot to the other, obviously ill-at-ease. "I've found the Earl to be a reasonable and honorable man, sir. As I say, I wasn't here in the beginning."

Caedmon and Agneta continued their tour, and came at last to the largest chamber, where they were standing when Lady Ascha entered.

"This must have been your chamber, mother, yours and my father's? It's only fitting you have it now. Agneta and I can—"

"Absolutely not," Lady Ascha exclaimed. "This is the chamber for the lord and lady of the Manor. That's you, Caedmon and Agneta Woolgar. There's another chamber I'll be perfectly happy with."

"Thank you, mother," Agneta said, clasping Ascha's hand. Caedmon wondered if his wife was aware she'd used the word *mother*. He sensed there was something about Agneta's own mother she'd never told him.

Tybaut's wife soon had water warming for baths. The stable boy carried up the buckets of hot water and poured them into the ornate wooden bathtub, which had been brought to the lord's chamber.

"My parents must have used this chamber, but I find I've no sense of them together. Of course, I never met my father."

Agneta sat on the edge of the bed, testing the mattress. "Your mother seems nervous about being back here."

He nodded. "Too many memories, I suppose."

***

Caedmon savored making love to his wife for the first time in their own home. As they lay together naked, her back snuggled against his chest, his body wrapped around hers, his hands cupping her breasts, his face in her hair, he felt content and mused about the future.

"I'll become familiar with the tenants, and Tybaut will help me with that. You'll need a lady's maid and we can deal with procuring her and other servants when Tybaut goes to the village. We'll need a cook—a good one. And clothes for you."

"There's plenty of time, Caedmon. We don't have to do everything in the first sennight. We're both tired from the eventful journey. You could have drowned. And we've Yuletide to plan in the next few days. I'm surprised we made it here in time."

"You're right. It will be good to celebrate Yuletide here for the first time. However, I can't take too long before I must travel to Ellesmere to confirm my allegiance to the Earl. Much as it galls me to serve a Norman, after all Montbryce has done for the Woolgar family I'm sure I'll be expected to provide some kind of service, now I've returned to claim my birthright. Perhaps I'll have to patrol the border against the Welsh. I'll need to recruit and train my own men-at-arms—men who are loyal to me. They say the Earl is a fair man, hard but fair."

"Speaking of hard men," she giggled, reaching behind her to touch him.

The huskiness in her voice inflamed him and his manhood surged. It seemed to have a life of its own when she put her hands on him.

She draped her long leg over his, opening herself. "You feel warm—and full. I'm tingling."

Caedmon stretched beside her and kissed the nape of her neck. "Turn to me, Agneta," he whispered.

As she turned her body to his, he kissed her lovingly on the mouth. She coaxed his lips with her tongue. He teased her with the tip of his tongue, but wouldn't open. He licked his way down her neck to her sensitive throat. She giggled and then clasped her hands to her mouth. "We mustn't make too much noise with all these people in the house."

"I don't care if you scream the house down, and you probably will," he teased.

She glared at him.

Caressing her stomach and thighs, he trailed his fingers to her throbbing bud. She gasped and whimpered, "That feels good."

He suckled her nipple and nibbled it. The whimpering sounds told him it aroused her. "You like that. I can tell." He moved his mouth lower and circled her navel with his tongue. She tossed her head from side to side, her eyes tightly closed, her breathing ragged as his fingers continued to play with her engorged bud. She pressed the back of her hand to her mouth.

"You're beautiful, Agneta. You make me want you too much," he whispered, his voice husky with need.

She opened her eyes. "My body aches for you, Caedmon. I never yearned like this till I met you. I need you inside me."

She cried out when he inserted his long fingers into her. He knew it partly satisfied her but she needed more. Sensing she was ready, he knelt and guided the head of his shaft into her. He trembled and gasped when the warm wetness of her sheath enveloped him and he buried more deeply as she wrapped her legs around his body.

Entering her filled him with a sense of coming home. With his finger he found her bud again and moved his manhood back and forth over it. She moaned with delight and lifted her hips higher to him. He withdrew, pushed back in and found his rhythm. As her need intensified he could barely keep up with her. The shuddering spasms of release took him and he heard his own guttural cry as his seed exploded into her. The pulsating throbs inside her told him she'd found ecstasy.

"Welcome home, wife," he whispered to her several minutes later as she lay in his arms.

But she'd already fallen asleep.

CHAPTER FIFTEEN

Their first Yuletide at Shelfhoc was a subdued affair, given the short amount of time they had to prepare for it. Nevertheless, the house was warmed by the atmosphere of relief and conviviality, and Tybaut made sure the larder was well stocked.

As the days went by and spring approached, Lady Pamela Brightmore and her sister, Lady Edythe Walwin became less formal than they had been on the journey.

"Their fear is gradually leaving them," Lady Ascha told Caedmon, when he remarked on their change of attitude. He and Agneta and Lady Ascha were enjoying a warm spring day in the garden.

He agreed. "That will be good for Coventina. They are too strict with her. The poor girl can't do anything without one of them criticizing her."

"Yes, it will be good for your friend, Leofric."

Caedmon turned to face his mother. "You've noticed it too, have you?"

Ascha smiled. "I believe Leofric is in love with Coventina, but he hesitates, because of his—injuries."

Caedmon frowned. "We need to know how Coventina feels about him. I don't want to see him hurt."

"Hmmm," Ascha pondered. "Does she confide in you, Agneta?"

Agneta shook her head.

"No? I could probably arrange to find out—subtly though."

Caedmon grinned at his mother and winked at Agneta. Lady Ascha seemed to be happy to be back in England, something he'd wanted for her for a long time. Yet, he sensed a nervousness about

90

her, and whenever he mentioned going to pay his respects to the Earl, she became morose and angry. He decided to pursue another topic. "What do the Brightmore women intend to do? Will they seek out their relatives in Wessex, or is that a lost cause?"

Ascha shook her head. "Lady Pamela has already sent messages, but no reply. They'll be here a long while. What about Leofric? Will he stay here with us?"

"I'd like him to. I've told him I want him to stay. I need men around me I can trust. I suppose it depends on what happens with Coventina."

They found a stone bench and sat for a while in companionable silence before Caedmon spoke. "I'm satisfied with the progress we've made. Tybaut has introduced me to all the tenant farmers."

"What's your opinion of them?" his mother asked.

"Mostly hard working Saxons. I don't foresee any problems. Tybaut and I have discussed increasing the provisioning of the manor house."

"Definitely no problem there," Agneta interjected. "He's a good steward. Very thorough."

His mother turned to look at Caedmon. "Have you seen the Church?"

"Yes, Agneta and I went together. Some minor repairs needed, but nothing too serious. It's a nice little wooden church."

"Yes, I liked it," Agneta agreed.

"The Woolgars were proud of it. Several of their ancestors are buried in the churchyard," his mother said wistfully, then suddenly shot a strange glance over at Caedmon.

It was the first time he'd heard her say anything positive about her husband's family. He decided not to pursue the matter. "Tybaut has seen to most of the repairs of the fortress gate, and we're in the process of improving the ditch and rampart."

"It's hard to believe all this labor is being provided free by a Norman earl," Agneta commented.

Lady Ascha stood up abruptly. "Excuse me, I need to speak to Enid." She left the garden.

Caedmon and Agneta watched her, wondering what had made her leave so abruptly. He took his wife's hand. "Aye, I'm getting more and more curious about this Earl."

Agneta hesitated then remarked, "Your mother seems nervous when you mention his name."

Caedmon had indeed noticed, but chose to say nothing. He curled his fingers more tightly round his wife's hand. "Tybaut and I have gone over the accounts and I have a good grasp on the income and expenses of the estate. While Tybaut, and the stewards before him, have done a surprisingly fine job, I have many ideas about how things can be expanded and improved."

Agneta smiled. "I've been busy too, with the servants Tybaut procured. I'm pleased with the improvements in the kitchen, and we've aired out the linens and draperies. We'll have to replace some of them that haven't stood the test of time."

Caedmon was gladdened by the optimistic sound in her voice. He put his arm around her shoulder. "Tybaut has also introduced me to the men-at-arms provided by the Earl. I'll definitely have to recruit and train my own men, who'll be loyal to me alone." He smirked. "They looked at me as if I had two heads—typical Norman arrogance."

***

Caedmon, Leofric and Tybaut went to Ruyton to buy more horses. They chose a magnificent red roan stallion for him and a sweet white palfrey for Agneta.

"I love her," Agneta gushed when she saw the horse's ambling gait. "I will name her *Abbey*."

Caedmon was pleased to have given her something she loved. "Wyvern saved my life at Alnwick, but he's never recovered fully from that experience and the long ride from Scotland to Ruyton. I'll let him retire and enjoy his oats. With Tybaut's expert guidance, I bought myself this fine new stallion."

"He's a beauty," she agreed, looking at the magnificent roan chomping at the bit.

Caedmon grinned. "I've named him *Abbot*." Agneta seemed unimpressed.

Tailors and seamstresses came from Ruyton, took measurements and returned with new clothing made from the bolts Caedmon and Agneta had chosen from the selections they brought. Her hair had grown quickly and was now to her shoulders. She looked like the lady of the manor. Caedmon felt a surge of pride at the sight of her. It was plain to see she'd been born to a good family.

They learned what pleased the other when they made love. However, while Agneta welcomed him to her bed with unbridled passion, he sensed an invisible barrier between them the rest of the time and he wondered if she would ever forgive him his role in the raid on Bolton. He sometimes felt she lavished more love and attention on her palfrey than on him. Leofric seemed to merit friendlier treatment.

"It was my plan to ride to Ellesmere soon," Caedmon announced to the ladies of the household and Leofric one day at the midday meal. "It's May already and I need to convey my thanks to the Earl and come to some arrangement about Tybaut and the men-at-arms. It's my obligation to offer to serve him in some capacity, though I hate the idea of serving a Norman."

"So you've said many times," Agneta retorted, banging her goblet down on the table. "You want me to forgive the Scots and the Saxons who aided them, including the two of you, for the murder of my family and destruction of my home, yet you can't bring yourself to forgive and build bridges with the Normans."

"I don't want to argue with you, Agneta," he replied, trying to keep a rein on his emotions. Leofric shifted nervously in his seat, and he wondered if his friend and his wife had ever discussed Bolton. Agneta evidently knew it was Leofric who'd stood at his side as he looked at the barn. "I'm willing to swallow my pride and serve the Earl, but I'll never have any love in my heart for the Normans. Leofric and I both know what it is to lose a parent to an invader. Anyway, I won't be going."

His mother's head jerked up, her face flushed and her shoulders tense.

Caedmon watched her as he explained. "Tybaut tells me the Montbryces have gone off to Normandie, for the summer. They apparently go every year. Won't be back until September at the earliest."

"Oh well, you'll get to meet the famous Earl eventually, I suppose," Agneta said with a degree of sarcasm, her face still showing traces of anger.

"Yes, I suppose," Lady Ascha whispered.

CHAPTER SIXTEEN

"We must get her fever down, Caedmon," Lady Ascha whispered as she wrung out the cold compress and placed it on Agneta's forehead. "And for goodness sake, stop pacing."

"I don't know what else to do," her son replied, running his hand through his hair. He came over to the bed where Agneta lay in a stupor and took hold of her hand. "What's wrong with her? She was well yesterday at the Harvest Festival, but during the night became delirious. And she's too hot."

Ascha shook her head and he could see she was worried. "It could be any number of things. Perhaps she ate something."

Agneta moaned, "I ache all over."

Speaking seemed to irritate her throat. She sat up and coughed uncontrollably. Lady Ascha comforted her by rubbing her back.

Caedmon's eyes were wild, and he was afraid to touch Agneta. "Do something, mother. She'll choke."

If anything happens to her.

Ascha looked at him with irritation. "She won't choke. You must be calm. Your upset won't help her. We must be patient and concentrate on getting the fever under control. I'll instruct Enid to make mint tea for the cough. Go to the garden and get a sprig of rosemary to hang around her neck."

At that moment Lady Edythe poked her head in the door. "I suggest burning juniper berries. It will ease the cough and ward off evil spirits."

They tried all these remedies, but for three days Agneta hacked and her nose ran. Her fever worsened. "I'm dying, Caedmon," she moaned.

He sat by her bedside throughout her ordeal, his head resting on the bed beside her, her hand in his. Despite his protestations to the contrary to Agneta, he was convinced his beloved wife's death was imminent and had never felt such helplessness.

"You must get some rest, my son,' his mother cajoled, laying her hand on his shoulder.

"I'll rest when she's recovered. I can't leave her. I'd planned to ride to Ellesmere this week. Tybaut tells me the Earl and his family are back from Normandie, but I can't go now."

"No, I agree. Better to wait," Lady Ascha replied. "I've told Cook to add thyme and chives to the broth we're feeding Agneta, and we'll try chamomile tea."

"My eyes hurt," Agneta moaned huskily.

Caedmon could see her eyes were red and inflamed and he clenched his fists, angry at his helplessness to ease her pain.

On the third day, when he woke, he noticed bright red spots inside Agneta's mouth when she coughed. He fled the room, shouting urgently for Lady Ascha.

"That's a relief," Ascha sighed when she saw Agneta.

Caedmon wanted to strangle his mother. "A relief?"

Ascha smiled. "Yes, it's rubeola. You had it as a boy. Agneta must never have had it as a child. She is ill but with care she'll survive."

Caedmon let out a sigh of relief and covered his face with his hands. He felt like sinking to his knees in thanks to the Almighty. "You're sure?"

Ascha nodded. "If, on the morrow, she's covered with a red rash, then I'll be sure."

By the following morning, Agneta's face was indeed covered with an itchy red rash which gradually spread over most of her body. But her fever was down and the coughing lessened. The Brightmore ladies were not pleased. Coventina was feverish and coughing.

"I'm itchy," Agneta complained.

Ascha thought for a while. "Caedmon, we need to trap mice. Ask Tybaut to help you."

"Mice?"

"Yes, we'll roast them."

"Roast them?" Agneta asked weakly.

Ascha hesitated. "Roasted mouse takes away itchiness."

Agneta struggled to prop herself up on her elbows. "I'm to eat them?"

Lady Ascha nodded.

"No, I refuse. I'd rather itch," Agneta exclaimed, bringing on another bout of coughing. She fell back on the pillow, and Caedmon could see she was exhausted. It pained him to see her fair face so ravaged.

"I feel terrible, and I'm sure I look terrible," she complained.

"You're still the most beautiful woman I've ever known," he whispered, cradling her face in his hands.

Ascha had been thinking. "The only other cure I know of is to rub a wolf skin over the rash, but where will we get a wolf skin? We could try boiling some white willow and dabbing it on. I'll talk to Cook."

It took another sennight for Agneta to be fully recovered, and meanwhile the Brightmore sisters and Lady Ascha were busy taking care of Coventina. Caedmon often bumped into Leofric pacing in the hallway outside Coventina's chamber.

"Don't worry, Leofric, she'll recover, like Agneta."

"They won't let me see her," his friend complained.

"Leofric, about Coventina," Caedmon began, not sure what he wanted to say. "I'd hate to see—"

"Caedmon, I love her. I can't help it. Surely you understand?"

"Yes, I understand," Caedmon replied sadly, putting his hand on his friend's shoulder. "But sometimes we want what we can't have. She may not—"

"You're a fine one to tell me this," Leofric retorted, shrugging away from Caedmon. "You couldn't have Agneta, but she's your wife now. I'll find a way. I don't have much to offer, but I love her."

"I know you do. I've known it for a while. Look, Leofric, you do have a lot to offer. I'll stand by you, whatever happens."

Once Agneta recovered, Caedmon found it more and more difficult to make up his mind about Ellesmere. He'd been shaken by her illness and didn't want to spend a single day away from her. He started making excuses about not going and suddenly time had gone by and Yuletide was upon them. Because they'd been unable to celebrate Yuletide properly the previous year, they planned to have a resounding celebration at Shelfhoc.

They decorated their home with ivy, holly, and boughs of evergreens. Tybaut procured ribbons in Shrewsbury and Agneta used them to embellish the garlands and wreaths and the Yule Tree. Morris dancers, mummers and sword dancers came from the surrounding communities to perform for them. Agneta clung nervously to Caedmon, her hand clasped over her mouth as she watched the dancers leap over the sharp swords and twirl intricate patterns in the air with them. The dance inevitably ended with a mock death, but the victim was *revived* by the *physician* who did the same for the dead hero in the Mummer plays.

Agneta remembered Caedmon's love of vegetables and had the kitchen prepare lots of winter chard and onions to accompany the venison. For their sweet they enjoyed marzipan and custard.

Lady Pamela fashioned a large Yule Wreath from cedar boughs. Everyone made a wish on it as they celebrated Epiphany gathered around a bonfire outside the house. Their faces reflected the glow of the flames and their breath on the cold air vanished quickly in the fire's heat. As lord of the manor, Caedmon had the first wish. He rubbed his hands together and put his right hand on the fragrant fronds of the boughs. "I wish for health and prosperity for us all," he proclaimed.

I wish for Agneta's love.

Agneta placed her hand on the wreath. "I wish for a babe," she whispered, blushing, her eyes downcast. Caedmon squeezed her cold hand. He'd hoped Agneta would be with child before this.

"I wish for a wife," Leofric said loudly, when his turn came.

Coventina reddened and cast a furtive glance at Leofric.

"I wish for a husband," the shy girl murmured, looking back at her toes.

The Brightmore women exchanged indignant glances that worried Caedmon.

"My turn," Lady Pamela said. "I wish the Normans had never come."

"No, Lady Pamela, you're supposed to wish for something in the future, not the past. We can't change the past," Lady Ascha said, and a wistful look stole over his mother's face as she looked at him.

I wish I could be sure she's happy. What is it that preoccupies her?

His mother took a deep breath. "I wish for an end to the enmity that divides this country."

"I echo that wish, Lady Ascha," came the sentiment from Lady Edythe.

They gathered closer to the flames to watch Caedmon lay the wreath on the bonfire. "I have one more wish, before this oath ring burns up completely," he laughed as the sparks flew. "I want to stop delaying my visit to Ellesmere and get it over with. I'm sending Tybaut to tell the Earl I'll be there two days hence."

Despite the heat from the flames that reddened everyone else's cheeks, the color drained from his mother's face. "Are you all right, mother? You look pale." He reached for her arm, to steady her and felt her tremble.

"I was too close to the flames," she stammered. "Or perhaps I have eaten too much over the last few days. Please excuse me. Time for me to retire to my bed. Goodnight. Thank you all for a wonderful Yuletide."

"Should I go with her?" Agneta asked. "She certainly seems to have no love for the Earl. When you mention his name—"

Caedmon clenched his fists. "Yes. I've noticed. If I found out he'd done anything to harm her all those years ago, I'd kill him."

CHAPTER SEVENTEEN

Ellesmere Castle, Salop, England, Yuletide 1095

Rambaud, First Earl of Ellesmere, and third *Comte* de Montbryce, didn't ride out on patrols to defend the Welsh Marches often nowadays. His favourite horse, Fortis, the steed that had helped him survive at Hastings, had died several years ago. Brindis, though a good horse, didn't have the same temperament.

He was content to visit the local market towns, continuing to promote trade and immigration from Normandie, and kept close track of the accounts of his various properties in the Marches and in Sussex, spending hours in sometimes tedious meetings with various stewards.

"I've decided I'm getting far too old to keep chasing Welsh rebels," he confided to his wife, Mabelle, as they relaxed in their comfortable solar. "Nine and twenty years is too long. Will the hatred and conflict between our peoples ever cease?"

His wife looked up at him. "Ram, don't be despondent. As our sons Robert and Baudoin have grown to be adults, they've developed an appreciation for the Welsh language and culture, despite the fact they were boys when they underwent their kidnapping ordeal at the hands of Welshmen. Our daughter, Hylda Rhonwen has a great fondness for the land of her birth. She often boasts of being born in the fortress of Cadair Berwyn in Wales."

Ram smiled. "*C'est vrai.* She likes being called Rhoni because it sounds more Welsh."

"Remember too that Rhodri ap Owain has made a point of not attacking your lands, since his marriage to Rhonwen, and she has visited us frequently, with her children. These are small steps. Change takes time."

"*Oui*, I was surprised Rhodri agreed to her visits."

"He loves Rhonwen deeply and is grateful that she agreed to marry him and share his life as a warrior, though she's a woman of peace."

Ram shook his head. "It's difficult to believe that eighteen years have passed since the kidnapping. You're a remarkable woman, Mabelle. It was only your strength that helped everyone survive that ordeal. I still keep your love letter close to my heart."

He patted his doublet, smiling at the memory of first reading the letter Mabelle had written on the last day of her captivity, avowing her love for him. He reminisced a lot these days.

I'm getting old.

He rubbed his knees. "I'm not as young as I was and my body isn't as capable of action as it used to be. And a pox on this cursed rheumatism."

Mabelle crossed the room to where her husband was seated, stood behind him and put her hands on his shoulders, kissing the top of his head. "Ram, be content. You and I share an intoxicating and erotic passion and our lovemaking is still a thrilling joy for us both, after all these years."

He reached up and took hold of her hands, drawing them around his neck, leaning his head back against her, inhaling the scent that was uniquely her. It had intoxicated him for nigh on thirty years. For as long as he'd known her, they'd been drawn to each other, the mere sight of her enough to arouse him.

His abilities as a diplomat and administrator had brought growth and prosperity to Ellesmere and the extensive lands to which he held title. Years ago, he'd been afraid his deep love for his wife and family would interfere with his ambitions and abilities, when in fact it had enhanced them. It had made him whole. He loved and was loved in return and had become one of the wealthiest and most influential men in England, with the help of his wife.

"You make me feel like a youth, Mabelle."

"You're still my stallion, Ram."

They remained locked together for several minutes until he drew her down on his lap, needing to feel the light friction of her body on his growing arousal. She leaned into him, cradled in his arms.

He kissed the top of her head. "My biggest regret is that we've never been able to return to Normandie to live. It's where we belong."

"We go at least once a year to see Robert, now that he has moved there permanently. I know he's a grown man of three and twenty and that, as the future *Comte* de Montbryce, he has to live in Normandie, to learn to administer the castle at Saint Germain, but I miss him and I worry about him."

"He must remain there. Those estates are of primary value," Ram replied. "Our second son, Baudoin, will inherit the lands in England, as well as the title of Earl of Ellesmere. Don't forget, my brothers, Antoine and Hugh, both now happily wed, are close by, controlling Belisle, Domfort and Alensonne. They are strong allies for Robert."

Mabelle chuckled. "It's hard to believe both your brothers have grown families of their own now."

"Harder still to believe Rhoni's eighteen. A woman."

"Soon, you'll need to look for a husband for her. In fact we've put it off long enough."

Ram wasn't looking forward to that prospect. Rhoni could be independent minded when she wanted to be—like her mother. Thoughts of his daughter reminded him of one of their visits to Normandie. They had gone to Bishop Eude's cathedral in Bayeux to see the magnificent embroidered display of the conquest of England. The boys were tremendously interested in the panels and the episodes they depicted, and Ram did his best to appear detached as he explained the events and phases of the Battle of Hastings. His sons were bursting with pride that their father had fought at Hastings and played a decisive role in the Norman victory.

Surprisingly, it was Rhoni who'd seemed to sense his unease. He continued to be haunted by the ghastly images of Hastings and feared he would be for the rest of his life. Several times he felt like rushing away to retch as the vivid scenes of the horror he'd witnessed, and participated in, assailed his memory. He relived the moment when he believed his own head had been severed from his body. He'd never told any of them about that terrifying episode.

"I can't believe it's been eight years since our beloved Conqueror died," he said. "It's incredible how much has changed since we were at his Coronation."

Mabelle nodded. "I remember that near-disaster well. Seems like only yesterday."

He laughed. "Those nervous Norman soldiers almost burned down Westminster Abbey."

They were silent for a while. He twirled his fingers absent-mindedly in her hair and stroked her leg, holding her tightly to him, his lips pressed to her temple. "We Normans have become the new English nobility, the new ruling class. We've lived in England close to thirty years. Thirty years! Castles are being built everywhere it seems. The church I commissioned for Ellesmere is a grand building. When I gaze up at the intricate rib vaulting, my heart swells with pride."

"But," Mabelle cautioned, "The Conqueror began his reign with words of conciliation, allowing those English who swore loyalty to him to retain some of their lands, but within ten years, he'd obliterated many of the higher echelons of the English nobility."

Ram agreed. "Some of our fellow Normans believe themselves invincible, and there's an inherent danger in that. After these many years, there's still tension between the conquerors and the conquered."

"But," she interjected again, "Your friend William kept good order, so that men of substance could travel about unmolested. If a man lay with a woman against her will, the King decreed he should have those parts of his anatomy with which he disported himself removed."

Ram glanced at her, a peculiar chill running up his spine. Then he saw the expression on her face. She had spoken in jest. His erection swelled and she raised her eyebrows and smiled, grinding into him.

"You look worried, Ram. I'm only playing with you and I love to do that."

She stood and took his hands, drawing him up from the chair. She fondled him, pressing her hand against the straining fabric of his hose and her breasts to his chest.

She was unaware that his serious demeanour was caused by the sudden unwelcome memory of what was *really* his biggest regret in life—he'd been unfaithful to her, during their betrothal. It was an infidelity that had bothered him since the aftermath of Hastings when he'd been taken, injured, to the manor house of a Saxon widow at Ruyton, in the Welsh Marches.

What bothered him most about the episode was that he hadn't had the courage to tell Mabelle about it. There never seemed to be a good time to bring it up. He was passionately in love with his wife and didn't want to hurt her. Yet he felt a compulsion to tell her. What a fool he was. He and Mabelle weren't married at the time, but he still felt he'd betrayed her. He only hoped she loved him enough to forgive him. It was the desire for her forgiveness that drove him to tell her. He was like a penitent thirsting for the Sacrament of Forgiveness.

"Much as I would love to stay here with you, I have to go speak with Bonhomme," Mabelle said.

He held on to her hand. "How long will you be?"

She kissed his fingertips. "Not long."

He couldn't bring the matter up in their private chamber. It wouldn't be appropriate in the room where they'd shared such fulfilling intimacy for many years. "Meet me in the gallery. I'll wait for you there."

As soon as she entered the gallery a short time later, his body responded in the usual way. He could tell by the suggestive smile and the fire in her eyes that she too was aroused at seeing him. He embraced her and kissed her on each cheek as he carefully took her hands in his. She broadened her smile and moved to arch her body to him, but he held her away, touching his fingers to the silver streaks in her beautiful hair.

"What's wrong, Ram?"

"I've something I need to tell you, Mabelle," he replied as calmly as he could. "Something about an occurrence at Ruyton, many years ago."

There was a tap at the door, and the steward entered.

"Sorry *milady*, I forgot—"

"Not now, Bonhomme," Ram said curtly, regretting, as the steward nodded and left quietly, that he'd been rude to the man whose family had served his for generations.

Mabelle's belly clenched. She'd wondered about Ruyton, suspecting that her husband had bedded another woman there in the period after Hastings, and before the Conqueror's coronation. She knew he'd been taken to the manor house of a Saxon noblewoman. At first rage had consumed her, but the more she thought about how anguished he must have been, and how little support she had provided him, the more inclined she was not to judge him. He'd never mentioned it and she sensed that, if it had happened, he regretted it.

We weren't married. I had released him from our betrothal. Why does it torment him?

Now she sensed what was to come. "You can tell me, Ram," she said, hoping she would meet this challenge with grace.

Ram took hold of her hands, but his head was bowed as he admitted, "It was after Hastings—I was—I'd been injured, as you know, in the skirmish with Rhodri."

He raised his head and looked at her face. "Mabelle—I broke my betrothal vows to you. I bedded another woman."

He expected her to pull away from him, but she didn't. Silence filled the room.

"Tell me about it, my husband," she whispered finally.

He looked into her eyes. He saw tears welling, but didn't see condemnation. He sighed, drew her over to a chair and bade her sit. He sat in the other chair, and leaned forward, his forearms on his thighs. He told her the story, pausing now and again to run his hands through his greying hair.

She was silent for a long time, and then asked, "Is she still in Scotland?"

"I suppose. As far as I know she's never returned to the manor in Ruyton, only because I've administered the estate, through a seneschal who keeps in touch with her, and have provided men-at-arms as security. I did that partly through a sense of wanting to protect a woman alone, and also to safeguard a vulnerable property in the Marches from the Welsh. But I made it known in no uncertain terms I wasn't to be bothered with any of it."

"You've never seen her since that day?"

"No. I've never wanted to see her. I felt no love for her, only compassion. I didn't force her, Mabelle, you must believe that. But she didn't force me either."

She rose from her chair, took his hands in hers and bade him rise. "Ram, I've sensed something happened at Ruyton, long ago that you regretted. I thought it had something to do with a woman, but I love you with all my heart. If you love someone, you can forgive them. I forgave you long ago for this."

He put his arms around her waist. "Mabelle," he whispered hoarsely, "What did I do to deserve you? You're my life, and I worship you. Everything I am, everything I have is yours. I'm sorry I've hurt you."

She encircled his waist, and drew his body to hers. "Ram, you're a wonderful man. A proud Norman, a credit to your country, a brave hero, strong, educated, loving, a good father, husband, and brother, a handsome and passionate lover. A true Montbryce. But no one is perfect. You'd endured the horror of Hastings. I was immersed in my own grief and confusion and failed to provide you with the love you needed, to help you deal with the toll that battle took on you. We weren't married then."

He shook his head. "But my heart told me you were my destiny, Mabelle. I knew it was a betrayal."

He drew her closer and they clung to each other. She held him tightly as the long pent up regrets shook him. It was a lament for the friends and comrades lost amid horrendous carnage almost thirty years before, for the anguish of their separation during her kidnapping, for his dead Conqueror, for his homesickness for Normandie, and for his betrayal of the woman he loved. But his tears were also ones of relief that she'd forgiven him.

"You must think me a coward," he sniffled, though he had to admit the experience had been a cleansing one.

Mabelle put her palm against his cheek. "Ram, a man who can't cry, who can't feel things deeply, isn't a man. One thing you could never be accused of is cowardice. Let's go to our chamber. It's getting late."

"Hmm. Did you say *handsome and passionate lover* a while ago? Is that what I am?" he said, smiling at her, feeling suddenly like a young stallion.

"Oh, *oui*—and more," she smiled back. "I should have added *insatiable*."

"*Non*, Mabelle, that would mean I can't be satisfied, and you more than satisfy my needs. Come, let me show you."

Two hours later, as he lay with his wife's warm body nestled against him, he remembered that their son Robert would soon be visiting from Normandie for the Yuletide celebrations.

"When is Robert arriving?" he asked lazily.

"Two days hence."

"It will be good to see him, but I worry about the amount of time he spends away from Normandie. His life is there. He'll be the *Comte*. He needs to get established."

"He knows that. He's happy to live in Normandie. He only comes because he misses us and his brother and sister, especially at this time of year."

CHAPTER EIGHTEEN

Robert de Montbryce, eldest son of the Earl and Countess of Ellesmere, strode into the Great Hall of his father's impressive castle in England with the confidence that was his birthright. His parents were immensely proud of him. As a boy he'd endured being kidnapped and threatened with beheading by a maniac bent on misguided revenge, yet he'd dealt with it all with courage and resilience.

He'd grown into a handsome man, the mirror image of his father. He was lithe, fit and strong, and had the same piercing blue eyes as his sire. He was a trained warrior who'd accompanied the Earl in skirmishes against the Welsh and had acquitted himself well. Aware of his inheritance, he'd assumed the mantle of the castle in Normandie and the lands there without qualm. He'd stepped smoothly into the role of *comte*-in-waiting. He loved Normandie.

"Robert. *Mon fils*." Mabelle cried, flinging her arms open wide when she saw her son enter.

"*Maman,*" he replied with a smile, hugging her.

"Robert. Good to see you my boy," said his father, coming forward to embrace him.

"Papa, it's good to see you too."

"Robert!" Hylda Rhonwen flung her arms around his neck.

"Ah! Rhoni, I'm content to linger in the warm embrace of my loving sister. You're growing up, little Welshwoman." Family tradition demanded they all tease Hylda Rhonwen about being born in Wales.

They talked for a long while, enjoying the easy warmth that only members of a loving family can share with each other. Ram felt good. He'd loved his own parents, and they'd loved him. He'd made a point after the kidnapping of making sure his children were aware he cared deeply about them and he was confident they loved him. They trusted each other, aware that a great family could only prosper if its members shared love and trust. Family treachery had divided many noble houses, as evidenced by Mabelle's own family, the Valtesses.

Robert brought them up to date on the news from Normandie, and Ram shared his opinions of King William Rufus.

"William hasn't been successful expanding our influence into Wales," he confided. "Though he's an effective soldier, he's a ruthless ruler who's disliked by those he governs. He's hateful to all his people, roundly denounced for presiding over what's held to be a dissolute court and questions have been raised about his sexual preferences."

He noticed his wife's look of disapproval. "Sorry Mabelle, my dear. He's a flamboyant character with a belligerent temperament who hasn't married, and hasn't sired any bastards, let alone legitimate heirs."

If Ram voiced these thoughts in some circles, he could be charged with treason, but he was safe here at home with his wife and children. "I'm the proudest and most stalwart Norman there is, but we have to embrace the culture of the English to a certain degree, if we want to rule here successfully and for the long term. After all these years, people still rebel against us. Have we learned nothing? William Rufus scorns the English and their culture. He's cruel, grasping, and arrogant and lacks tact and discretion. As you know, he's frequently in conflict with his elder brother Curthose, Duke of the Normans."

"But the worst situation is with the Church. With the death of Lanfranc, the Archbishop of Canterbury, the King lost his father's advisor and confidant. After Lanfranc's death, he delayed appointing a new archbishop for many years, appropriating ecclesiastical revenues in the interim."

A servant entered with refreshments. Everyone stopped talking. Robert indicated to the girl that he would pour the wine for his parents. She nodded and left. Robert handed his father a goblet of wine.

"*Merci, mon fils.*"

"Go on, Papa," Robert said, pouring for everyone else. "Only sit. Your pacing is making us all nervous."

Ram laughed, and sank down into his favourite chair, rubbing his knees. "Gladly. In a panic when he was seriously ill, Rufus nominated

Anselm of Bec as Archbishop, but this has led to animosity between Church and King. Anselm can't condone the King's actions. Rufus feuds with his bishops and confiscates church revenues for his own extravagances."

Ram glanced at Mabelle, and sensed her irritation. "I know we talk of naught else, but—"

Mabelle interrupted him. "It's important you discuss these matters. Don't worry."

Ram nodded his gratitude and continued. They discussed the situation in Scotland and agreed it was confusing and volatile. Robert had heard much of this before, but was tremendously interested in his father's opinions. What happened in England affected his position in Normandie. The politics of both countries had become inextricably intertwined.

"*Alors*," the younger Montbryce commented, "William Rufus has succeeded in consolidating his power during these early years of his reign, but has done so largely by bad faith and brutality rather than by military skill and diplomacy. But the underlying problem remains that we have a ruler of the Normans, Duke Robert Curthose, and a ruler of the English, King William Rufus, which results in us Normans trying to serve two masters."

"*Exactement!* You have it exactly, Robert. That's what some of us have attempted to achieve, one ruler for both. Otherwise there's too much instability. Our Conqueror's half brother, Bishop Eude, has often pointed out that if we serve Duke Robert Curthose of Normandie, we'll offend our King William Rufus and he may deprive us of our revenues in England. However, if we serve King William Rufus, Duke Robert Curthose may confiscate our lands in Normandie."

Ram shook his head, exasperated with the political games that seemed to swirl around them constantly. Sometimes he wished he could withdraw to Saint Germain and enjoy his apple orchards.

"I see your *Maman* has finished her wine, and she and Rhoni are getting bored with all this talk of politics."

He suspected Mabelle wanted to steer the conversation in other directions, especially to when Robert intended to marry and produce heirs. "Baudoin will be here soon to join us for the meal," he informed Robert. "He's meeting with some of the tenant farmers."

Mabelle suggested they take their places for the meal the servants were about to serve. "Trésor has prepared your favourite foods,

Robert, let's go enjoy them. You know how she is if we don't appear for meals when she has them ready. She rules here, not your father."

They all laughed, knowing she spoke the truth about the cook who'd been trained in Normandie to come and serve them in England many years ago. Trésor had boxed Robert's ears on more than one occasion.

CHAPTER NINETEEN

"Do you want me to accompany you to Ellesmere?" Agneta asked on the eve of Caedmon's departure.

"No, I prefer you stay here. It will be difficult to be apart, but I don't know what to expect there. I've been told the Earl is a fair man, but you might be safer here. I've sent Tybaut ahead to tell the Earl of my intention to visit."

"I'll miss you in my bed," she murmured coyly.

He hoped she would add *and in my heart*, but it was a forlorn wish. He took her by the hand and led her to their chamber.

There was a hint of melancholy about their lovemaking. It would be the first separation since their marriage. He slowly kissed her mouth and tasted her lips, then feathered kisses down her neck. He spiraled his tongue around the whole globe of her breast in teasing circles until he reached her nipple, repeating the ritual with the other breast.

Agneta writhed in pleasurable anticipation. His tongue found her navel and he ran the tip of it round and round then pressed hard below her navel. Her moans of delight were music to his ears.

He sucked each of her toes in turn and then licked the soles of her feet. She stretched, arched her back and opened her legs in invitation. He kissed her thighs, beginning behind her knees and ending at the place where he knew she ached for him. He lifted her hips. His tongue pressed between her legs and licked. She rose to the challenge and pushed against him. He lapped her, savoring her essence. He sensed her rising to a crescendo and she screamed his name in surrender. The notion passed through his mind that he could postpone yet again the journey to Ellesmere.

When her breathing had steadied, she motioned for him to lie on his back, climbed on top of him, cradled his engorged manhood between her breasts, and rocked.

"Feels good," he crooned.

Then she engulfed him with her warm mouth and moved on him.

"I can't wait any longer," he rasped after a minute or two.

"Come inside me," she whispered.

He turned her over onto her back and entered her warm wet centre, pounding into her, his loins on fire. His ecstasy reached its pinnacle and he filled her.

They fell asleep in each other's arms. He wondered how he could survive a three or four day separation.

As Agneta drifted off to sleep, she acknowledged that she would miss Caedmon terribly, and not only in her bed. She had to reluctantly admit yet again that she was in love with him. It confused her that she could trust Caedmon with her body and share the most intimate of touches and caresses with him. He wasn't a trustworthy person. He'd been partially responsible for the deaths of her family, but her heart knew he wasn't an evil man. In fact, he was gentle and kind, strong and brave. He deeply regretted his part in the Bolton raid. She recalled how he'd looked that day as she peered, with terrified eyes, through the chink in the planking of the barn. His heart had not been in the deed. She resolved to tell him of her forgiveness, when he returned from Ellesmere.

***

Tybaut had already left to inform the Earl of Caedmon's imminent arrival. When the steward arrived at Ellesmere, he discovered the Earl was away and wouldn't be returning until later that night. He wouldn't be available until the morrow—the day Caedmon planned to meet with him. Tybaut couldn't wait until the next day. He'd made arrangements to meet with someone in Shrewsbury that same night, on his way back to Ruyton, to procure more ribbons for Lady Agneta.

He sought out his friend and fellow steward, Martin Bonhomme and found him in the kitchens. "My friend, I need your help to convey a message to the Earl," he said as he swilled down the ale Bonhomme offered him.

Bonhomme raised his own tankard to his lips. "I'll see to it. What do you want me to tell him?"

"I've been assigned to the manor at Shelfhoc for some time now."

"*Oui*, lucky dog. Off the beaten track, not much work," teased his easygoing friend, whose father Mathieu had in fact procured the post for Tybaut.

Tybaut took another big gulp, smacked his lips and carried on, "It's true there hasn't been much to do there, but I've done my best to carry out the Earl's wishes. Anyway, out of nowhere, maybe a year ago, comes the thane, Sir Caedmon Woolgar and his lady wife, to take up residence."

"Huh. A year ago?" was all his friend could apparently say.

"I suppose I should have come tell the Earl, but my strict instructions have been not to bother him with anything to do with Shelfhoc and all is in order."

"Hmmm."

"Anyway, be that as it may, he's a pleasant fellow, albeit a Saxon. But he wants to see the Earl on the morrow. Come to pledge his service, no doubt, and give his thanks. I was supposed to tell the Earl about his coming."

Bonhomme slapped his companion on the back. "Leave it with me, Tybaut. I'm to meet with the Earl early on the morrow. He plans to return late tonight and I'll tell him about his visitor. I doubt the matter will take much time?"

"Probably not," Tybaut replied, swigging down the last of the dark ale and swiping his sleeve across his mouth. "Obliged to you, my friend. I'll be off now. Want to make it back to Shrewsbury before dark. There's something bothers me about this Sir Caedmon. He reminds me of someone, but who?"

"Never met him, therefore I'm no help with your quandary. Sir Caedmon Woolgar. These strange Saxon names! I'll remember it. Good journey, *mon ami*."

As Tybaut left the kitchens he bumped into Robert de Montbryce. "Beg your pardon, *milord* Robert. It's good to see you back from Normandie. I trust all is well at the castle there?" he asked, bowing deferentially.

"Steward—Tybaut, isn't it? Things are relatively good in Normandie," Robert replied, with a grin, walking away quickly. "I'm looking for Trésor and I can't be deterred from my errand. She usually has something good to eat tucked away for me."

In that instant Tybaut found the answer to the question that had nagged at him since he'd met Sir Caedmon. "I have it," he murmured gleefully. "Sir Caedmon could be *milord* Robert's twin brother—except Sir Caedmon is older. They look much alike."

***

When Bonhomme met with his Earl the following morning they discussed matters concerning Ellesmere that needed immediate attention. He suddenly remembered the message his friend had asked him to pass on.

"Oh, *milord* Earl, it slipped my mind. Tybaut, the steward appointed to Shelfhoc Manor, was here yesterday with a message. He wanted to inform you that the thane, Sir Caedmon Woolgar, and his lady wife, have returned to the manor."

The Earl's reaction wasn't what the steward expected. He jumped out of his chair. "Sir Caedmon Woolgar? He's dead. He died at Hastings. It can't be him. His lady wife? Did he mention her name? Was it Lady Ascha?"

Bonhomme searched his memory. "No, *milord*, he didn't mention the lady's name. Anyway, Tybaut said Sir Caedmon is coming here to see you today—to thank you—for the manor and all."

The Earl scratched his head. "Today? He's coming here today?"

Bonhomme wasn't sure why the Earl was visibly upset by this news.

"Is the Lady of Shelfhoc expected?"

"Not that Tybaut mentioned, *milord*."

The Earl seemed relieved at that news, but started pacing the room, his brow furrowed.

"Will there be anything further?" the steward asked.

"*Non*, Bonhomme, *merci*. I need to speak with my Countess. Do you know where she is?"

"I believe she's in the kitchen with Trésor, *milord*."

Ram ran to the kitchens to find Mabelle, leaving a perplexed Bonhomme behind. He asked her hurriedly to meet him in their chamber as soon as possible. Trésor bit back a grin as the flustered countess left the kitchen. "Our Earl can't keep his hands off his wife," she chuckled to the scullery wench. "They've always been that way. Rushing off to their chamber this early in the day. What I wouldn't do for a lusty man like that."

When Mabelle arrived, Ram paced the room nervously.

"What is it Ram? What's wrong?"

He took hold of her hands. "I'm not sure. I've received a message that Sir Caedmon Woolgar has returned to Shelfhoc Manor and is coming here to see me today."

"But you said—"

"*Oui*, Mabelle, Lady Ascha believed her husband died at Hastings. Perhaps he didn't. But where has he been all these years? The news gets worse. Apparently, he didn't return alone. His lady wife is with him. I'm sorry, Mabelle, but I don't know if she'll accompany him."

"Ram," she replied calmly. "We'll receive them together. You're the Earl and I'm the Countess. They are vassals for whom you've done a great deal. They can only be grateful. If Lady Ascha is coming here she's probably more worried about it than you are. Her husband may not be aware of your interlude with her."

"That's what I'm afraid of," he confessed.

CHAPTER TWENTY

Impatiently cooling his heels in the courtyard garden of Ellesmere Castle, Caedmon rehearsed over and over what he would say to the Earl. How much longer would he have to wait? He was anxious to return to his beloved Agneta. A young Norman nobleman sauntered by, evidently looking for someone.

"Robert de Montbryce," the young man introduced himself, bowing his head slightly. "I'm the Earl's son."

"Sir Caedmon Woolgar," Caedmon replied. "I'm waiting to speak with the Earl." There was something familiar about this nobleman. "Have we met before, Lord Robert?"

"I don't believe so—though—there's something—my father is in the Map Room with my mother. He sent me to fetch you. I got the mistaken impression you were an older man. And you have a Scottish burr. If you'll follow me, I'll show you the way."

Caedmon entered the room and Ram saw him.

Robert started to introduce the visitor, but stopped when he saw the shocked look on his father's ashen face. His mother's hand went to her mouth and she let out an involuntary startled cry, grasping the arm of a chair.

"What is it, Papa? Are you ill?" Robert asked worriedly.

Ram had to sit down, as did Mabelle. Neither of them took their eyes off Caedmon.

"What is it, Papa, *Maman*? I'm sorry, Sir Caedmon, I don't know what's wrong. I'm embarrassed."

"I admit this isn't the reception I envisaged," Caedmon muttered.

Ram was the first to get hold of his emotions. He could see no point in denying or avoiding the truth that had slapped him in the face. He stood. Bitterly aware of the hurt he was about to inflict, he said to Robert, "You can't see it, can you?"

"See what, Papa?" Robert followed his father's gaze to Caedmon and turned to look fully at the man he'd escorted into the room. He gasped and his jaw fell open. "You look like my father," he exclaimed. "Who are you? Are you a Montbryce?"

At the same moment Caedmon looked more closely at the Earl. His hand went to the hilt of his sword. He tore his gaze from the Earl and looked at the Countess. Ram saw his reaction to the compassionate and stricken expression on her face. He felt Caedmon's eyes on him as he turned to his wife and said, "I didn't know there was a child, Mabelle. I swear I didn't know."

She nodded.

Had Caedmon heard? Ram saw the truth sink into the newcomer's befuddled mind. The young man drew his sword and strode angrily toward him. "How can it be, Norman beast, that your face is my face? You must be a rapist, a violator of women. Did you rape my mother? Now I understand why she didn't want me to come here. You raped a defenseless widow. Was it not enough that Norman dogs slew her husband?"

Ram stood rooted to the spot, shaking his head. Robert recovered from his shock and ran to stop Caedmon. But Mabelle moved calmly to stand between the enraged young knight and her husband.

"Sir Caedmon," she said quietly, "If you kill my husband, it's likely you would be killing your own father. I'm sure we can agree that wouldn't be the best thing. You would regret it for the rest of your life, if you escaped the noose. My husband isn't a rapist."

Caedmon lowered his sword, but didn't sheathe it. "You can hide behind a woman's skirts, high and mighty Earl of Ellesmere, but that doesn't change the fact you shamed my mother." He spat the words out. "I came here today to thank you for taking care of my estate. Hah, I often wondered why you were so generous. Now I know it was guilt at work. You shamed my mother and you've shamed me. I came into this room a proud Saxon knight, the son of a war hero who gave his life in defense of his country. I'm leaving as the bastard of a filthy Norman pig."

He hurried from the room, sword still in hand.

Robert went to follow, but his mother stopped him. "Let him go, Robert. You need to stay here. We must talk. Go find your brother and sister."

Robert looked angrily at his parents. "I sense whatever we'll *talk* about won't be good."

He left to find his siblings.

When they were alone Mabelle turned to Ram who had slumped into the chair, pressing his fingertips into his forehead. "He's a fine boy, Ram. In truth, he's not a boy. He's a man. He's your son and you mustn't be ashamed of him or make him feel ashamed. It has obviously been as much of a shock for him as for us."

"Why didn't she tell me? I had no idea. I would have acknowledged the boy. I would have supported them." He shook his head. "He won't wish to see me again, he made that clear."

"He's angry and confused. So is Robert. Baudoin and Rhoni will be too. But they love you. They'll come to understand. You must reach out to Caedmon. We must both reach out."

Slowly, he came to his feet to embrace her, and rested his chin on the top of her head. "All those years ago when I watched in disbelief as you threw my sword into the lake, the thought ran through my head that you were stronger than you looked. Little did I know. You've proven to be the strongest half of our union. I thank you for your strength."

***

Caedmon wasn't sure how far or in which direction he'd ridden, but as he rode his fury grew to encompass not only the Norman who'd sired him, but the woman who had birthed him. As he went over and over the events of the fateful meeting in his mind, he recalled the Countess saying her husband wasn't a rapist. To his confused brain that must mean his mother had consented. She was a strumpet, a whore, bedding a Norman before her husband's grave had gone cold.

Head pounding, he slowed Abbot to a walk then reined the horse to a halt. Sliding dispiritedly from the saddle, he barely noticed he was in a clearing in a copse. He tied Abbot's reins to a tree, sank to his hands and knees in the rustling carpet of dead leaves and twigs and sobbed until he retched.

Everything he'd believed was suddenly not true. It would have been better if he'd never recovered after Alnwick, or, better still, why hadn't he died on that field?

"I'm nothing," he cried to the uncaring trees. "Less than nothing. As a bastard, I don't have a right to the manor I claimed as my own. I can offer Agneta nothing."

His wife's name on his lips intensified his pain and he sobbed until he lay exhausted on the forest floor, full of loathing for himself and the man and woman who had sired him. When he could cry no more, he struggled to his feet, found a blanket in his saddle bags and curled up in it. He lay awake watching as darkness fell and stars appeared in the sky.

"What do the stars portend for me now?" he wondered aloud. "I can't live off the income of a house I've no right to. I can no longer take money from my whore of a mother. I'll have to make my living as a mercenary. It's no life for a woman. I will lose Agneta."

It was more than he could bear. "But where will she go? I'm all she has, and I'm nothing. How can I tell her I'm base born? She hates me already. She will despise my bastardy more."

Exhaustion claimed him and he slept fitfully beneath the winter canopy.

***

By the time Robert returned to the Map Room with Baudoin and Rhoni, he'd told them about the events that had occurred there and his suspicions that the unknown knight was their father's bastard.

"You both seem rather calm," Robert said to his parents with some irritation.

Ram clutched the wooden arms of his chair and squared his shoulders. "*Mes enfants*, I'm sincerely sorry you had to find out about this in such a manner. I take full responsibility for what has happened. I didn't know of the young man's existence. I was unaware my indiscretion many years ago had produced a child."

"*Mon père*," Robert replied, "You need to tell us what happened."

Ram sighed, noticing his son had addressed him more formally than usual. He told the story, deciding to leave out nothing, to tell the whole truth about his fears during the battle, his emotions, his stupid bravado with Rhodri and his resulting humiliation, his frustrations, his worry for his brother, Hugh, Ascha's pain and longing—all of it. They were surely mature enough to understand about fears and emotions. He hoped so.

He remained seated in his chair and Mabelle stood behind him, her hands on his shoulders, indicating, he thanked God for it, that she still loved their father, that she'd forgiven him, that this painful experience wouldn't destroy their family.

Robert paced as the silence dragged on. Baudoin sat on the edge of a bench staring at his feet. Rhoni fidgeted with her braids.

Ram watched his children struggle with their new found knowledge. Finally, he spoke again. "I intend to recognize him as my son. You all need to be aware of that."

Robert stopped pacing and looked at his father. "*Mon père*," he managed to say, "What to say to you? This is a lot to digest. I'm not sure what Rhoni and Baudoin think—"

"I think," the taciturn Baudoin interjected unexpectedly, "That this family has undergone some terrible ordeals, but we've survived because we've faced them together. We have today learned things about our father. About our mother, too."

Ram was moved by the maturity of his youngest son, and the compassionate look in his eyes.

"Papa," Baudoin continued, his voice strong, "I know you to be a loving father and husband. Discovering I have a half brother doesn't change that. While I may not approve of your infidelity towards my mother, it's evident she has forgiven you and I can't find it in my heart to condemn you. You are still my father. Some noblemen sow their seed at random and sire bastards with impunity. You've never been that sort of man. You're the kind of man I've aspired to be, and still aspire to be. You are my liege lord and I am your loyal man."

Ram rose from his chair as Baudoin walked towards him and the two men embraced. He could see Robert was still conflicted.

"Robert," Mabelle now spoke, tightening her grip on Ram's shoulders. "Your father and I hadn't spoken our wedding vows to each other when this happened. If it was a mistake it's one that will obviously have repercussions for many people. But we need to do what we've always done as a family. We must turn this to our advantage. You're hurt, but think about the young man who just left us. Everything he has ever believed about his birth is suddenly not true. He has Montbryce blood in his veins. We must help him see the value in that. At this moment he sees himself as nothing, but he's a Montbryce. He's your half brother. You need to be man enough to accept that. We can't cast him out. I know what it is to lead the life of an outcast, and I have experienced the destructive power of anger."

"*Maman*," her son replied, aware of his mother's difficult years of exile wandering around Normandie with her father. "I suppose my problem is I have too much Montbryce pride. I expected my father to be perfect and of course that was naive and unfair of me. No one can truly understand the burdens and adversities another person has to face and therefore shouldn't sit in judgment."

Turning to his father and looking him in the eye, he said in a strong voice, "Papa, as your heir, I should have been the one to voice the sentiments Baudoin has spoken. My younger brother has put me to shame with his maturity, and I bow to him. I too have no greater aspiration than to be the man you are. You are my liege lord and I am your loyal man."

Ram clasped the hand Robert proffered and they embraced. Then the Earl turned to his daughter. She ran to her father and embraced him. "I don't understand why you feel guilty about it, Papa, if you and *Maman* weren't married?"

Ram stroked his beloved daughter's hair. "I'd given your mother my troth, my pledge. And my heart told me she was the only woman for me."

Rhoni looked up at him. "I love you, Papa. I'll learn to love my new brother."

Ram and Mabelle had never been prouder of their children. He found it difficult to speak as he watched them struggle with their emotions. "I'll offer Caedmon the name FitzRam. He may not accept it, but I'll offer it. We'll decide between us what lands and titles to confer on him and what he will inherit when I die."

The three Montbryce children nodded and left together, arm in arm. Ram and Mabelle stood together, locked in an embrace, his chin resting lightly on the top of her head.

She reassured him. "They understood in confirming their allegiance to you in this matter that it would mean sharing with their newly discovered half brother."

"I know, but it pains me that Robert felt it necessary to remind me he's my heir, though he's no longer my eldest son."

CHAPTER TWENTY-ONE

Caedmon had been gone a sennight and Agneta worried about her missing husband. Tybaut had assured her he'd given the Earl the message about his visit and, as far as he knew, Sir Caedmon had met with the Earl. Where was he and why had she heard nothing? He'd said it would be two or three days at the most. Why hadn't he returned or sent a message?

Lady Ascha was acting strangely and scurried off to her chamber when Agneta broached the subject of Caedmon's prolonged absence. She took all her meals in her own chamber. Leofric paced and Agneta could see the concern etched on his face as he returned from several fruitless rides out into the surrounding countryside to find his friend.

By the tenth day everyone was beside themselves with worry. Sleep for Agneta had been elusive. She sat by the window, as she did every day, watching the distant hills, praying to see Caedmon come over the rise. Leofric had gone off on another search. Agneta hadn't seen Lady Ascha for three days.

She fell into a doze, but suddenly became aware of a commotion in the courtyard. She hurried out, but stopped abruptly at the sight of Caedmon dismounting. He was swearing at the stable boy and seemed to be having difficulty standing.

She rushed to embrace him, relief flooding her heart. "Caedmon, I've been worried."

He swayed, barely able to remain upright. She stepped back. He'd sprouted an unkempt beard and his body odor was offensive.

An oxcart, rain, a spile in my hand.

She also detected the strong smell of ale. "Caedmon? What's happened to you?"

"Agneta—my beautiful lady Agneta," he gushed then hiccupped, falling over.

She tried to steady him. "Caedmon. Are you—have you been drinking?"

He looked at her, but she could tell he wasn't seeing her. "Do you mean am I drunk? Aye, I'm drunk. I've drunk. I mean, I've been drinkin'—for days—"

He slumped to the ground.

"Tybaut," she shouted to the steward, her mind reeling. "Sir Caedmon is unwell, please help me get him to his chamber."

The steward emerged from the house and ran to her aid. Agneta suddenly noticed Lady Ascha leaning heavily on the doorpost, her hand pressed to her mouth. She scurried back into the house when Agneta looked at her.

Tybaut and another servant had to carry Caedmon to the chamber, where they deposited him on the bed.

What will the steward think of my husband coming home like this? And the Brightmores.

Out of breath, the steward made a suggestion. "Perhaps an herbal tisane, *milady?* I'll get Cook to see to it."

"Thank you, Tybaut, but first we must get him out of these filthy clothes."

She muttered nervously, not sure what to make of the drunken spectacle passed out on her bed. It wasn't the passionate reunion she'd envisioned. With difficulty, they stripped him as he raved in a drunken stupor.

Such a man should not be bound.

"We need to get him into a bath, but how will we manage it?"

"I'll get the stable boy."

Tybaut returned in short order with a burly lad and Leofric entered with them. His voice betrayed his shock. *"Godemite!* It's not the first time I've seen Caedmon suffer the effects of one too many ales, but I've never seen him like this. Where's he been?"

"I don't know," Agneta murmured.

Tybaut's wife had filled up the tub with hot water. Tybaut and the lad and Leofric picked up Caedmon with difficulty and deposited him in the hot water. He protested loudly, but Agneta soothed him. "Hush, Caedmon, hush, let me bathe you."

"Leave us," she whispered to the others. "He'll be calmer if there's just me."

"Are you sure?" Leofric asked, looking doubtful.

She nodded and the other men left. She cleansed Caedmon's body with the soft linen cloth. He suddenly burst into song, but evidently couldn't recall the words and laughed a silly laugh that set her teeth on edge. The memory of his genuine laugh rolled over her. Gradually he calmed and let her minister to him. How would she shave off the grubby beard he'd acquired?

He liked me to shave him in the infirmary.

It would have to wait until he'd sobered. Her mind was in turmoil. She couldn't imagine what had happened to cause this change in his behaviour. He passed out in the tub and she had to call Tybaut and Leofric to help her get him out and deposit him on their bed. His wet body was more difficult to manhandle, especially with Leofric's damaged hand.

She sent them away with her embarrassed thanks and set about drying his body, the beautiful body she loved, the body that had given her such intense pleasure. She blotted him dry, tears welling as she lovingly dabbed the scar on his thigh. She was careful not to disturb his manhood curled in its black nest, not wanting to arouse him and have him try to make love to her in this condition.

"Caedmon, what has happened to you? Where have you been?" she whispered.

"I'm nothing, Agneta, nothing." He said it so quietly she barely heard it.

"What do you mean, Caedmon? You're everything to me."

"I'm less than nothing," he murmured as he lapsed back into a stupor.

She donned her night gown and lay beside him, cradling him in her arms. "I'm here, Caedmon. I'm here," she whimpered, struggling to hold back her fear.

He woke at dawn and vomited into the chamber pot. She wiped his face with a wet cloth and he fell back to sleep. How could she help him if she didn't know what had happened? Two hours later he vomited again and then sat on the edge of the bed for another hour staring at his feet, his head in his hands.

"Caedmon?" she ventured, coming to sit beside him and putting her arm around his shoulders.

"Leave me be, woman," he shouted, pushing her away. "Leave me be." He slumped back down on the bed, his knees clasped to his belly.

She was angry now. She'd done nothing to deserve being pushed away. She jumped to her feet. "Caedmon stop it! Stop this! You're not a drunkard. Why are you behaving this way? Don't push me away. You're hurting me."

He became instantly contrite and sat up. "Agneta, my beautiful Agneta. I don't want to hurt you. But I'm not the man you married. I'm nothing."

She clenched her fists, longing to touch him, to bring comfort, but afraid. "Stop saying that."

He continued to sit on the edge of the bed with his head in his hands.

"Did you meet the Earl? Did he say something to bring on this—this state you are in? I demand you tell me, Caedmon. You're making me afraid."

He slowly raised his head and looked at her, his eyes red rimmed. "Oh, aye. I met the Earl. And surprise, surprise. It turns out I'm the man's bastard son. Me, the proud Caedmon Brice Woolgar, son of a martyr of Hastings, I'm the by-blow of a Norman pig."

Agneta's mouth fell open. She frowned and shook her head. "I don't understand, Caedmon. How can you be his son?"

"It seems my wonderful, caring mother was a strumpet who bedded the Norman dog before her husband's grave had grown cold. I'll send her to a nunnery."

"Not so loud," Agneta gasped, looking anxiously at the door. "Caedmon, your mother's not—"

He tried unsuccessfully to stand. "Enough! Bring me some ale."

Agneta clenched her hands together. "No, Caedmon, no more ale. You've had enough."

He managed to get to his feet and thumped his chest with his fist. "I'll be the person who decides that. I may be the bastard of Norman filth, but I'm still the master here—oh, no—that's not true is it—I'm not the master here—I don't have the right to this manor—it probably belongs rightfully to some other *legitimate* Woolgar relative."

"Caedmon, stop," she pleaded desperately as he swayed. He walked unsteadily to the *armoire*, shoved back the curtain and with difficulty donned the clothing he grabbed from within. She was afraid to offer assistance.

"Agneta, it's over. I'm a dead man, a man without honor. I've lost everything important to me. I can't be your husband. I don't have the right."

He staggered out of the chamber, thundered down the stairs and she heard the front door slam.

"No, Caedmon," she whispered. "You haven't lost everything. I'm still here." The tears streamed down her face. What to say to make him stay? She cried herself to sleep alone in their bed.

***

Caedmon slowly came to his senses in Abbot's stall. What in the name of all the Saints was he to do? His heart ached at the possibility of losing his beautiful wife, but he had nothing to offer her now. He stripped to the waist, doused his head in the horse trough and splashed the icy water over his body.

When he looked up, his mother stood in front of him, swaying nervously, her fists clenched. Leofric stood a few paces behind.

"Strumpet," he exclaimed. She winced. Leofric's good hand went to the hilt of his dagger.

"Caedmon—"

"Silence. Go to your chamber." He splashed water from the trough at her. She gazed down at her soaked gown in shock. Leofric rushed to support her as she swayed.

"Caedmon—" Leofric tried, his eyes burning.

"Be gone, all of you. Get out of my sight," he shouted, catching a glimpse of the Brightmore sisters peering nervously through the partly open front door. "And get those interfering hags out of my sight too."

Ascha gasped and with a backward glance of disbelief at Caedmon, let Leofric assist her as she fled, sobbing.

Dragging his feet, Caedmon slowly climbed to his own chamber and tapped lightly. Hearing no invitation to enter, he opened the door and crept inside. Agneta was still asleep, amid a tumble of disheveled bed linens. He found a clean shirt, dragged it over his head and moved silently to the bed, where he sat down, trying not to disturb her, but wanting to watch her in repose.

Her eyelids fluttered open. "Caedmon," she whispered, reaching out her hand. "Caedmon. You've come back to me."

He shook his head. "No Agneta. I can't be with you. I'm not worthy of you."

She sat up beside him, and his manhood swelled as her thigh touched his, adding to his misery. He edged away.

She put her hand on his thigh. "Caedmon, please don't shut me out. I'm your wife. I'll decide if you're worthy or not."

He lifted her hand, kissed her fingertips and put her hand back in her lap. "Agneta, I'm no longer the man I was. I'm less than nothing. I am in fact the embodiment of all I've despised my whole life. And from the look on my true father's face when he saw me, I would venture to guess he's as ashamed of me as I am of him."

Agneta took hold of his head in both hands and turned his face to her. "Caedmon, you're a gentle, noble and honest knight. You must find it in your heart to forgive what has happened—"

"Forgive," he shouted, leaping to his feet. "You speak to me of forgiveness and yet you can't forgive me my part in the raid on Bolton."

Agneta flushed. "It's true," she conceded. "We both need to find the path to forgiveness. But we must help each other to find peace. I've already—"

"I'll never find peace here in this manor house. I believed it my birthright, but it's not. I must leave."

"Then I'll go with you."

"No," he shouted. "I don't know where I'm going, or what I'll do. I plan to sell my sword to some lord who has need of it. That's no life for a woman. There's no reason you can't stay here and enjoy the security of the income of this house."

"I have no wish to live here without you," she whispered, lowering her eyes to the floor.

He turned and left, his heart breaking.

***

Leofric returned to the manor house with news that Caedmon was seen regularly in Ruyton, drinking and carousing, causing disturbances. He came back to the house at night, stumbling into the stables and nothing Leofric could say to him seemed to make any impression.

Agneta was distraught, at a loss. Lady Ascha refused to leave her room and could be heard sobbing. The Brightmores made themselves scarce. Agneta wondered if she should appeal to the Earl, but what would she say? Caedmon would be angry. The decision was taken out of her hands when Tybaut told her he would have to report the situation to the Earl.

"It's my duty, my lady. Sir Caedmon is neglecting the estate. If he keeps on squandering the money from the rents on—"

She held up her hand. "Do what you must, Tybaut. You have the best interests of the manor at heart. I myself—"

While he might have his suspicions, the steward wasn't aware of the real reason for Caedmon's behaviour and must be perplexed by it. It disturbed her to see the effects his loathing was having on Caedmon. She wondered about the changes her own hatreds and resentments had wrought in her.

***

Tybaut journeyed to Ellesmere and sought an interview with the Earl. He explained what had been happening at Shelfhoc. The Earl listened attentively and thanked the nervous steward, assuring him he would travel to Ruyton, then went to find Mabelle.

She was sewing with some of her ladies. He dismissed them. She rose to greet him and he saw the look of concern on her face. He told her of Tybaut's news. "I intend to ride to Ruyton to face Caedmon, something I should have done sooner, but I want to be sure you approve of this decision."

She would agree. They'd already made the determination together that they would endow Caedmon with three of the manor houses in Sussex and that he would inherit three more on Ram's death. The properties they'd chosen were lucrative estates which would ensure a prosperous future for Caedmon and his family.

Mabelle drew him down into a chair and sat opposite him. "Of course you must go."

He rode with a company of his men-at-arms. As they entered the courtyard of her home, Agneta came out to see who'd arrived. "My lord Earl," she croaked, curtseying.

Ram dismounted. "You know who I am?"

She looked up at him. "My lord, your face—is Caedmon's face."

Caedmon had married a beautiful woman, and Ram sorrowed for the pain she suffered. He took her by the hand and bade her rise. "Lady Agneta, you must not bow to me. I'm the cause of your grief. You're the wife of my son, a daughter to me. Where is Caedmon?"

She rose, gripping his hand. "He's probably gone to Ruyton. I don't know when he'll return. It's difficult these days."

"Tybaut has told me of the problems. I'm here to try to resolve some of them. May I enter and tell you of the circumstances that have brought us to this point?"

He kept hold of her hand, sensing she needed his reassurance. The two of them went into the hall of the house and Ram shared with her the story of his liaison with Caedmon's mother. It felt strange to be back in this house where it had all begun.

"My wife, Mabelle, has forgiven me my infidelity to her and my children have accepted that Caedmon is their half brother. I didn't know of his existence until he came to Ellesmere, but he's my son and I want to recognize him as such."

She turned to face him. "But he's angry," she whispered. "Forgive me, but he despises Normans."

Ram frowned and nodded. "I suspected as much from what he said when we met. I hope to change his mind."

Without warning a loud bang heralded Caedmon's arrival through the front doorway of the house. He burst into the room, his face flushed with anger. "Well, well, great Earl. Not content with taking advantage of my whoring mother, now you turn your attention to my wife while my back is turned."

"Caedmon!" Agneta gasped, taking her hand from the Earl's. "That's not why the Earl is here. Have you taken leave of your senses?"

Ram's heart thudded. He wanted to embrace this young man, his son who looked like him, obviously a Montbryce. "Caedmon," he said softly, trying to maintain his composure. "You may say anything you wish about me, but your mother isn't a whore. If you'll but allow me to explain the circumstances of what happened—"

"Circumstances?" Caedmon cut in. "I know the *circumstances*. You shamed my mother then rode away, leaving her to fend for herself and her child."

"I swear to you, I didn't know I had a third son until I saw you at Ellesmere."

Silence hung in the air. When Caedmon said nothing, Ram decided to continue. "Caedmon, I want to recognize you as my son. My family is of the same mind. I wish to offer you the name of FitzRam, if you'll accept it. I also wish to—"

Caedmon strode to within a pace of his father, and hissed into his face. "I want nothing from you, Earl of Ellesmere. I wouldn't consider bearing a Norman patronymic. You're everything I despise."

Agneta took her husband's hand, trying to pull him away from his confrontational stance. "Caedmon, he's your father. You can't despise him."

"You'll not be the one to tell me what I can or can't do, wife," he shouted, red in the face, shrugging off her hand, keeping his eyes on Ram.

"Caedmon," Ram said, raising his hands, palms towards Caedmon, trying to calm the situation. "You may not accept it at the moment and you may not like it, but you have Montbryce blood in your veins, blood from an honorable family lineage. Montbryce men don't shout at their wives in that manner, particularly when she hasn't been the cause of pain. If you wish to shout, shout at me."

"Aye, father," Caedmon spat out the words with great sarcasm. "Was it in *this* room you fornicated with my mother, or perhaps in the chamber where I've lain with my own wife? Your whore is upstairs now. Why don't you go up and see her?"

The slight upward glance Ram gave betrayed him. Caedmon thrust out one hand towards the door, the other on the hilt of his sword. "Get out of this house."

Ram felt there was no use arguing further. He'd made the first move. It was up to his son now. For all his skill as a diplomat he felt he'd failed. He bowed to Agneta, bidding her farewell, nodded to Caedmon and left.

Caedmon turned to his wife. "You had no right to allow him to enter this house, Agneta."

She could find no words to say to him. She'd on the one hand hoped the Earl would come, and on the other dreaded he would. She wanted to know what kind of man he was. When the Earl dismounted and she saw the resemblance, it made her weep.

Relief had washed over her like a cleansing rain when the Norman nobleman called her *daughter*. She could scarcely believe she'd heard him say these words. She'd been an orphan since her own parents had been murdered and Caedmon had been the rock she'd come to rely on, but now he seemed lost to her. To hear words of support and love from the Earl of Ellesmere was more than she'd hoped for.

She left the room and went to her chamber, where she wept alone, marvelling at the depth of forgiveness that had enabled the Earl's family to survive this blow and to accept Caedmon. That was the kind of family she wanted. She prayed she might be able some day to overcome her own hatred for the Scots who had killed her parents and brothers and that her husband would survive the depths of despair into which he'd sunk.

***

Caedmon had been missing for another sennight. There was no sign of him in Ruyton. When a rider cantered into the courtyard with a message, bearing a seal with the imprint of Caedmon's ring, Agneta's hands shook violently as she tore it open. She crumpled to her knees on the cobblestones as she read the missive.

My dearest wife Agneta,

I regret the agony and grief I've caused you. I no longer know who I am. I have to come to terms with the reality of my parentage, but I'm too full of anger. I need to make amends, to cleanse myself of the hatred and resentment burning a hole in my heart.

I've decided to join Pope Urban's Crusade to rid the Holy Land of the Saracen menace. I hope in this way to restore honor to my name, and perhaps return a richer and saner man. By the time you read this, I will have taken ship for Normandie—ironic isn't it! From there I will make my way to join with the Crusaders in Constantinople. I'm confident the income from the estate will meet your needs. I miss you. Forgive me, for everything.

Your unworthy husband, Caedmon

She clenched her fist and pressed it to her mouth to stifle the scream that threatened to burst forth. The bile rose in her throat. She didn't know which emotion to succumb to first. Anger, fear, desolation, sorrow, all raged within her, but the most overwhelming pain was that he'd left as she'd come to the full certainty that she was with child.

"Not one word of love, Caedmon. Not one word of love. But then why should I expect that? I told you I could never love you, but I know now that I do. Perhaps if you'd known of my love, this torment you're facing might have been easier for you to bear."

She could pursue him and beg him to return. But she would be a pregnant woman, alone in foreign lands. She went to her *armoire* and stood in front of it for many minutes, finally taking out the bundle she'd brought with her from the Abbey. Trembling, she unwrapped the dagger that had taken her mother's life, spread the cloth on her bed, lay the weapon atop it and crawled to sit cross-legged on the bed.

131

She stared at the dagger for more than an hour before she could touch it. Gingerly, she ran her trembling fingers over the walrus ivory handle then withdrew them quickly, as if she'd been burned. A sob tore through her and she curled up in a ball on the bed.

She awoke some time later to the sound of someone banging on the door.

"Agneta," Leofric shouted. "Open this door, Agneta."

The dagger was still there, taunting her. She lunged and grasped it in both hands, pressing the sharp point to her breast. Her body shook, sweat poured from her.

"Agneta!" Leofric shouted again.

The steel of the long blade made the dagger feel heavy in her hand, though it wasn't large. It was a weapon made for a woman. Her thumb felt the raised edges on the elaborately carved steel guard. She looked down and, through her tears, noticed, for the first time, the Viking warrior carved into the front of the guard.

The banging came again, more insistent, and she heard Lady Ascha's sobbing voice. "Please open the door, Agneta."

Agneta looked back at the dagger—a gift to her grandmother from her own Danish grandfather. Was this a carving of him, striding out of his longship onto some foreign shore? Onto the shores of Northumbria, long ago? The blade too was carved with mysterious designs which she didn't understand, but which somehow spoke to her.

"Mamma," she whispered, tears streaming down her cheeks. "I now have some understanding of why you did what you did. Why you couldn't face life without my father. I can't accept the prospect of life without Caedmon."

Absentmindedly, she traced her fingertips over the Viking warrior. "Help me, brave grandsire from ages past. I don't have the courage to raise a child alone."

The Earl won't allow you to face it alone. He will help you.

Trembling uncontrollably, she put the dagger back down onto the bed and stood on unsteady legs. She went to the door, opened it and collapsed into Leofric's arms.

"Agneta," he whispered, holding her tightly.

They were all there. Lady Ascha looked like she had cried for a sennight. Agneta had never seen her mother-by-marriage look disheveled, even during the long journey they'd undertaken in their flight, yet now the woman was a wreck.

132

Coventina stared at her wide-eyed and it was obvious she too had been crying. Agneta leaned on Leofric who eyed the dagger in her hands. She gave him a reassuring smile and handed him the weapon. "Call Tybaut, Leofric. He must ride quickly to the Earl with this message from Caedmon."

She gave the missive to Leofric and he and Lady Ascha read it together. Caedmon's mother fell to her knees and wailed. Coventina knelt beside her to bring comfort.

Agneta turned to Leofric. "I must add a postscript, to tell the Earl about our child."

Ascha looked up. She and Coventina and Leofric all spoke at the same time. "Child?"

"I'm carrying Caedmon's child," she whispered.

Ascha struggled to her feet and took Agneta's hand. "Dear daughter, I beg your forgiveness for what has happened. I should have told Caedmon. I should never have lied."

"Lady Ascha, I'm not the one to whom you should say these things. Perhaps one day you can tell me, but now I'm too distraught. We must think only of getting Caedmon safely home. Go to your chamber and rest. Lady Pamela, help her."

Edythe and Pamela, who'd stood gaping at the proceedings, both scurried to assist Lady Ascha to her chamber.

"I'll ride with Tybaut," Leofric stated. "Bastard of a Norman or son of a Saxon martyr, makes no difference. Caedmon is like a brother to me."

Agneta nodded and held out her hand for the dagger. When Leofric hesitated, she reassured him. "It's all right."

He handed it to her. She went back into her chamber, penned the note to the Earl, resealed the parchment and gave it to Leofric. "Go, quickly."

She climbed into bed, clutching the dagger, her thumb caressing the Viking warrior over and over. She prayed her unborn child wouldn't grow up without a father. It became her mantra, the dagger her talisman.

CHAPTER TWENTY-TWO

Caedmon was surprised to be one of the few English people among the motley horde of pilgrims gathering from many nations to join the crusade. Most of them were peasants with whom he had nothing in common. They were armed in large part with farm tools and crude weapons and had no fighting experience or skill.

As the days went by, an ironic truth dawned on him. He travelled mainly with the group of Norman knights in the throng, men who had experience in warfare, men like Fulcher of Chartres and Walter Sans-Avoir. He was drawn to them and soon established an easy camaraderie with several.

As he and Walter rode side by side one day, Caedmon asked, "Where are these multitudes coming from, and why are they eager to join this crusade?"

His new comrade answered, "Peasants from many lands have suffered through drought, famine and plague. They are fleeing those ills and hope to find redemption, and perhaps riches, by participating in a crusade against the unholy Turks occupying the holy city of Jerusalem."

Caedmon nodded thoughtfully. "It's a revolution, isn't it? Serfs and peasants have usually lived out their lives in the village where they were born."

"*Oui*, then in April of last year, a shower of flaming lights in the heavens was taken to be a divine blessing for the crusade, and the darkening of the moon which occurred in the following February confirmed their belief."

"I've heard outbreaks of St. Anthony's Fire across the land caused people to convulse in spasms. They were seen as a sign of witchcraft at work. People believe the world is coming to an end, and have rushed to join the crusade."

"What can you expect? They're peasants," Walter replied derisively.

***

Caedmon resolved to keep an account of his adventures in a Coptic-bound codex, obtained in a market. He was also lucky to find and purchase a tooled leather pouch with several good quills, attached to which was an inkpot with a firm lid, full of *encaustum*.

One good thing about the interminable miles is that I have time to think on my problems. As time goes by, some of my anger is draining away. Day to day survival has become the biggest priority.

In the beginning, the atmosphere in the camps was one of optimism and fervour. Women have joined the march, either to follow husbands and sons, or as camp followers. Many of these are gypsy women who offer their favours to any man who will pay. Though I ache for a woman, it's Agneta I want.

The lively Romanies provide relief from the hardships and suffering of the march with their music and dancing. I marvel at their ability to bring life and merriment where there's growing despair and doubt. They have learned to combat discrimination and persecution with laughter and abandon. No one in the camp trusts them, yet many come to their campfires.

Agneta and I have never danced, not even at Yuletide.

The masses are drawn by the monk, Peter the Hermit, from Amiens. Peter rides a donkey and dresses in simple clothing. He preached the crusade throughout Normandie and Flandres. He claims to have been appointed to preach by Christ himself and that he has a divine letter to prove it. Some of the peasants believe Peter, not Pope Urban, was the true originator of the crusade.

***

Peter the Hermit led the multitudes following him to Köln. He planned to wait there for more crusaders to arrive.

Caedmon attended a council of French knights held in Walter Sans-Avoir's tent.

"What is your opinion, Walter?" Caedmon asked the man who'd emerged as a leader among his countrymen. "Will you wait with Peter in Köln, or go on?"

Walter replied without hesitation. "I'm encouraging the French knights to go on. I see no benefit in waiting for more rabble to arrive. They are not warriors."

135

Others nodded their agreement, but he was undecided. "Köln is a bustling city, a centre of trade. It might be beneficial to stay here a while."

Walter looked at him squarely and placed his hand on Caedmon's shoulder. "It will be in your best interests to come with us, my friend. We're knights like you. You don't belong with the poorly armed masses."

Many, including a group of French knights led by Walter Sans-Avoir, want to move on and not wait in Köln for more crusaders. Though I see the wisdom of Peter's plan, I believe Walter is right—it is in my best interests to go with the French knights. I pray I've made the right decision.

Thus it was that Caedmon joined thousands of French crusaders who completed a wearying, dusty journey through Hungary, without major incident, and arrived at the river Sava, the border of Byzantine territory at Belgrade. The long trek gave him more time to ponder his situation.

I'm very homesick, and can barely recall the reasons I left England. I ache for my beautiful Agneta. I'm a fool for abandoning the only woman I've ever loved. I know now I've loved her from the first moment I saw her in the infirmary.

But she won't want me now. I've hurt her terribly. I behaved like a child. How often in my life have I wished I had a father? Why wasn't I willing to at least listen to the Earl? I think often about my newly discovered Norman father. He could have turned his back on me, and who would blame any of them for doing so? He wanted to embrace me and I insulted him. I've been consumed with hatred for Normans, and yet here I am with Norman knights as my comrades and they are noble men to the last of them. My own problems seem paltry in the face of what some of these people have endured.

***

His scribbling one day, as he rested in the shade of a plane tree after a long day in the saddle, was disturbed by the shouts of a fellow knight. "The Belgrade commander is taken by surprise, having no orders on what to do with us. He's refused entry. We'll need to pillage to find food."

Provisioning was a constant problem. They had all looked forward to being able to enter Belgrade, a sizable town, and hoped food would be provided. As the horde had grown, settlements had become increasingly reluctant to honor the holy obligation to feed and shelter pilgrims. Having to pillage some poor peasant's land for sustenance was more than Caedmon could bear, but he went off with other knights and aided in the theft of meager pickings from local farmers. He was to be glad he'd made that decision

.

Sixteen knights, who opted to rob the market in a village across from Belgrade, were caught and stripped of their armour and clothing, which was then hung from the castle walls. How can they survive without armour and clothing? What am I doing here?

***

The crusaders were allowed to carry on to Niš, one of the most ancient towns in the Balkans, where they were provided with food. There they waited to hear from Constantinople, the embarkation point for the Holy Land.

I long to hear my own language spoken again, but I've become adept at communicating with the Normans in their language. In Scotland I wasn't forced to learn to speak it, as English Saxons were after the Conquest. I suppose if I'm half Norman, I should learn to speak the language. I'm regaining some of my sense of humor. Praise God!

My quills are done. I'll need to learn how to make them if I can't find any in a market. I traded some of my food for ink. It is hotter than Hades—high summer. They say July is the hottest month here.

In Niš, Caedmon's group joined Peter the Hermit's larger group once more and were soon acquainted with what had happened to them in the interim.

.

When the larger army with Peter the Hermit arrived in Zemun, they became suspicious when they saw sixteen suits of armour hanging from the walls. It's said tensions resulted in a dispute over the price of a pair of shoes in the market, which led to a riot, which then turned into an all-out assault on the town by the crusaders. Four thousand Hungarians were killed. Four thousand—over a pair of shoes. I can scarce believe it.

The Hermit's crusaders then fled across the river Sava to Belgrade, but only after skirmishing with Belgrade troops. The residents of Belgrade fled, and the crusaders pillaged and burned the town. This noble endeavour has deteriorated into a murderous rampage. At first I was proud to bear the red cross of Christ on my right shoulder, but now—

I must not utter such words out loud, however. In these foreign lands they burn 'heretics' on a whim.

***

The commander of Niš was worried about the size of the rabble following Peter the Hermit. He summoned the monk. "We congratulate you on the success of your bold endeavour, Brother Peter, but we do not have the wherewithal to shelter all your crusaders. There could be trouble."

"We all want to avoid that," the monk replied. "Perhaps if you provided us food?"

The commander nodded, rubbing his chin with his thumb and forefinger. "It will be done, but I prefer you not stay in Niš. I will provide an escort to Constantinople, if you agree to leave right away."

Peter thought for a few minutes, stroking his beard, then nodded. "I will prepare my army to move as soon as possible."

Two days later, the well-provisioned throng was ready to set out. They hadn't gone far when they came to a large mill. A group of German knights dismounted and strode into the building. They emerged minutes later bearing several heavy sacks on their shoulders. They were pursued by an indignant miller, protesting the removal of his property. "You cannot take my grain," the miller said in his language, gesticulating wildly.

"Your commander has agreed we can have food," came the reply in German.

The miller appealed to the escort from Niš, his arms wide in supplication. "They cannot steal my grain. They have food aplenty already. See!"

"You cannot take the grain," the captain of the Niš escort confirmed, barring the way for the Germans, who promptly dropped the sacks and drew their swords.

"We were guaranteed food," they cried, shoving the indignant miller into the swift stream.

The Norman contingent had been following close on the heels of the Germans and had at first watched this scene with a degree of ridicule. "Here we go again," Caedmon said. "The German knights are never happy unless they're fighting or arguing."

"You're right, *mon ami*," replied Amadour de Vignoles, who'd become Caedmon's frequent travelling companion.

The miller struggled to stay afloat. Things were escalating.

"*Mon Dieu*," Amadour cried. "They'll drown him over a few sacks of grain to which they're not entitled. We were given enough supplies when we left Niš."

"Good, here comes Brother Peter," Caedmon said with relief. "He'll sort them out."

"It will be too late for the miller. That German coward is holding him underwater with his boot."

With two or three others, Caedmon and Amadour dismounted quickly and ran to the aid of the miller, shoving the belligerent German into the water. As Caedmon proffered his hand to the miller, he too was pushed into the swirling water and drawn to the millwheel. Though he couldn't understand the miller's language, he understood his desperation. Caedmon held him up, but he flailed his arms and panicked, pulling them both under. Caedmon recalled his fear when Agneta had struggled to pull him out of the river at Chester. He hadn't drowned then, and he didn't intend to drown now.

"Stop struggling," he spluttered. "Amadour—help me fish him out."

They managed to get the frantic Balkan out of the water. As the three men struggled up the slippery bank, the miller suddenly shouted, pointing to the mill.

"*Sacrebleu!* They've set fire to the mill," Amadour exclaimed.

Caedmon swore under his breath. "Quick! Get him away from here, it's going up like a torch. That wall will collapse soon, and we don't want to be under it when it does."

"*Attention*, Caedmon, we must be careful. The soldiers from Niš have attacked the main group of crusaders. The cowardly Germans must have run back there."

They stood, panting heavily, watching in disbelief as the skirmish carried on down the road. Caedmon raked his hands through his wet hair, combing it back from his face. The poorly armed peasants were no match for the soldiers, panic soon set in and bodies piled up.

"Come with me. Get your horses and come with me," cried the miller, gesturing to make them understand. He led them away from the burning mill, up and over a steep embankment into a copse, indicating they should stay hidden there. He turned to leave them. Caedmon grasped his sleeve. "Where are you going? Stay here with us. It's too dangerous."

The miller looked into Caedmon's eyes, smiled briefly, shrugged his shoulders, shook Caedmon's hand, then Amadour's, and left.

They sat for an hour until the sounds of conflict abated.

"Sounds to me like they've sent out the whole garrison. This is unbelievable," Caedmon hissed. "I'm totally disillusioned with the whole idea of the Crusade. I've probably killed more men in my own defense while on this religious pilgrimage than I did at the great Battle of Alnwick. Too many lives lost through misunderstandings, stupidity and hatred, and we're nowhere near Jerusalem yet."

Amadour nodded sadly. "I agree, but we have no choice now."

Ten thousand souls lost, because of an argument over grain. Amadour and I were lucky to survive. The miller we rescued is probably dead.

We regrouped and soon reached Sofia where we met our Byzantine escort, which brought us safely the rest of the way to Constantinople.

I pray Agneta is safe and well. She's my talisman, an image I carry in my head. I'm convinced she has protected me, my guardian angel. It's the only thing that keeps me going. My goal in life is to stay alive long enough to return to her and beg her, beg her to forgive me, for Bolton and for my sheer stupidity. She told me in Chester how foolhardy I was. She would scold me now if I told her I came close to drowning in Niš.

I long to hear her laughter again.

My other goal is to master the making of these cursed quills.

It seemed to me the Byzantine emperor, Alexius Comnenus, was astounded at the size and composition of this huge unexpected army that descended upon Constantinople. He'd petitioned the Pope for a crusading army, but I don't think this motley horde was what he had in mind. I suspect he didn't know what to do with us, so he quickly ferried all thirty thousand of us across the Bosporus.

Once in Asia Minor, we pillaged towns and villages on the way to Nicomedia. There, yet another argument broke out between the Germans and Italians on one side and the French on the other and I again saw the folly of divisiveness. The Germans and Italians have split off and elected a new leader, an Italian named Rainald. The French chose Geoffrey Burel, of all people, to take command. Many of us are not sure it's a wise choice. But I must go with them.

***

The French group reached the edge of Nicaea, a Turkish stronghold, where they pillaged the surrounds. It was a suicidal idea, but they had to have food. He'd taken to the Norman habit of shaving the back of his head to help cope with the heat and the lack of facilities for bathing.

Lice are an ever-present scourge. As the 'army' has grown, conditions in the camps have deteriorated. The movement of the horde and horses stirs up enough dust to choke a man, and I wear rags across my face to protect myself from the suffocating air. Thirst is a constant problem. My skin is baked onto my bones.

"Rumors are flying now about a group of six thousand Germans who captured Xerigordon from the Turks," Amadour told him. They were sharing the raw root vegetables they'd dug up.

Caedmon smirked. "I don't believe anything about the Germans any more, not after Niš."

Amadour spat out some fibrous bit of food he couldn't chew. "The counter-rumor has it the Turks recaptured the city from the Germans, who were forced to drink the blood of donkeys and their own urine, when their water supply was cut. Some of the captured crusaders converted to Islam and were sent to Khorasan, while others who refused to abandon their faith were killed."

The rumors about Xerigordon are enough to make the hairs on the back of my head stand up—except I have no hair. I remember the first time I saw Agneta's beautiful hair. It was very short! It's a bittersweet memory. I ache for her, in my heart and my loins.

I've had a recurring dream. I ride up to a castle. Agneta is there, but she's been transformed into a tree—a beautiful lush green tree. She smiles at me as I approach, and then I hear a sound. It's birdsong. I frown, not knowing where the sound comes from. Agneta slowly raises her arms and they become branches. I look up at the branches, and see two birds nesting.

I wish I could fathom what the dream signifies. I asked a Romany, but all he was interested in was my coin. He mumbled something about the castle foretelling great wealth. That surely can't be true. Maybe I didn't understand his language properly.

***

"They say now the brave Germans have taken Nicaea," Amadour told Caedmon a few days later.

Caedmon could see his friend was pale and had lost a lot of weight. He wondered about his own appearance. It was a long time since they'd eaten a good meal. "That rumor must have been started by Turkish spies."

Amadour shifted wearily into the shade of the palm tree they sheltered beneath. "Maybe, but it has people excited to get there as soon as possible."

Caedmon absent-mindedly scratched a drawing of a tree in his codex. "Aye, so they can share in the looting, no doubt."

"You're probably right," Amadour sighed. "The trouble is, Burel has popular support among the masses and he's arguing it would be cowardly to wait. He wants to move against the Turks right away."

"He's a hothead. The rumor can't be true."

Next to the tree Caedmon drew two birds.

We advised caution, but Burel's will has prevailed. I have a feeling of foreboding about the whole enterprise. I've no faith in Burel and even less in the veracity of the rumor about the fall of Nicaea. Nevertheless, I can't remain in the camp with the women and children.

Pray for me, Agneta.

***

On the morning of the twenty-first day of October, the crusading army of twenty thousand marched out toward Nicaea. Caedmon, Amadour, and several other Norman knights positioned themselves near the rear of the column. As they marched, they caught sight of a derelict fortification on a hill overlooking the water, about half a mile to the west.

"If we're attacked, make for the ruin over there. We might have a chance if we reach it," Caedmon suggested. The others nodded in grim agreement.

Three miles from the camp, the column entered a narrow, wooded valley near the village of Dracon. Caedmon felt uneasy, and could tell the other Normans were nervous.

"Burel doesn't have enough power of command or common sense to have the army march quietly. We're making too much noise as we approaching the valley—"

His words were interrupted by a hail of arrows.

"*Oli Crosse!* As we suspected," he cried. "The Turks have lain in wait for us here."

"The vanguard has already started to panic and retreat. They're in full rout," Amadour shouted. "We'll be trampled if we don't head for the ruin."

"They're cutting down those fleeing back to camp," Caedmon yelled. "Hopefully they won't pay attention to the few making for the ruin." He wheeled his horse and shouted to the main body. "The ruins." He pointed the way with his sword. "It's the only chance."

A few Turks broke away and pursued them up the hill to the ruined fort. Caedmon wheeled Abbot to face them. He lopped off the head of one Saracen, and the arm of another. Blood spurted over him. Screams of anguish filled the air.

Alnwick.

Satisfied that at least part of the main Crusader army had broken away in the direction of the ruin, he turned his horse and rode at full speed through the gate, only hoping some of the others might make it to the sanctuary. The Normans struggled to close the massive gates when the last of the fleeing crusaders had ridden in.

"These gates are rotten, they won't keep anyone out," Amadour shouted desperately.

His friend was right. "Pass the word," he shouted. "Pile up as many shields as we can."

The wall of shields rose rapidly as panicked knights rushed to throw anything they could find at the gap.

"Bring rocks too," another knight shouted.

After terrifying minutes, the group of Turks who had pursued them drew back under the barrage of slingshots, lance blows and arrows from the desperate Crusaders.

"They'll be back," Caedmon ground out, wiping the blood from his face.

"How many do you reckon we are?" Amadour panted.

Caedmon looked around at the crowd of exhausted men packed inside the compound. "About three thousand, I would guess. At least the walls are intact and will provide us some protection. I'll climb up and survey what's happening."

It took them a few minutes to find a way up. Many of the ladders were broken or rotting.

"*Mon Dieu!*" Amadour gasped as he looked out. "Look at the fires in the main camp. They're slaughtering everyone."

Neither man mentioned the ghastly screams they could hear from three miles away.

"*Merde!*" Amadour exclaimed, turning away from the horror to look down into the fort. "Burel has made it to the sanctuary."

Caedmon grimaced. "Look at him, issuing orders already. It turns my stomach. I'll not obey him."

From their vantage point, they watched the arrogant Norman strut around for a while

"Looks like you're not the only one," Amadour smirked. "No-one is paying any attention to him."

"It's only a matter of time," Caedmon said with grim finality, looking back over the scene of the ongoing massacre. "When the Turks are finished slaughtering our main army, they'll turn their attention to us. They'll starve us out."

Amadour nodded in tacit agreement. Their reprieve was a temporary one. Caedmon sensed every man there was reminded of the Germans who had drunk their own urine.

My throat is already parched, my lips dry and cracked. Will I ever again taste the sweetness of Agneta? I despair of it. At least there are no donkeys here. We have horses. I hope I won't have to eat Abbot.

CHAPTER TWENTY-THREE

After receiving Agneta's message, Ram de Montbryce immediately set about organizing a contingent of two hundred of his best men-at-arms and making arrangements to sail to Normandie with them, in pursuit of Caedmon.

They gathered in the Map Room at Ellesmere to lay their plans. Robert would go with them as far as the Montbryce family castle at Saint Germain. Baudoin told his father he wanted to accompany him in his quest to rescue Caedmon.

Ram looked up from a chart. "It won't be easy, Baudoin. If Caedmon had been thinking normally, he wouldn't have embarked on this foolhardy venture."

"Papa, I've done many foolish things in my life too. We can't allow his folly to kill him. For Agneta's sake, as well as the babe's."

Ram slapped him on the back, wondering what foolish things his shy son might have done. "Thank you, Baudoin. I would like you with me on this journey. I blame myself for not going to Caedmon immediately. He has a head start on us. It won't sit well with me if anything happens to him. Before we depart, we must see to it that the documents are drawn up regarding the land we're deeding to Caedmon. I leave that in your capable hands."

"I'll have the scrivener prepare the documents and bring them for your signature."

***

The night before the departure, Ram and Mabelle shared a night of tender lovemaking. He kissed his beloved wife's lips, then her neck and throat, then slowly worked his way down to her breasts. He circled each nipple with his tongue and whimpering moans escaped her lips. He suckled and she ran one hand through his hair, holding her breast to his mouth with the other. His knowing fingers found where she loved to feel his touch, and a low throaty moan escaped her lips. She opened her legs and dug her heels into the bed, crying out with squeals of ecstasy he never tired of hearing. He entered her and she wrapped her legs around his waist, pulling him deep inside.

"Straighten your legs, Mabelle," he whispered.

Gripping him inside her, she did as he asked, until he lay with his weight on her, his phallus against her sensitive bud. He raised up and gently pressed her breasts together, then lowered his body back onto hers.

"You've always borne my weight. I want to cover you completely as I possess you," he whispered hoarsely.

He was inflamed with the feel of her body beneath him and it took but a few strokes for him to find his release and he filled her.

"I want to stay joined to you as long as I can, my love. It might be many months before we see each other again. This journey is a perilous one, and we might never meet again in this lifetime. You know I love you, have always loved you."

"As I love you, Ram," she whispered, tears flowing freely down her cheeks as she pressed her face to his chest.

The next morning he bade his beautiful wife farewell, gazing at her for long moments, trying to engrave this last image of her face on his mind. She told him she would ask Agneta to come to Ellesmere. "I'll ask Lady Ascha too, if that's all right with you?"

He sighed heavily, wondering how he'd been lucky enough to have been gifted with such a wife. "You're an amazing woman, Mabelle."

He kissed her lovingly. Baudoin silently embraced his mother for long minutes. They embarked on their desperate journey.

**

Their trek to the south coast was uneventful, but they had a stormy crossing to Normandie and were in danger of being shipwrecked. Two horses suffered broken legs in the panic and had to be destroyed, but they'd brought extra in the event of such an occurrence. Once regrouped and underway they had no difficulty coming across large numbers of people headed for the Holy Land. News of the People's Crusade, of Peter the Hermit, of Walter Sans-Avoir was on everyone's lips.

"It's hard to separate fact from rumor," Ram said to Baudoin. "I've heard word of thousands of crusaders, a mighty army."

"There's persistent talk of Belgrade, of the armour of crusaders hanging from castle walls," Baudoin added. "You're right. It's hard to believe some of the stories."

Ram's private army made good progress. They'd taken on provisions at Saint Germain. Whenever they passed through the lands of a baron or magnate, Ram made a point of presenting himself, and his son, as goodwill emissaries of the King of the English. He would deal later with any objections from Rufus, if they came.

"I don't want to be perceived as a threat. This way we can make good connections and allies which might stand us in good stead on the return journey."

More often than not, they were treated with the hospitality nobility obliged. If they needed food when none was available, they traded for it. Ram gave orders there was to be no pillaging. They followed what they deemed to be the most reliable rumors. But as the sennights went by, Ram became frustrated they could never be sure they were on the right road.

"I don't want to have to go all the way to Jerusalem to rescue Caedmon," he complained. "Who knows if he'll want to be rescued? Perhaps he's dead anyway."

"Don't despair, Papa," Baudoin urged. "I have a good feeling we'll find him."

Everywhere they saw evidence of the passing of huge hordes of people. Ram sensed his men were shocked and disgusted at many of the sights they encountered.

"This crusade is a disaster, Baudoin," he lamented frequently. "Crops have been devastated, village after village pillaged, women raped, human waste and detritus soil the landscape."

"Surely this isn't what the Pope had in mind when he called for the crusade," Baudoin often remarked.

After six fruitless sennights they passed the rusting armour still hanging from the walls of Zemun. Baudoin gaped at the sight. "Well, that story was true at least. Let's hope Caedmon wasn't one to lose his armour that day, if he came this way. Survival is hard enough *with* armour."

When they arrived at Niš, Ram again presented himself to the Commander as a wandering emissary from the King of the English, not a crusader. He confided to the commander that he was merely a distraught father, seeking news of his son who had been naive enough to join the crusade.

The Commander agreed, through an interpreter, as he entertained his important guest with a sumptuous meal. "I too have children. Sometimes we must save them from their own folly. And this crusade is pure folly. There was a great slaughter here, caused by a senseless argument over grain. We were forced to kill thousands in an effort to restore order. But I don't know if your son was among the dead. Though—I did hear tell of a knight from Scotland who saved the life of a miller."

Hope surged in Ram's heart. "Scotland?"

"Yes, he and a Norman knight rescued the miller from drowning."

"A Norman knight? The Scottish knight was with a Norman?" Ram wanted to make sure there was no misunderstanding because of the language differences.

Having been reassured that such was the tale, Ram told him, "We'll press on. My hope is renewed."

The commander raised his eyebrows, obviously not understanding what had given the Earl new hope. "As you wish. The horde moved on to Constantinople. I'll provide you with an escort."

Ram bowed in acknowledgment of the generous offer. "We're in your debt."

They arrived in the great city and, after several fruitless attempts, Ram managed to secure an audience with the Byzantine Emperor. Once in the Emperor's presence, he used the same tack he had in Niš, pleading the case of a distraught father.

His face grim, Alexius replied, "My dear Earl, I wanted the Crusade. We must rout the Saracens from the Holy Land. But we must do it with a properly equipped army, not a rabble of poorly armed peasants. I warned their leaders not to proceed against the Turks. I told them this peasant army would be slaughtered if they insisted on moving into Asia Minor.

But they didn't wish to heed my warnings. I arranged for them to be ferried across the Bosporus. I can only offer you the same advice and service if you choose to go. But it's dangerous. Though you have a well equipped contingent of your men, you don't wish to meet up with the Turkish army. They are a deadly force."

Ram had become increasingly worried about this talk of a poorly armed host of peasants. "I sometimes wonder, Baudoin, what Caedmon has become involved in?"

"There were knights too. Don't you think Caedmon would have allied with them, rather than the peasants?"

Once across the strait, they heard of a split in the army, of the loss of authority of Peter the Hermit and the creation of a French faction.

"I'm not sure why, but I feel Caedmon would have joined the French. His Norman blood would draw him to that group. I'm more convinced than ever of it after hearing the tale of the two knights who saved the miller."

Baudoin nodded his agreement. "I also believe it was Caedmon who saved the miller."

As fragile hopes were blossoming, they stumbled across a handful of traumatized women and old men who had escaped the massacre in what had been the Crusaders' main camp. It was the worst news— news they'd hoped never to hear. The whole crusading army had been slaughtered on its way to Nicaea.

"It's too dangerous to continue," Ram said quietly, standing dejectedly by his horse, looking at the ragged skeletons who were all that was left of the People's Crusade. "We must accept there's no choice but to turn back. We'll take these people back with us."

He issued the order to one of his men to assist the unfortunates. Turning to Baudoin, who was still on his horse, staring in disbelief at the condition of the survivors, Ram swallowed hard. "Caedmon must be dead. The odds against his having survived this horror are too great. We'll ask the Emperor if we might rest a few days in Constantinople, before setting out on the long journey back to England. Hope is dead."

Baudoin dismounted wearily and went to embrace his father. They stood together for long minutes in silence, sharing their grief.

CHAPTER TWENTY-FOUR

The abandoned fort had no roof and the besieging Turks rained a series of arrow attacks on the Christians, killing many. Then the Turks sat back to starve the defenders out. The Normans huddled together to discuss their options.

Caedmon had emerged as a leader. "Many men and horses have already died, not only from the attacks, but of thirst. Our only chance is to get word across the strait to the Emperor, and hope he'll rescue us. I'll try to slip out tonight and find a boat."

"I'll come with you." It was Amadour de Vignoles who'd spoken.

"It may be suicide, Amadour."

"It will be my honor, then, to die with you, brave Englishman. If I stay here, I'm a dead man anyway."

Their Norman friends agreed. "God go with you both. We've no other chance. We'll search for a place in the walls where you can slip out, without alerting the Turks. There's always a bolt hole somewhere in a castle. At least in every Norman castle." They laughed, but there was no humor in it.

My father would be proud I can now converse with my Norman friends. Hopefully my attempt to reach help will succeed and I will see them again.

This may be my last entry. If I don't return and some kindly soul finds this journal, know that my name is CAEDMON BRICE WOOLGAR, son of Lord Rambaud Montbryce, Earl of Ellesmere in England, and Lady Ascha Woolgar in Ruyton, England. I am the husband of Lady Agneta Woolgar of Ruyton.

I WOULD WANT MY WIFE TO KNOW I LOVED HER.

He closed the codex, screwed the lid back on the inkpot, held the journal to his heart for a few moments while he prayed for God's blessing, kissed the book and placed it carefully in his saddlebag. He said goodbye to Abbot, who seemed to sense Caedmon's quiet desperation as he nuzzled his master.

"Thank you, worthy stallion. You've helped keep me alive. Hopefully we'll see each other again," he whispered as he stroked the horse.

They found a gate at the back of the ruin, overgrown with vegetation. When all seemed relatively quiet in the Turkish camp, Caedmon and Amadour slipped through it and slid carefully down the steep hill, away from the Turks. The enemy was camped on the other side, at the approach to the ruin, but it was probable they would send out patrols. They crept slowly away from the sea that was their ultimate goal.

They could hear Turkish voices, smell the pungent odor of the food cooked in their camp and didn't want to bump into some wandering Saracen accidently. It was a still night and the blue smoke from the smouldering campfires hung in the silent air. Any noise might carry to the enemy.

Caedmon hoped the occasional muffled moans of pain and despair from the exhausted wretches huddled in the ruin would mask any sounds they might make. The slippery grass made it difficult to keep their footing in the dark. They ran their hands over the grass and assuaged their raging thirst by licking the meager moisture from them.

When they judged they'd gone far enough, they doubled back in the direction of the water and away from Nicaea. They found a pool of fresh water in a ditch and fell into it face down, slaking their rampant thirst, then staggered on for another hour.

"There," Amadour exclaimed, pointing to a small rowboat pulled up on shore.

Caedmon's spirits lifted. "This should take us down the strait. There seems to be no one about. Let's get it in the water."

"I pray I have enough strength left to row," Amadour wheezed.

"The wind has come up. Let's hope this stretch of water isn't as treacherous as that between England and Normandie. This is a flimsy craft."

A journey that should have taken them about an hour took two.

"The city seems to get nearer, and then further away," Amadour complained, and Caedmon suspected the Norman's tired muscles felt like they were about to rupture, as his did. They were exhausted by the time they dragged the boat out of the water. Two guards accosted them as they staggered up on the rocky shore. They feared they would be thrown into the dungeon, but finally managed to get the burly Byzantines to understand they were crusading Christians in need of help.

***

The Emperor and his guest, the English Earl, were breaking their fast, when a message was brought. Ram intended to leave at first light.

"Highness, pardon the interruption, there are two Crusaders who wish to speak with you. They tell a tale of escaping from the ruins near Civitote. They say there are many desperate crusaders who have taken sanctuary there and are trapped by the Turks. One of them is an Englishman, the other a Norman."

"English and Norman? Good that you're here, my dear Earl, to help me speak with them."

When Caedmon and Amadour were ushered in, Ram didn't at first recognize the filthy wretch spattered with blood, though the messenger's news had drawn his interest. Caedmon was completely bald, his beard dirty and unkempt, his bronzed face gaunt. He was exhausted and desperate to get his plea to the Emperor. He didn't pay attention to the other man sitting near Alexius.

"You bring a message, young crusader for Christ?" the Emperor asked.

"Your Highness," Caedmon said hoarsely.

Alexius appeared startled. "I was told you were English. You sound more like a Scot."

Ram jumped up from his seat and walked towards his son. "Caedmon? Can it be you? You're a sight I've longed to see for many a day."

Disoriented, Caedmon turned his attention to the man who'd spoken his name. It took him a moment to recognize him. He couldn't believe his father was there, looking overjoyed to see him. The implications of what he must have gone through to get there, and why he was there, hit Caedmon full force. He collapsed to his knees in thanksgiving for his father's forgiveness.

"*Mon seigneur?* Father, I can't believe—you came for me—you came to search for me, the most ungrateful wretch anyone could have for a son."

The man who had risked death to accompany him from the ruin ran to his aid.

"Amadour, *c'est mon père,*" Caedmon explained to the confused Norman, at the same moment that Ram said to the Emperor, "He's my son."

Ram moved quickly to embrace Caedmon, dragging him to his feet.

"Caedmon, Agneta is with child. We must return to England with all possible haste."

Caedmon rose with difficulty. "With child?"

The Emperor, who by now had risen to his feet, held up his hand and interrupted. "First, what of this abandoned ruin and the besieged crusaders languishing there?"

Amadour explained, "Your Highness, there are thousands trapped there who managed to reach the safety of the ruin. We slipped out and crossed the strait to fetch help. The Turks have them under siege. There's no food or water."

Alexius summoned a servant and dispatched an order. He turned to the Earl and explained, "I've commanded a battle squadron be sent on the morrow under the command of Constantine Katakalon."

"I would like to accompany them, if possible," Ram asked.

The Emperor acquiesced to his wishes. "I'm delighted you've found your son. I invite you to take him to your accommodations. I will send servants to attend to his obvious needs. You have many things to speak about. We will take care of his companion."

"Thank you, your Highness."

Ram clamped his arm around Caedmon's shoulders and escorted him to his quarters, muttering, "I can't believe it. We had abandoned hope."

Baudoin had been making final preparations for departure and was startled to see his father with an unpleasant smelling and unkempt ruffian. He'd never met Caedmon.

"Baudoin," Ram's voice broke. "This is your brother, Caedmon. God has seen fit to deliver him to us. Caedmon, your brother Baudoin."

Baudoin's jaw dropped open then he smiled. "Caedmon?"

Caedmon was astonished Baudoin had also risked his life to find him. What kind of family was this he suddenly belonged to? He hung his head. "Baudoin, I've been a selfish fool. Can you forgive my stupidity and blind hatred?"

"There's nothing to forgive, Caedmon. You were lost and now you're found," Baudoin replied, raising his right hand, his palm open in a gesture of brotherhood. Caedmon returned the gesture and they clasped hands, gripping each other fiercely.

"You need a bath, brother," Baudoin grimaced with a smile.

"Aye, for certain," Caedmon chuckled. "I've got used to it, but I know—"

Two servants came to prepare a bath and his father reassured him he should bathe and get some rest. There would be plenty of time to talk on the long journey home, after they'd helped to rescue the unfortunates trapped in the ruin.

***

The following morning, the Turkish commander in charge of the siege of Civitote woke early and, as he stretched his cramped muscles, seemed dismayed to see a battle squadron of the Byzantine Navy docked in the bay below him. Weighing his options, and satisfied he'd managed to kill most of the infidel dogs in the so called People's Crusade, he decided to withdraw his troops and allow the escape of those trapped in the ruin.

The Christians came ashore when they saw the Turks had withdrawn and relieved the besieged crusaders. Caedmon was reunited with Abbot. Both Montbryce men went with the rescue party and when Caedmon was greeted by his Norman friends with embraces and effusive thanks in Norman French, and responded with equal ease, Ram and Baudoin were amazed.

"It seems you're a Norman after all, Caedmon," Ram jested.

His son smiled and shrugged his shoulders. "Wait until you read my codex," Caedmon said, extricating the journal from his saddlebags.

The survivors were ferried back to Constantinople, the last remnant of an 'army' that had started out forty thousand strong. Many of them were on their last legs and had to be carried from the ruin.

CHAPTER TWENTY-FIVE

Mabelle missed Ram terribly. It was the first time they'd been separated for any length of time since her captivity in Wales, and recalling that terrible episode brought back some difficult memories. But when Ram returned, he would be overjoyed if a healthy grandchild awaited him. She prayed daily for the safe return of her men. After she saw Ram off on the expedition to recover Caedmon, she immediately sent a messenger to Shelfhoc Manor, inviting Agneta and Ascha to come to Ellesmere. Agneta accepted and travelled to Ellesmere with Tybaut and some of the men-at-arms. Ascha opted to stay at Shelfhoc, citing the presence of her house guests, the Brightmores. Mabelle greeted Agneta warmly.

Agneta curtseyed. "My lady Countess, I'm indebted to you for inviting me here. It's hard to be at Shelfhoc without Caedmon. I'm sorry we've brought this trouble to your door."

Mabelle proffered her hand to Agneta and helped her rise. "Lady Agneta, these are difficulties we'll overcome with prayers and goodwill. We'll keep each other company as we pray and wait for the men we love to return. All we can do is keep faith and support each other."

Agneta was given a chamber and a lady's maid assigned to take care of her needs. She'd brought some clothing with her, which the maid unpacked from her trunks. Because she was with child the clothes would soon not fit her, so she had brought only a few things. The dagger lay among her belongings. She felt somehow it had become a talisman, a symbol that perhaps there was hope for Caedmon's return. She concealed it in her chamber.

Gradually she and Mabelle got to know each other. One day she felt bold enough to say, "My lady Countess, Caedmon isn't your son. He's your husband's illegitimate son and yet you've accepted him, and me, and allowed your husband to look for Caedmon in a place he may not want to be found, a place of many dangers."

Mabelle looked up from her sewing. "Agneta, I learned long ago that if you love someone you can forgive them. To live my life without Ram would be no life. He has regretted what he did for the past thirty years. If I refused to forgive him, I would be harming myself."

"I told Caedmon I could never forgive him for something he did," Agneta whispered.

"What did he do?" Mabelle asked quietly.

Agneta told the story about the death of her parents and Caedmon's part in the raid. "I could tell from my hiding place that he regretted what had happened. But I've continued to make him suffer for it."

Mabelle watched Agneta for several minutes then asked. "Do you love him?"

Agneta fidgeted with her embroidery. "I love him with all my heart. If he doesn't return—"

"Have you ever told him you love him?"

Agneta hung her head. "No, if I had he might have been better able to cope with the shock of finding out the Earl is his father. He believes I don't love him. When he despised himself, he had no love to cushion his fall."

Mabelle reached out and patted Agneta's hand. "You can't blame yourself, Agneta. But now you've a child to consider. You must make sure that you take care of yourself, then, God willing, your baby will be born healthy and you'll survive. When Caedmon returns, you must tell him how much you love him."

"I will," Agneta sighed.

She decided the Countess was right. She took good care throughout her pregnancy and kept a positive outlook about Caedmon's return. The alternative couldn't be borne. In her ninth month, when she'd grown large, she walked daily and ate the good food Trésor prepared for her. She was determined her baby would grow up with at least one parent. After all, her mother-by-marriage had raised Caedmon alone in difficult circumstances.

Mabelle provided Agneta with the best of care. The younger woman had many questions and the Countess was able to allay some of her fears. The day her labor started she wasn't as afraid as she had been, and took it all in stride. As she strained in the birthing stool, fighting the pain, she concentrated on Caedmon—his smile, his face, his hair, his hands, his body, the sound of his husky voice. She envisaged welcoming him home, showing him his child for the first time.

She was comforted by the presence of Mabelle, who insisted on being the one to support Agneta's shoulders during most of the labor. Agneta jested she would tell her son as he grew that he'd been brought into the world with the aid of a Countess.

The last leaves were clinging to the trees outside as the cool autumn winds assailed them. Agneta had never been as hot in her life as she travailed to give birth, and in the afternoon of her second day of labor, she heard the cry of her first born child.

"It's a boy," cried Mabelle. "A beautiful strong boy. He has Caedmon's black hair."

The midwife was worried. "My lady, there's another babe," she whispered to Mabelle.

"What is it?" Agneta whimpered. "My son?"

"*Non*, Agneta," Mabelle soothed, wiping Agneta's brow. "Don't worry. But we'll need to mark him in some way. There's another babe. I need a knife, something to mark him with."

The midwife handed over a knife, but Agneta stopped her. "No, go to the *armoire*. In the bottom, there's a dagger, wrapped in cloth. Use that. It's an heirloom, from my Viking ancestors."

Mabelle quickly found the weapon and nicked the baby's forearm to mark him as the first born. Minutes later, Agneta gave birth to a tiny girl. Though she was exhausted, the good care she and Mabelle had taken with her health came to her aid and the midwife assured her everything was as it should be. They cleansed Agneta and helped her to bed. After a while, they brought the two newborns to her, swaddled and hungry. Mabelle laid the girl to Agneta's breast.

"She's not first born, but she's tiny and needs you first," she said, tearful at the thought of Ram's blue eyes glowing with pride at the sight of these grandchildren. "Now October will have a happy memory associated with it."

CHAPTER TWENTY-SIX

"We'll rest a few days before beginning the journey back," Ram decided. "Your ordeal has taken its toll on your body, Caedmon, but you're strong, and you'll soon regain your strength. You have good bloodlines."

Caedmon smiled at the wink his father gave him. "With the Emperor's lavish hospitality, I'm confident you're right," he replied, putting his feet up on an ottoman.

"Baudoin and I have met with the Norman knights who survived with you. All expressed their gratitude for your saving their lives. They praised you as a man of fortitude who bore the trials and ordeals of the journey with courage and forbearance. I'm proud of you, my son."

"I couldn't have done it without Amadour de Vignoles," Caedmon replied.

"I've invited Amadour and the others to join our forces if they wish. They were honored, recognizing the Montbryce name. Allying themselves with our family may bring them renewed hope after the terrible failure of this crusade. Once we reach Normandie, if they meet our standards, they can either remain at the castle in Saint Germain or go with us to England."

Caedmon suddenly jumped to his feet. "Is Burel among them?" he asked.

Ram raised his hand to reassure Caedmon. "*Non*, all spoke of his incompetence and arrogance."

Caedmon sat back down, but not before he grabbed another handful of grapes from the groaning board set out by the Emperor. "It's as it should be."

Ram helped himself to a sweet confection and joined his son on the divan. "Baudoin is making sure the men-at-arms sharpen their weapons, repair armour and prepare horses before we set out. It won't be an easy journey back to England."

"Abbot has weathered the ordeal remarkably well. I might not be alive today if he hadn't kept going. Thank God for Tybaut's keen eye for horseflesh."

Ram nodded. "I understand how you feel. My stallion Fortis kept me alive at Hastings. Perhaps one day I'll tell you about it." Ram was surprised he'd uttered those words. He'd always avoided talking about Hastings.

After a few days rest, all were anxious to be on the road home.

"You look like a Byzantine knight," Baudoin mocked when he first saw his brother in his new equipment, provided by Alexius. Caedmon wore a fine new chain mail hauberk, a lamellar leather cuirass over it, metal arm and leg braces, and a helmet, clothing and boots. His own were beyond repair.

Tens of thousands of people were still flocking to join the next crusade and Ram deemed it best to keep to the routes those travellers were taking, though in the opposite direction. While there were risks, it would be safer than journeying through sparsely travelled territory where they might be vulnerable.

Instead of following the Danube we've decided to go overland through Macedonia to Dyrrhacium, which ironically fell briefly to Norman forces many years ago. From there we'll take ship across the Adriatic to Bari in Italy.

"I'm not sure why I want to go the sea route," Ram complained as they made their plans. "I'm a terrible sailor."

"So am I," said Caedmon.

Just as at the outset of my journey, I couldn't stop retching throughout the voyage across the Adriatic, but now I know from whom I've inherited this malady. The Earl was as sick as I was. Baudoin deemed it amusing. Bari was shrouded in fog from the sea and the landing was difficult.

From the heel of Italy they made their way to the Duchy of Naples. At first they traversed rolling hills, but the terrain became more difficult as they followed trails through high rounded mountains, sometimes catching sight of villages perched right on the top.

The magnificent Arch of Trajan in Beneventum is a testimony to the ancientness of these towns we're passing through. The Earl seems to have made an ally of the Archbishop here in this Papal stronghold. He has gifted us with some of the fine wine from this region. We've packed it well and the Earl hopes we can get it back to Ellesmere safely. He wants his Countess to taste it. He talks about her as much as I talk about Agneta.

I'm developing a taste for olives.

***

Ram and Caedmon and Baudoin had many hours to get to know each other and their respect and liking for each other grew. The conversation one day turned to the Battle of Alnwick where Agneta had found Caedmon wounded on the battlefield.

"I must tell you, my lord Rambaud," said Caedmon, "Sometimes I wish I'd never regained my memory of that event. I can still hear the screams of the injured and dying. I'll never forget the fear. It's not very Norman of me to reveal such a thing to you."

Ram shifted in the saddle, and it was a while before he replied. "Caedmon, a warrior who says he has never been afraid is a liar. I can tell you that during the Battle of Hastings, I was terrified all the time. At one moment I thought my head had been severed and I was looking into my own dead eyes. Then the horror struck me that the blow had felled the knight who rode at my side."

It suddenly occurred to Ram he'd never told anyone about his near decapitation before. But Caedmon had fought and fallen in an equally horrific battle.

"The memory of that day has haunted me all my life. But courage isn't the absence of fear. It's acting in spite of the fear. When you made the decision to flee the abandoned ruin and sail for help, were you not afraid?"

"Aye, I was afraid. But you're right. I had to act in spite of the fear. Though I could hear Turkish voices in their camp, I kept going."

"That makes you a man of great courage," Ram answered proudly. "You saved thousands of lives."

"But I was a coward when I first found out you were my father. I ran away from my fears then," Caedmon lamented.

Ram was thoughtful for a while, contemplating the landscape around them. "My belief is that when we experience a tremendous shock of some kind, violence, bad news, something completely unexpected, our bodies have a number of ways to react. Yours chose to forget when you were at Alnwick. When you understood you were my son, it chose denial and flight. After Hastings I chose to try and overcome my emotional turmoil, and the frustration of losing the confrontation with a Welsh rebel, by seeking solace with your mother who was also in need of comfort. She'd suffered a loss and was faced with a future filled with fear."

It was the first time the two men had ever spoken about Ram's coupling with Ascha.

Caedmon was silent for long minutes and then said, "I'm ready to hear the whole story."

Starting with the preparations for the invasion and omitting nothing, Ram told his son the story of how he'd come to be, ending with his discovery of Ascha's flight to Scotland. He didn't try to make excuses for what he'd done.

"You were not conceived in violence, Caedmon. In fact, I recall it as a brief time of beauty amid a sea of despair and horror. I didn't love your mother, but we filled a desperate need in each other. It was a mutual joining. Neither forced the other. I took care of her afterwards, made sure the manor was safe."

"But when you recognized the moment you saw me that I was your son, you didn't choose to fight, or flee, or deny. You immediately chose to face the reality and embrace it."

"That's because, my dear boy, I'm much older, and thus wiser than you," Ram replied, smiling. "And I've had the great good fortune to be that most unusual of things—I'm a nobleman married to a woman who loves me and who has helped me see that without love, life means little."

"I would wish for such a love from Agneta, but I doubt she'll want to see me when we get home. This is the second thing I've done to give her unbearable pain."

He told Ram about the attack on Bolton.

"Do you love her?"

For a few minutes, Caedmon couldn't speak, then he swallowed hard and admitted, "She's all I've thought about during this long odyssey. In the midst of the hardships, the stupid quarrels between the different groups, the mayhem, the slaughter, it was the memory of Agneta that kept me sane, kept me going. She was my beacon of hope."

Ram nodded, glad his son had found a great love. "Have you told her you love her?"

"No. I knew when I asked her to be my bride that she could never love me, because of my part in the raid. I was willing to settle for the passion we share."

Ram laughed. "This sounds remarkably like history repeating itself. Mabelle and I spent many years trying to deny the fact we love each other. It took a cruel kidnapping and separation to make us see that without the other life meant nothing."

When Caedmon looked at him questioningly, Ram told him the story of Mabelle's kidnapping by Rhodri. Baudoin rode up to travel at their side while Ram told the tale.

Caedmon suddenly reined his horse to an abrupt halt. "Rhodri ap Owain? It was he who kidnapped your family?"

Ram halted his horse, as did Baudoin. "*Oui*, why do you have such a surprised look on your face?"

Caedmon shook his head. "You won't believe this, but Rhodri ap Owain saved my life."

He told Ram and Baudoin the story of how Rhodri had rescued him from near-drowning.

"It's strange the twists and turns life sometimes takes, isn't it?" Baudoin remarked. "Papa, tell him the rest of the story about Rhodri and Rhonwen."

They set the horses in motion again. "Rhodri ap Owain and I have a sort of tacit understanding. He hasn't attacked any of my lands since the kidnapping."

"Part of the agreement for the ransom?"

"*Non*. He married Rhonwen Dda, the healer from Ellesmere who was kidnapped with my wife and sons. Rhonwen was like a daughter to my wife. Though we call our daughter Rhoni, her name is Hylda Rhonwen, and Rhodri's eldest child is named Myfanwy Mabelle. Rhonwen has visited us numerous times at Ellesmere, often bringing her children. They have five now, three boys and two girls. Baudoin can likely tell you their names."

Baudoin smiled. "*Oui*, besides Myfanwy Mabelle, there's Rhys, Rhun and Rhydderch, who are twins, and Carys. Rhodri taught me useful raiding and defense tactics during my captivity. I liked him."

Caedmon had been nodding as the account was told. Now he smiled. "Rhys helped rescue me, and Rhodri told me about his wife Rhonwen and her friendship with your wife. No wonder he looked at me strangely when I told him he would be welcome at Shelfhoc. Come to think of it, he told me then I reminded him of you."

Ram shook his head and laughed. "The wily old fox has probably already guessed your parentage."

"Rhodri actually saved all our lives by killing Phillippe de Giroux as he was about to behead Robert," Baudoin said. "I for one will never forget that experience."

Ram added, "Rhodri could easily have finished me off at Ruyton, but he chose not to."

"You didn't mention the name of the rebel you fought with at Ruyton. I didn't know it was Rhodri."

"*Oui*, anyway, the first thing I told Robert and Baudoin when I saw them again, after the ransom was paid, was that I loved them, and I discovered it wasn't that hard. Fortunately, Mabelle wasn't abused during her captivity, but if she had been, it wouldn't have made a difference in my feelings for her. If you want a father's advice," he winked at Caedmon, "You'll tell Agneta you love her."

"What if she doesn't love me in return?"

"You keep telling her. Over and over. Show her you love her. I barely know Agneta, but I think you'll find she cares for you deeply. A woman may say she's only marrying for passion, but—perhaps Agneta was as afraid as you to avow her love, fearing you didn't love her in return."

I've much to learn from the Earl—should I be calling him Father?

I was impressed by his demeanour during our encounter with Bohemond, who is engaged in recruiting a large army, mostly Normans, to join the next Crusade. This giant of a man, son of the celebrated Duke Robert Guiscard, appears to have been overcome by the zeal to crusade. He abandoned the siege of Amalfi he was embarked on when he encountered the hordes of Crusaders passing through. He was interested in what we had to tell him of our adventures since he plans to cross the Adriatic, as we did, and go on to Constantinople.

However, my Father is of the opinion Bohemond's true purpose is to carve out for himself an eastern principality. He and Alexius have a history. Alexius won't be glad to see him.

I've seen a volcano for the first time, the mighty Mons Vesuvius. They say it hasn't erupted for two score years, but it's a daunting sight. Dramatic clouds of smoke still rise from the mouth of the beast.

***

Leaving Naples they followed the coast, heading north. In Roma, the Earl sought out members of the powerful Frangipani and Pierleoni families. Afterwards, lounging in an opulent chamber provided by the Frangipanis, he explained his ideas to Baudoin and Caedmon.

"I'm pleased with our talks with them. They'll make excellent contacts. The world is changing. The Crusades will open up trade and commerce like never before. Look at the three of us. Like thousands of others, we're crossing lands we've never visited before."

He got a pear from a bowl of fruit and sat down again, rubbing his knees.

"I have to start eating more fruit. Too much rich food in Constantinople. It made my rheumatism worse. Travel doesn't help, either. Anyway, what was I saying? Oh, yes. People used to live in one place and never leave it. The wealth of these two patrician clans comes from trade and commerce, not lands. We need to make allies of such people. Then England and Normandie can take advantage of the new trade routes which will open up."

Caedmon watched his father trying to ease the pain in his knees. "This city has recovered well from the sacking the Normans carried out over ten years ago," he replied. "I never understood what that was about?"

Baudoin jumped into the conversation. "*Alors*, Guiscard and his men set fire to Roma after the populace revolted against his army's cruelty. The Duke had gone there to rescue Pope Gregory from the Holy Roman Emperor."

He turned to his father. "I understood Frangipani and Pierleoni are bitter enemies."

Ram put his forefinger on his lips and whispered with a smile, "They are. That's why I met with them separately. However, they both understand the power of money. It's ironic the Pierleoni family, descendents of Jews, are the strongest protectors of the Popes."

Rome has risen from the ashes like the phoenix in the myth of old. Will I be able to rebuild my life with Agneta, after destroying her hopes and dreams?

***

The weather turned cold, windy and wet as they crossed Tuscany, through Siena and on to Firenze, where they attended mass at the Basilica di San Miniato al Monte. They came out into the bright sunshine and were watching artisans and masons working on high scaffolding on the exterior of the neighbouring Baptistery. Baudoin wandered off to explore the other side of the renovations.

"This is incredibly decorative work," Ram commented to Caedmon, his hand shielding his eyes from the glare.

"Aye. It is indeed."

Their attention was suddenly drawn by a frenzied shout from high above them. A portion of scaffolding had collapsed and a large slab of marble had tumbled from it. Baudoin was directly below.

Caedmon sprinted towards his half-brother, waving his arms. "*Baudoin!*"

As Baudoin turned, Caedmon leapt forward, knocking him out of the way of the falling marble. The block shattered on impact, inches from where they lay, and shards sprayed over them. Caedmon shielded Baudoin and a sharp sliver struck him on the shoulder, embedding itself in his flesh.

"*Mon Dieu,*" Baudoin gasped. "*Qu'est-ce qu—*"

"*Mes fils,*" Ram shouted as he reached them. "My sons, *grâce à Dieu,* you're safe. *Godemite,* Caedmon, you're hurt. Your shoulder is bleeding."

"What?" Caedmon said with a chuckle.

Ram looked at him strangely. "What is amusing?"

"That's the first time I've ever heard you utter a Saxon word."

Ram laughed. "You're right. Here's another. *Oli Crosse,* we must get that taken care of."

Caedmon hadn't felt anything until he looked at the wound and then he swooned. By now a frenzied crowd of animated Florentines had gathered, making apologies, offering assistance. Several of Ram's men had also run to the scene, ready to protect their lord from harm.

"*Vite,*" Ram ordered one of his men. "Fetch our own physician."

"*Oui, milord.*"

***

"I owe you my life, Caedmon."

"You would have done the same, Baudoin."

Caedmon had been dozing in a giant bed in the opulent villa of a Florentine nobleman who had witnessed the incident. He'd offered the Earl and his family his hospitality, and the Earl had expressed his delight at the establishment of another good ally in Italy.

"Let's hope that's true." Baudoin wandered around the room, picking up ornaments and examining them. Then he turned back to

Caedmon. "This is the first time you and I have had the opportunity to be alone together. To speak our minds."

Caedmon turned to lean on one elbow. "Speak it now, Baudoin. We should have no misunderstandings between us."

Baudoin perched on the edge of the bed. "When I first learned of your existence, I shared my brother Robert's misgivings and resentments."

Caedmon shrugged, but shouldn't have. It hurt. "I can understand that. It was a natural reaction. Look at me. I came close to destroying myself with resentment."

Baudoin shook his head. "But I decided quickly that harboring those resentments in the long term would only harm our family."

Caedmon bit his bottom lip. "You're a wiser man than I, Baudoin."

His half-brother hesitated, then went on, "But—still—I never thought I would come to like you, love you even, like a brother."

Caedmon felt his face redden and his heart race. "You don't have to—"

Baudoin stood. "*Non*, Caedmon. I'm not saying these things because you saved my life. Time after time as we've journeyed, I've found myself drawn to you. You're a man to be respected, and I'm honored to have you as a brother."

Caedmon was overwhelmed. "The honor is mine, Baudoin. *Merci*."

They clasped hands.

"The physician says you'll be ready to travel on the morrow. How do you feel? It won't be easy travelling with your arm strapped to your body."

"I'll be ready."

Four days later they were in the seaport of Genova. The physician from Montbryce examined Caedmon's shoulder, and declared it sufficiently healed to allow the removal of the bindings.

"You're lucky, my boy. You seem to heal quickly," the trusted Norman said.

"Like most of us in the Montbryce family," Ram remarked. "I remember when Hugh was wounded at Hastings, he recovered remarkably quickly. He accompanied me to Ellesmere the first time I ever went there. What a shock that was, I can tell you. The *castle* the Conqueror had granted me was a derelict earthwork."

Anyway, enough reminiscing. I seem to do a lot of that these days. As I was saying, ostensibly it's the Bishop of Genova who rules here for the Emperor, but Frangipani told me that merchant families like the Adornos have the power. This city has one of the largest and most powerful navies in the whole Mediterranean."

I wish Agneta could see some of these places. The Mediterranean isn't like any body of water I've seen before. It evokes memories of Heysham, though I doubt this sea is as cold! I wonder if Leofric and Coventina have married yet.

The Romans arrogantly called this Mare Nostrum, 'Our Sea' but where is their empire now? The Normans should pay heed.

They continued to follow the coast, passing through the Genovan colony of Monoikos before heading inland. This way they hoped to avoid the rigors of crossing the Alps. Still, it took four days to get to Arles, from where they struck out for the north, hugging the banks of the Rhone to Lyon, the Massif Central looming to the west and the mighty Alps to the east. They were cold, wet and hungry by the time they arrived in Lyon. They located a lodging house with a large communal bathhouse and took advantage of it to get warm.

Ram admitted, "I was tempted to break open the wine from Beneventum as we struggled along against the wind. In fact, we should have brought a bottle in here to enjoy, instead of this swill."

Caedmon and Baudoin agreed, but they kept on drinking the inferior wine.

"It's a pity we weren't travelling in the other direction. We could have let the vicious Rhone current carry us down to the sea," Ram jested, relaxing in the hot water. He let out a long sigh. "This is good for my knees. Now if I had your mother here, Baudoin, to take care of my other needs, I'd be a happy man."

Baudoin glanced at Caedmon and reddened. "Given both your tendencies to *mal de mer,* it's better we're going the other way," he teased them both. "How's your shoulder, Caedmon?"

"The cold makes it stiff, but it's healing. The hot water does help."

The route became flatter and easier and in a sennight they'd reached Alensonne, where they intended to stay with Ram's brother, Antoine, who now governed that castle on Ram's behalf.

"A lot of memories here," Ram observed as they approached the castle. "First time I came here, Antoine and I were faced with solving the mystery of the sudden death of the *seigneur*—my wife's half-brother, Arnulf. I'll tell you the tale later."

"Does Antoine know about me?" Caedmon asked as.

"Robert told him when he came back to Normandie."

"What will be his reaction?"

"Antoine will be accepting. He's a compassionate man. I could tell you tales of him and my other brother Hugh, whom you'll meet in a few days at Domfort, but I'll leave it for them to tell."

As Ram predicted, both Antoine and Hugh, and their families, were welcoming. Caedmon was surprised to learn both Hugh and Antoine had married women who were not Normans.

When they reached the Calvados, Ram wanted Caedmon to see the ancestral castle Montbryce at Saint Germain. He too wanted to spend some time there, though he was anxious to get back to Mabelle.

Robert was in residence at the castle and he and Caedmon met again. It was an opportunity to get to know each other. They shared a tumbler or two of the Montbryce apple brandy, and Baudoin told his brother about the events of the crusade and the rescue.

"That's an incredible story of bravery, Caedmon. I salute you," Robert said, after hearing about the abandoned fortress.

"Not only that, *mon frère*, Caedmon saved my life in Firenze."

Robert never took his eyes off Caedmon as Baudoin told the story. "And how is your shoulder now, *mon frère*," he asked.

"It's healed. If I'd been wearing my metal arm braces, I wouldn't have been injured, but we'd been to Mass. This is fine apple brandy."

"We should also salute Baudoin," Ram said with a smile, sensing Caedmon's discomfort with the attention. "This has been a life changing experience for you, *mon petit*, hasn't it?"

"*Merci*, Papa," the shy Baudoin replied.

"It will stand you in good stead when you become the Second Earl of Ellesmere."

Baudoin and I have become friends on this journey. He's a quiet man, but one of keen intelligence and fortitude. Our father has seen strengths in him he didn't see before. I believe he has lived in Robert's shadow somewhat. Many of the Norman Crusaders who returned with us have chosen to remain at Saint Germain, and the rest are travelling on to England with us. Amadour is staying at Montbryce. It was hard to say goodbye to him.

***

"Yuletide is drawing nigh and I want to get home to share the season with Mabelle."

"And I'm anxious to see how Agneta fares, with the baby. I've been away eleven months. I pray the child safely born and my wife hale and healthy."

"The babe must be about three months old. My first grandchild."

As they rode away from Ram's childhood home, Caedmon said, "I understand now your pride in your heritage, my lord Rambaud. Normandie is a beautiful land."

"*Oui*, my pride is in the land, but it's much more than that. I haven't been able to live in my own country for thirty years. It's the blood I'm proud of—Montbryce blood—the same blood that flows in your veins, Caedmon. But we each bring two families to our birth. You also carry noble Saxon blood. It's not the blood of the Woolgars, as you believed, but the blood of your mother's proud family. You're the future of your mother's country, a joining of our two great heritages. You're aware, of course, that our great Conqueror was bastard born? But did you know that when he was Duke of the Normans, he invariably signed official documents *Ego Willelmus Cognomine Bastardus*? He made his bastardy his greatest strength. Make it yours, Caedmon, then it can never be used to hurt you."

Caedmon bristled. "I can accept I'm half Norman, and take pride in it, but I'll never accept the brutality with which the Conqueror ruled my mother's country. He's not a man I would wish to emulate."

They rode in silence for a while, then Ram said, "I don't reveal this to anyone other than members of my family, but there have been many times I too have been appalled by the brutality of some of my fellow Normans, William included. If the King had insisted, I would not have been allowed to ransom Mabelle all those years ago. He firmly believed I should not be financing rebels. It would probably have cost my family their lives.

But I knew William, fought with him. I would have given my life for him willingly. He was a great warrior, a man who saved Normandie from anarchy and brought her to greatness. I was proud he called me his friend."

Caedmon pondered his father's words as they crossed the water to Dover. He'd thought never to see England again and it moved him because the Earl was right—he represented the future, and there was nothing to be gained dwelling on hatreds. Tomorrow couldn't be carved from tombstones. Trying to reach the future through the past was futile. He prayed Agneta would accept him back. Together they could carry his England forward.

Ram's voice broke into his thoughts. "By the way, Caedmon, we need some other way for you to address me, instead of *my lord Rambaud*."

"Aye, my lo—Sorry. It's become a habit."

He wanted to call Rambaud *father*, but was still mindful that this man was one of the most powerful men in England and Normandie. "How would you like me to address you?"

"*Father* would be fine," Ram said with a smile. "Or *mon père* if you feel like practicing your French."

They exchanged a smile as they took up their positions with Baudoin to help bring the boat ashore.

CHAPTER TWENTY-SEVEN

*T*o *Lady Ascha Woolgar at Shelfhoc Hall,*
  I am pleased to send you the good news that your
  daughter-by-marriage, Agneta, has been safely delivered. I
  believe it is important for you to come to Ellesmere. You will
be welcomed here.
  Mabelle, Countess of Ellesmere.

Mabelle had a mischievous smile on her face. "What's your opinion, Agneta? I don't want her to learn of the twins until she arrives."

Agneta eyed her curiously and read the letter again. "You would welcome her here? She's the woman your betrothed bedded."

"She's no threat to me, Agneta, nor to any of us. She must be devastated about Caedmon and no doubt longs to meet you and her grandchildren. What a surprise the two of them will be."

The letter was dispatched and a reply received three days later.

To the Countess of Ellesmere,
  I am indebted to you for the good news of my Agneta. At your suggestion, I will travel to Ellesmere. I thank you, Countess, for your kind consideration. I wish to express my regret that I never disclosed Caedmon's existence to the Earl, and for the shock it must have been to you and your family to learn of it. I humbly beg your forgiveness. No malice was ever intended. I pray for the safe return of your husband and son, and thank God for the delivery of a healthy child who might take Caedmon's place, if my son can't be found.
  In penitence and the hope of forgiveness,
  Lady Ascha Woolgar

And so it was that Lady Ascha Woolgar came to Ellesmere Castle a sennight later. She was ushered into the Great Hall where the Countess greeted her. She prostrated herself before Mabelle. "My Lady Countess, forgive me my sin. Forgive my wantonness that has caused this terrible grief."

"Please rise, Lady Ascha. None of us here bear you any malice. I'm sure the aftermath of Hastings must have been a nightmare for you. You must be anxious to see your daughter-by-marriage, and meet your grandchildren."

Ascha rose slowly and straightened her skirts. Then Mabelle's words seemed to penetrate. "Grandchildren?"

"*Oui*, there are two of them, a boy and a girl."

Ascha looked stunned. "My father, Sir Gawain Bronson, was a twin, but his sister died at birth."

Mabelle smiled at the news. "The girl Agneta birthed is tiny, but I believe she's a survivor."

"And what news of the Earl, and your son, and Caedmon?" Ascha asked tentatively.

"We have no news yet. But we must keep faith. Agneta is anxious for you to meet the children."

As they entered Agneta's chamber, she rose from the chair where she'd been resting. Ascha embraced her and Agneta took her by the hand and guided her to the cradles where the infants lay sleeping contentedly. Ascha could no longer hold back her tears, and wept with joy at the sight of her grandchildren, and with sadness for her missing son, who wasn't there to rejoice in his children and who might never return.

***

The Winter Solstice came and went and preparations were under way at Ellesmere for the Yuletide celebrations. The three noblewomen didn't have their hearts in the process, but went about doing the customary things automatically. They were interrupted by the appearance of a breathless page who came running into the Hall, where Mabelle was supervising the hanging of cedar boughs. Agneta had her son on her hip and Ascha held her granddaughter.

"My Lady Countess," the boy gasped, bowing.

"What is it, Edmond?" asked Mabelle.

"Riders, my lady, a large group of riders—sighted three miles out. It's the Earl and Lord Baudoin, and from all reports a Byzantine knight accompanies them."

Mabelle felt relief wash over her. She wondered if she could run three miles.

"I can't go out to meet them. If Caedmon isn't with them—I—" Agneta stammered.

Ascha said, "My lady Countess, by your leave, I'll go with Agneta and the children to her chamber. It's not seemly for me to greet the Earl with you. Go to welcome him home. If there's bad news about Caedmon, you can send word to us. We'll grieve together."

They left and Mabelle hurried to don a warm cloak so she could greet Ram in the chilly courtyard. His horse had barely come to a halt before he vaulted from the saddle and she ran to press her body against his. He enfolded her in his cloak. She felt his need as she sobbed against him.

"Mabelle," he whispered into her ear, nibbling on her lobe, "Yet again, I've only to set my eyes upon you and my body betrays my need."

"*Maman*," Baudoin shouted as he strode towards her, joining his parents in their embrace.

"Baudoin, my darling Baudoin," she whispered.

There's something different about him. He seems more mature, more self assured.

"I've missed you both. But what about Caedmon? You didn't find him?"

Ram released her, put his arm around her shoulders and turned her to face the other knight, still mounted on his horse—waiting—unsure. It was a moment before she recognized this man in the foreign uniform as Caedmon. She laughed out loud and kissed her husband, relieved for him that his son had been found, the perils of the long journey not in vain. She smiled too at the surprise the young man was about to receive.

Caedmon dismounted and came to stand before her. "My lady Countess, I hope the words come out of my mouth the way I've rehearsed them a hundredfold in preparation for this moment. I beg your forgiveness for the grief my folly has caused you and your family." He went down on one knee, took her hand and kissed it.

"Caedmon," she replied. "Please do not kneel to me. You're part of this family. The Montbryces would go to the ends of the earth to protect one of their own."

Ram laughed. "In fact that's what we did. Let's go inside. It's cold out here."

Once inside the hall, Caedmon turned to Mabelle and blurted out, "What of Agneta—and the child?"

Mabelle decided to prolong the young man's agony for a few minutes. His face betrayed his need. She knew that look. "A moment, Caedmon."

She summoned a servant and whispered, "Ask Lady Ascha to join us and tell her to bring only the baby girl."

A few minutes later, Ascha came into the room carrying Caedmon's baby daughter. She stumbled when she saw Caedmon and he rushed to embrace her. "Mother, you're here? And this child?"

Ascha glanced nervously at Ram, who nodded to her. She returned her smile to her son and said, "Caedmon, this is your daughter."

Nervously he took the babe and cradled her to his breast, kissing her forehead and taking her tiny fingers into his big hands. His heart beat erratically as he looked upon a squirming miniature of his beloved wife. He was afraid to voice his emotions, afraid of the answer he might receive in response to his next question. "Agneta?"

"She's in her chamber. I'll take you to her."

Ram eagerly took the infant from her father, gazing with awe at his beautiful granddaughter. "Leave the child with me, Caedmon. Go to your wife. What are you looking pleased about, Mabelle?"

Ascha led her son to Agneta's chamber, but wouldn't enter with him. She sobbed as she embraced him then pushed him to the door. He entered, closed the door behind him, turned slowly and saw his wife, standing in the middle of the room, waiting.

If he'd rehearsed his speech to Mabelle a hundred times, the words he wanted to speak now had gone through his mind a thousand times. He and his wife stood looking at each other and his thoughts fled. All he could think of was how much he loved her, how much he'd missed her.

"Agneta—my Agneta. I've longed for this moment, and now I'm afraid."

Suddenly his father's words came to mind and the simple truth tumbled out.

"Agneta, I love you more than I can ever tell you. I accept you can't love me—will probably never forgive me for—"

"Caedmon," she gasped, rushing across the room to embrace him. "Caedmon, all I care about is that you've come back to me. My love for you overwhelms me. I thought I would go mad if you didn't return. I've ached for you."

"You love me?" he asked incredulously.

She kissed his face, his hands, and then his face again. "I've loved you from the first moment I saw you, on the moor at Alnwick."

He pressed her body tightly to his, burying his face at her neck. "And I've loved you since I first saw you in the infirmary. What a fool I've been. I've wasted much of our lives because of my pride and hatred. I failed you, Agneta. I wasn't here when you brought our beautiful daughter into the world."

At that moment, a faint wail came from the corner of the chamber. Caedmon cocked his head, confused as to the source of the sound. He loosened his grip on Agneta. She took his hand and led him to the cradle where his son was making his demands known.

"Your son wants to be fed," she said, picking up the baby. Caedmon was dumbfounded, and it took him a moment to understand.

"Twins?" he murmured with bemusement. "You birthed twins? My grandfather was a twin."

Agneta nodded and undid the child's wrappings to proudly show him his son's maleness.

"My son," he breathed, touching the baby's head and stroking his wife's hair. "The two birds."

"What?" Agneta asked.

He told her about the dream as she prepared to feed her son. He watched his child happily suckle on his wife's heavy breast, and was overcome with emotion and had to blow his nose.

"Your daughter is probably getting hungry too, if you want to go get her and bring her to me," Agneta suggested with a smile.

He didn't want to take his eyes off the scene he'd been watching with rapt attention and walked into the door as left. He hurried back to the main hall, where the infant had indeed started to fuss. Ram handed the child to him, beaming as he told Caedmon, "I've always been good with babies, but I can't satisfy her needs at the moment. And I hear I've yet to meet her brother."

Caedmon strode back, holding the child carefully, afraid to drop this speck of life he held in his hands.

"Agneta, no man was ever more blessed than I. You've given me a priceless gift, two of them, and I thank you for it."

"They are our gift to each other, Caedmon," she replied, blushing. "I can't take my eyes off this magnificent bronzed warrior in the strange uniform—in case I discover he's not actually here."

Caedmon shifted the baby to another position in an effort to stop the wailing. "I'm here, Agneta. And I'll never leave you again. What did you name them?"

"We had to choose without your help, for their baptism. I hope you approve of my choices."

"I'll love whatever you chose."

"Our son is Aidan Branton, after my brothers, and our daughter is Blythe Lacey, a Saxon name and a Norman name."

"Blythe is getting hungry," he said loudly, over the squirming infant's screams. He placed her carefully at Agneta's other breast, brushing his hand lovingly over the milk-swollen globe and experiencing an immediate erection.

"And so am I. Do you have enough milk for both?" he asked shyly.

"They have a wet nurse, but I wanted us to share this first time together," she whispered, smiling at his discomfort.

"Thank you," he said huskily, ashamed because he felt jealous of his own children.

CHAPTER TWENTY-EIGHT

"You're still a beautiful woman, Ascha."

Ascha had been sitting alone in the gallery, lost in her thoughts. She hadn't heard Ram enter.

"My lord Rambaud! It's not—" She slipped from the chair and sank to her knees, bowing her head. She clenched her fists, trying to quell the feelings raging in her breast.

"Don't worry, Ascha. Mabelle knows we're speaking with each other. Do not kneel before me. It's I who should grovel at your feet."

She looked up at him and could see by the stiffness of his shoulders, and the expression on his face, that he too struggled with intense emotions. He was as handsome as she remembered. The silver in his hair made him more attractive.

He seemed unsure. "I would assist you to rise, but it's as well if we don't touch. I don't want to offend."

"Your touch would not offend me, my lord."

She offered her hand, hoping desperately she would feel nothing when their fingers touched. It was a forlorn hope, but she determined not to let her reaction show as he helped her to rise.

He let go of her hand quickly. "I thank you, Ascha—for Caedmon. He's a fine man."

"He's like his father," she whispered.

"I wish you'd told me, but I understand why you couldn't. You're a woman of remarkable courage to have survived the journey to Scotland, and to have prospered there, alone with a young child. You never married?"

She shook her head. "There was never anyone I wished to marry. I survived on my memories and on my love for Caedmon. You and your Countess are generous to recognize him as you have. You won't be sorry."

"I know. We're immensely proud of him. Caedmon *Brice*, eh? Clever."

Ascha reddened and smiled. "Yes, it was my secret."

Ram laughed and the warm sound rolled through her. "What will you do now, Lady Ascha?"

"I'll return to Shelfhoc with Caedmon and Agneta and help them with the children. I have nowhere else to go, and Shelfhoc is a comfortable manor, big enough for all of us. I thank you for your stewardship of it for all these years."

Ram nodded. "I hope you find contentment, *milady*."

"I've found it already, Ram. I'm content Caedmon has found happiness with Agneta, and now knows, and is proud of, his true heritage. I no longer have to keep hidden secrets. I will devote myself to being the perfect grandmamma."

And I will always love you.

"I too am a doting grandsire," he laughed, then sobered. "That's something else we share, Ascha. They'll never want for anything. I swear it. I regret the burdens you've had to bear alone."

"You're an honorable man, Ram, and I'm confident these children will bring more honor to your name and your household. Caedmon was never a burden."

"Have you talked with him since our return?"

"Only briefly. I couldn't speak."

"He's waiting for you. Will you take my arm, Lady Ascha, and I'll escort you to him?"

Ascha inclined her head, and placed her hand on Ram's arm. "Thank you, my lord Earl."

***

"Caedmon, forgive me."

He took his mother's hands and pulled her back to her feet.

"There's nothing to forgive, mother. Come, sit with me."

Ascha sat in the chair by the hearth, facing her son. "But I lied to you. It was my wantonness and lies that almost destroyed you."

He leaned forward and took her hand. "I understand why you did what you did. My father told me what happened after Hastings, what it was like—for both of you. I humbly beg your forgiveness for the way I treated you."

She looked away. "I deserved it. I was weak."

He squeezed her hand. "Look at me."

Ascha lifted her eyes.

"You've never been weak, mother. Your courage has made me the person I am."

She choked back a sob.

"What was your husband like?"

Ascha's eyes widened with surprise. "He was a brute," she whispered.

"He beat you?"

She shifted uncomfortably and looked away again. "Sometimes, when he was angry. He was a difficult man to please. I found it hard. My father was a warrior, but he was never a violent man. I wasn't used to it."

Caedmon rose, drew his mother up from her chair, put his arms around her trembling shoulders and embraced her. He suspected her husband had not cared much about pleasing her either and his heart ached for her. He understood why his mother had lain with Ram de Montbryce.

"Don't cry, mother. I should have known brutality is not solely the purview of Normans. I'm glad I'm not the son of such a man. Better he died at Hastings."

Ascha nodded. "You're a son to be proud of. I've never regretted your birth for one moment."

He put his hands on her shoulders and held her away from him, smiling. "And you've no doubt taken secret pleasure from my middle name."

She too smiled and blushed. "It was wicked of me. I wanted some small part of you to bear a trace of your real father."

"It means more to me now. There's something else you probably aren't aware of. The thirteenth day of November is Saint Brice's Day."

"I don't understand."

"That's the day the Battle of Alnwick took place."

"Oh, Caedmon."

He sensed his mother still loved Ram de Montbryce, and he grieved for her that it was a hopeless love. He silently thanked the saints he was a man whose deep love for his wife was returned in full measure.

***

Ram gave orders for a special feast to celebrate everything they had to be thankful for—the Yuletide season, their safe return, the birth of two healthy children, and the reunion of Caedmon and

Agneta. The hall was filled with the Ellesmere men-at-arms and their commanders, and local noblemen and women. The aging Trésor, still the doyenne of the kitchens, outdid herself and they feasted on roasted lamb, pigeon pie and trout. Trésor always acknowledged her debt for the secret recipe to the now dead *La Cuisinière*. The ale and wine flowed freely.

Caedmon and Agneta proudly carried Aidan and Blythe around for everyone to see. At the end of the meal, Ram stood and raised his hand. The Hall fell silent.

"This day, it's my honor to recognize, before all, Sir Caedmon Woolgar as my son. He's a child begotten of my seed and the body of Lady Ascha Woolgar not long after the battle of Hastings."

He nodded to Ascha, who was also seated at the head table. A murmur of surprise rippled through the crowd, and they looked at Mabelle, sitting next to Rhoni—both continued to smile regally.

Ram came down from the dais to stand at the front of the assembled gathering. Baudoin stood at his side, trying to look serious, a rolled and beribboned parchment in his hands.

"I call Sir Caedmon Woolgar to stand before me." Ram's voice was authoritative.

Caedmon came to stand before his father. Ram looked at this younger replica, the same stance, the same set of the shoulders, the same face.

"Sir Caedmon." He paused and coughed, momentarily overcome with emotion.

"Sir Caedmon, as Baudoin and I travelled with you through many countries this past autumn, we came to know you as a man of courage, honor and fortitude. I'm proud to call you my son, and we welcome you to our family. I bestow upon you the right to bear the name FitzRam."

He paused, unsure whether his son would accept the gesture, whether Caedmon understood the enormous honor he was granting him in Norman eyes. An imperceptible nod from Caedmon reassured him, and he continued. "As a token of our love and esteem for you, and your family, I also deed to you the manor houses and estates of Pagham, Tangmere and Slindon in Sussex."

With a flourish and a smile, Baudoin handed Caedmon the official document, prepared before they'd left on the quest.

"I feel I've been struck by lightning, and am perhaps imagining all this," Caedmon said as he broke the seal and unfurled the parchment. He scanned the document then looked at his father.

"You ceded these lands to me and my family before anyone knew if I would ever return. You wanted to take care of Agneta."

Ram nodded.

Caedmon whispered, "The Romany spoke true."

Ram looked at him enquiringly, but Caedmon shook his head.

Caedmon went down on one knee and his father held out his right arm, palm down, fist clenched. Taking a firm hold on Ram's wrist with his left hand and placing his right hand over his heart, Caedmon swore his allegiance, keeping his eyes fixed on his father's face.

"Since my lord Earl of Ellesmere has asked me to acknowledge to him my fealty and homage for the manors with which he has today gifted me and my heirs, in the name of the Lord, I, Caedmon Brice FitzRam, knight of Ruyton, in the presence of my mother, Lady Ascha, my son Aidan and my daughter Blythe, and my wife, Agneta, my brother, Baudoin, my sister, Rhoni, my lady Countess Mabelle de Montbryce, and of the nobles and other honorable men here gathered to honor our return, and the birth of our children, I acknowledge to you, my lord Rambaud de Montbryce, Earl of Ellesmere, that you are my liege lord—and my father, and I am your loyal man."

He took out his sword and handed it, hilt first, to his father, laying the blade across his arm. Ram nodded, took it from him, held it up, turned it and gave it back, never once averting his eyes from Caedmon's.

"Let the feasting begin," the Earl commanded.

Applause and cheering filled the room.

***

"Lady Agneta FitzRam, please come forward."

Agneta felt sure everyone in the hall must have heard her gasp as her head shot up in surprise. The Earl of Ellesmere had summoned *her* to the dais as the remains of the meal were being cleared away. She turned in her seat to look at Caedmon for some clue, but he seemed as surprised as she. She rose and walked on unsteady legs to stand in front of the Earl, head bowed.

"My lord Earl," she whispered.

"Lady Agneta, it has come to my attention you are the rightful owner of a manor in Northumbria known as Kirkthwaite Hall."

She looked up at the Earl and saw kindness in his eyes. She stole a glance at Caedmon whose expression told her nothing. She cleared her throat. "Kirkthwaite Hall belonged to my parents. It was built by my grandparents."

"And you are their only surviving issue?"

"Yes, with my children."

Ram cleared his throat. "I have sent messengers to the King, establishing your right to the manor and all it entails. I'm confident of a positive reply."

The tears came unbidden and rolled down Agneta's cheek. "It's a ruin," she choked.

"I've also asked for his assistance in rebuilding the hall and manor house. Rufus will recognize the benefits of a prosperous estate in that area of Northumbria, now Roger de Mowbray has been disgraced and imprisoned. I'm sure you and my son can restore it to its former standing."

She looked up again at the Earl. His smile filled her heart and she could barely speak.

"*Thank you* seems little to say in return, my lord Earl."

Caedmon rose from his chair, nodded to his father and escorted his wife back to her place. Agneta felt his hand tremble at her elbow.

***

They'd retired to their chamber. Caedmon sat, gazing at Blythe cradled to his chest. Whenever he looked at the child he couldn't believe how much she already resembled Agneta. His daughter slept peacefully, unaware of the thudding of her father's heart as he waited for Agneta to finish reading his codex.

Finally he heard his wife sigh and plucked up the courage to steal a glance at her and saw her tears. He rose and lay the child carefully in her cradle, then strode over to where Agneta sat, the closed codex on her lap, her hands folded atop it. He put his hands on her shoulders and kissed the top of her head. As soon as he touched her, the blood rushed to his groin.

"Don't cry, Agneta. I didn't want to make you sad."

"I'm not sad, Caedmon. I'm filled with a happiness that makes me want to weep. You truly love me."

He sat down beside her, took her hand and placed it on his erection. "Did you ever doubt it?"

She giggled. "No. I'm fortunate to have a lusty man like you for a husband." The smile left her face. "I grieve for the torments and trials you underwent on the Crusade."

He put his hand on her thigh. "But the experience made a better man of me, though it hurt you when I left."

She put her hand atop his. "But I'm stronger too. I've learned not to let my hatred and resentments rule me. I thank God for bringing you back safely to my side."

"And our children will perhaps benefit, if we teach them the futility of hatred."

She smiled. "The best way to do that is to preserve this book of yours and make sure they read it as they grow older. I'll make a new cover for it."

"And I'll teach you how to make quills, but first—"

She screamed with laughter as he pushed her back onto the bed. The codex fell to the floor.

"Your journal," she spluttered.

"Later," he replied.

***

"Caedmon," Agneta whispered as they lay skin to skin in each other's arms that night, listening to the steady breathing of their sleeping infants. "Your father has given us the Sussex manors, but when Kirkthwaite Hall is rebuilt, would you want to live there? You've said often you would like a piece of Northumbria for yourself."

He looked at her with surprise. "I would like that very much. I'm a northerner at heart. And my mother wants to return to Shelfhoc, though she'll be without a knight."

"Leofric will be more than happy to stay there, with his wife."

Caedmon sat up abruptly. "His wife?"

"He and Coventina married."

"The devil! Her mother approved?"

"She didn't have much choice. Coventina finally stood up for what she wanted."

Caedmon lay back down and cradled his wife again, chuckling.

Agneta put her fingers on his lips. "Will you promise, if we go to Kirkthwaite, to do something for me?"

"I'll do anything for you," he whispered, nibbling her earlobe.

Agneta rose and went to the *armoire*. She didn't unwrap the bundle she retrieved, but knelt on the bed beside Caedmon with it in her hands.

"I was proud of you this evening as you pledged yourself to your Father. My heart was ready to burst."

He sat up, pulling the linens around his hips, his arms resting on his bent knees. "I was proud of myself too. I'm a better man than I was."

She paused, trying to gather her thoughts. "When we left the Abbey, Mother Superior gave this to me. You've never asked me about it."

He looked into her eyes. "I trusted you would tell me."

She unfolded the wrapping and held the dagger out to him with both hands, like an offering.

"It's a ceremonial dagger," he said, leaning forward to take hold of the walrus ivory handle, examining the workmanship. "Danish, I think? Someone labored long over this."

"It belonged to my mother, who inherited it from her mother, who received it as a gift from her grandfather. He made it."

"Your great, great grandfather," he calculated.

"Yes. My mother took her life with it."

There was a long awkward silence as he sat looking at the dagger. Finally he raised his eyes to meet her gaze. "After Bolton?"

"Yes."

"I'm sorry, Agneta," he whispered, shaking his head. "Sorry for the pain I caused."

She struggled to continue. "At first I refused to take it, but Mother Superior insisted. She told me it's good to have a reminder of past sorrow."

Reaching forward, she took the dagger from his hands, and pressed the point lightly to her breast. "When you left on the Crusade, I intended to take my own life with it."

"No, Agneta," he cried, rising to his knees, trying to wrest the dagger from her.

She held his warm hand over the cold dagger at her breast as they knelt, their bodies pressed together, the dagger between them. She smiled and shook her head.

"I'm not telling you this to make you feel guilty. I knew then I loved you and didn't want to live without you. I truly understood, for the first time, something of what my mother felt on that fateful day when she took her life. The dagger brought home to me many things. My pride in my ancestry, my love for you, the sure knowledge you are a good and true man, a noble man, a man of value. When I saw you at Bolton, your actions showed you were sickened by what happened there. The way you cradled Aidan—"

She pressed her lips together, unable to continue.

"I'm not worthy of you," he choked.

"Caedmon, I'm the one who hasn't been worthy of you. I insisted on making you feel guilty for something you'd atoned for long ago. I failed to provide you with the love you needed to cushion the blow when you found out—"

Caedmon put his fingertips on her mouth, took the dagger, placed it beside them, then drew her back into his arms. "You'd suffered such a great loss."

"Our conversation about your codex made me think about what I want to pass on to my children. When we return to Kirkthwaite, I want you to find a place of honor to display my dagger. After my death, I want you to give it to Blythe. I will tell our children its history when they are old enough. It will be a reminder of pain and sorrow, but also love and endurance. We marked Aidan as firstborn with it. The dagger saved my life, and perhaps yours. It sent me to your father for help."

They clung to each other for long minutes, thighs to thighs, belly to belly, breasts to chest, her head resting on his shoulder. His breathing quickened and she felt his hard male length against her. She moved one leg to press against his hip. He kneaded her thigh and she wrapped her legs around him. He lifted her slightly and she impaled herself on his shaft.

"You're my heart," she whispered, rocking against him.

"And you my soul."

***

Later that night, the faithful steward of Ellesmere Castle, Martin Bonhomme, was making his final rounds through the darkened castle to ensure all was well. As he passed the chamber of the Earl and Countess, he smiled. Judging from the squeals of delight coming from the room everything was back to normal at the castle.

He carried on past the chamber assigned to Sir Caedmon and Lady Agneta, and after pausing briefly to listen to the happy commotion inside, chuckled, "Like father, like son."

He hurried off to his own chamber, where his wife awaited him.

EPILOGUE

The heroes and heroines of this story outlived King William II (William Rufus) who died in a bizarre hunting accident in the New Forest, in the year of Our Lord Eleven Hundred, after being king for only thirteen years. He was *accidentally* shot with an arrow, by a hunting companion renowned throughout England as an expert bowman. Rufus might have lived had he not fallen from his horse and driven the arrow deeper.

He was succeeded on the throne of the English by his brother, Henry, co-conspirator of the chamber pot incident, who coincidentally was also present in the New Forest on the day of the accident. We must bear in mind the New Forest covered a vast area.

The dramatic lives of the descendants of Ram and Mabelle, Rhodri and Rhonwen, and Caedmon and Agneta form the lore and legend of the next generation and the beginning of the turbulent twelfth century. But those are other stories in the Montbryce Legacy.

ABOUT THE AUTHOR

Anna Markland is a Canadian "Indie" author who writes medieval romance about family honor, ancestry and roots. Her novels are intimate love stories full of passion and adventure. Following a successful career in teaching, Anna transformed her love of writing and history into engaging works of fiction. One of the things she enjoys most about writing historical romance is the in-depth research required to provide the reader with an authentic medieval experience.

Born in England, Anna has lived most of her life in Canada. Besides creating intimate stories about the lives and loves of her characters, her other passion is genealogy, and she has written histories of many of the families she has researched. This has had a big influence on her fiction writing.

The mother of four grown children, she spends her time enjoying the beauty of Vancouver Island and the incredible beaches of Panama.

Twitter @annamarkland
Facebook Fan Page~Anna Markland Novels
Website: www.annamarkland.com
Email:anna@annamarkland.com

Conquering Passion
The Montbryce Legacy~ Book One
Copyright Anna Markland 2011

CONQUERING PASSION covers a span of over ten years and is rich in details of 11th century England. The first book of the Montbryce Legacy introduces the three Montbryce brothers, Rambaud (Ram), Anthoine and Hugh, and follows Ram's journey with Mabelle de Valtesse through the labyrinth of dangers that existed in the aftermath of the Norman Conquest.

Mabelle, a strong heroine, is more than a match for her warrior hero, Ram. The passion quickly flares between them, but both are reluctant to admit their love. Can a man like Ram, who demands obedience in a wife, find love with the wilful refugee brought to his bed in an arranged marriage? Mabelle is an independent woman who has learned to live by her wits during a six year exile with her psychotic father.

Only through trials and tragedy do they finally realize that they can no longer deny what their hearts have always known—love conquers all.

Lovers of medieval romance and English history during the time of King William the Conqueror will enjoy this intimate story of passion, betrayal, ambition, vengeance, and of course love.

If Love Dares Enough
The Montbryce Legacy~Book Three
Copyright Anna Markland 2011

Hugh de Montbryce, is haunted by a deep fear, rooted in his experiences at the Battle of Hastings, that violence arouses him. He avoids women, but is drawn into the life of a Saxon noblewoman, Lady Devona Melton, a victim of abuse at the hands of her Norman husband. Can Hugh overcome his demons and the political and religious implications of abducting the wife of a Norman nobleman?

The rake of the family, Antoine is faced with the dilemma of what to do with Lady Sybilla Sancerre, the pregnant widow of an enemy he killed in battle. He is expected to send her for execution as the wife of a traitor, but finds himself driven to protect her and the deformed child she bears.

William the Conqueror's anger at both brothers could endanger all the Montbryce family holds dear.

Enjoy this excerpt from

If Love Dares Enough

Hugh sometimes wished he could find a woman to interest him, a woman to take away the constant ache for release he'd felt since Hastings. But his fear held him back whenever he got too close. It amused him whenever a new servant girl brought his repasts to his chamber. He wondered if there was some kind of wager going on in the kitchens to see which wench could tempt him. But no matter how brazenly they thrust their breasts and fluttered their eyelashes, they left him cold with the dread that, if he let down his guard, the bloodlust that had surfaced at Hastings would rear its ugly head, and he might—

They don't know the monster lurking within!

He brought release to himself. It seemed the right thing to do, and he became resigned to his fate never to bed a woman he loved, or any woman. He thought often of his brother, Ram and his wife, Mabelle. It was easy to see the sparks of passion that flew between them. Hugh longed for that kind of love, but it could never be. He couldn't take the risk, couldn't let his passion rule him. How ironic it was. He'd been the devil-may-care brother, the carefree family clown. Who would have suspected the dark side that lurked beneath? It would destroy him to find a woman he loved, only to hurt her in some way, unable to control himself.

He wondered if he should perhaps become a monk, but had grown fond of Domfort, and had plans to make it a better holding. In any case, ordinary monks couldn't involve themselves in war and politics, and Hugh sensed turbulent times ahead in Normandie. As soon as the Conqueror had been crowned King of the English, his enemies had begun attacks on Normandie. As a Montbryce it was Hugh's responsibility to defend his homeland against any enemy, and Domfort wasn't far from the lands of the treacherous Angevins. His Duke depended on him. But it was a lonely life!

CPSIA information can be obtained at www.ICGtesting.com
Printed in the USA
LVOW10s2157060416

482510LV00010B/103/P

9 780987 867360